Celebrity Skin

Celebrity Skin

Fame Unlimited

Liane Bonin

nal
jam
books

NAL Jam
Published by New American Library, a division of
Penguin Group (USA) Inc., 375 Hudson Street,
New York, New York 10014, USA
Penguin Group (Canada), 90 Eglinton Avenue East, Suite 700, Toronto,
Ontario M4P 2Y3, Canada (a division of Pearson Penguin Canada Inc.)
Penguin Books Ltd., 80 Strand, London WC2R 0RL, England
Penguin Ireland, 25 St. Stephen's Green, Dublin 2,
Ireland (a division of Penguin Books Ltd.)
Penguin Group (Australia), 250 Camberwell Road, Camberwell, Victoria 3124,
Australia (a division of Pearson Australia Group Pty. Ltd.)
Penguin Books India Pvt. Ltd., 11 Community Centre, Panchsheel Park,
New Delhi - 110 017, India
Penguin Group (NZ), 67 Apollo Drive, Mairangi Bay,
Auckland 1310, New Zealand (a division of Pearson New Zealand Ltd.)
Penguin Books (South Africa) (Pty.) Ltd., 24 Sturdee Avenue,
Rosebank, Johannesburg 2196, South Africa

Penguin Books Ltd., Registered Offices:
80 Strand, London WC2R 0RL, England

First published by NAL Jam, an imprint of New American Library,
a division of Penguin Group (USA) Inc.

First Printing, February 2007
1   3   5   7   9   10   8   6   4   2

LIBRARY OF CONGRESS CATALOGING-IN-PUBLICATION DATA:
Bonin, Liane.
Celebrity skin: fame unlimited / Liane Bonin.
p. cm.
Summary: Two high school students, one a major television star and the other under constant academic pressure
from her Korean-born parents, remain best friends in spite of loss, love, and the spotlight.
ISBN-13: 978-0-451-22032-5
ISBN-10: 0-451-22032-3
[1. Fame—Fiction. 2. Best friends—Fiction. 3. Friendships—Fiction. 4. Interpersonal relations—Fiction.] I. Title.
PZ7.B64164Cel 2007
[Fic]—dc22   2006025067

Set in Bembo
Designed by Spring Hoteling

Printed in the United States of America

Acknowledgments

Much love and mushy stuff to the 'rents, Lou and Mary Bonin. Thanks for everything!

Great big thank-yous to Faye Bender, Anne Bohner, Sammy Buck, Christine Carr, Nina Malkin, Grace Straus, Ronda Whaley, and Steve Yu. I'm grateful for all your time, advice, and support.

I save the best for last. I love you, Brad.

Chapter One

You wouldn't believe what a geek I was as a kid. A raging geek. I got picked on a lot, too. Terrorized, actually. But hey, success is the best revenge, you know? I mean, where are those kids now? Knocking over 7-Elevens? Hell, that's probably giving them too much credit. I doubt any of them are bright enough to open the cash register.

—TAYLOR CHRISTENSEN in *Vogue* magazine

Everyone thinks they know Taylor Christensen. All those *Star* and *Us Weekly* subscribers think they've got the whole dish, even the dirty secrets. They've read about which celebrities Taylor's supposedly slept with, her real hair color (dark ash blond, *not* platinum), the time she got wasted off her ass and danced on the tables at Butter with Paris Hilton. Not all of the stories are wrong, even though her "people" always deny them, soulless liars that they are. It's just that there's so much more, true stories no one will ever, ever read about. I know it all, but I'll never spill, especially not to some scumbag reporter.

See, Taylor and I have known each other since we were kids. She would probably die if I told a tabloid she was so shy she used to eat her lunch in a toilet stall inside the girls' bathroom. And I'm not even sure anyone would believe me if I told them that Taylor—perfect, gorgeous, A-list Taylor—used to have buckteeth. And I'm talking about serious, point-and-whisper-behind-her-back buckteeth. They were cute when she was little and got her plenty of TV commercial gigs, but she had to wear monster metal headgear for almost two years of middle school. It's funny to think about now that we're adults, but I bet she would agree that was the toughest time of her life. Yes, even after all the hell she's been through. I think it's because when you're a kid, you're still so soft, so vulnerable. Taylor hasn't been either of those things for a long, long time.

I hope it doesn't seem like I'm slamming Taylor, or that I'm jealous. Sure, I used to be when we were younger—I'll cop to it. As a teenager she was beautiful and blond, while I was, well, cookie-cutter Asian. Skinny, flat-chested, always too short, and stuck with a big moon-shaped face I absolutely hated. I'd see Taylor getting ready for a premiere, a stylist fluttering around her like a fairy godmother while a makeup artist covered up her zits with some high-tech airbrushing gizmo, and I'd wish just once someone would lavish that kind of attention on me. I used to feel that way, but not anymore. Everyone thinks they want to be famous, but that's only because they haven't seen what being a star is like close-up. And believe me, for all the glamour and hype, it's not as great as you'd think.

When I met Taylor, she still went by her real name: Maryanne Fedderbit. Yes, that's the name on her birth certificate, which sounds about as Hollywood as an Iowa cornfield. But back when we were in seventh grade, it sort of fit. Maryanne was going through an "awkward stage," according to her mom, Sheila. Mrs. Fedderbit tried to be cool by letting everyone, even her daughter, call her by her first name. But she was never, ever cool with me. Even then I thought she was a witch with a capital *B*, which was a pretty big insult by my geeky seventh-grade standards.

I still remember Maryanne—I mean Taylor—walking into class looking like she was being led to her own execution, her eyes darting around the room and her face deathly pale. If you squinted, you could see some of the things that landed her on *People* magazine's "50 Most Beautiful" list last year, but it was hard to put the pieces together back then.

Sure, she had the silky blond hair (a little darker and stuck in a prissy ponytail) and the enormous green eyes (which were, as I already mentioned, darting around like a crazy person's). But that all took a backseat to the stuff that was wrong. And there was a lot that was really, really wrong.

She was wearing a plaid skirt and this horrible blue sweater with a cartoon duck on the front. Seriously. A big yellow duck, like something you'd see on a baby. Oh, and don't forget the headgear, although Taylor would love it if you did. Go to Taylor's house in the Hollywood Hills now, and there are tons of pictures of her from magazine covers and movie posters, but you won't find a single one of her wearing her headgear or braces. She even tore her face out of all our old class photos, if you can believe it.

Anyway, Mrs. Simpson, our old gargoyle of an earth sciences teacher, made Taylor stand in front of the class so she could introduce her. That's the worst, and I know because I went through it myself two years earlier when my parents moved to Beverly Hills from San Francisco. I still remember looking out into this sea of cold, pitiless eyes and feeling like everyone was furiously hating me. Taylor must have felt the same way, because her face turned whiter and whiter the longer Mrs. Simpson yapped.

"And Maryanne comes to us from—where is it, sweetheart?" You could tell Mrs. Simpson was either having a good day or feeling sorry for Taylor, because she called her sweetheart. Usually she just yelled your full name. "ERIN KIM, where is your homework? Bring it up NOW," that sort of thing.

"I'm from Oxnard," Maryanne muttered, putting a hand over her braces as she opened her mouth. She spoke so softly I almost didn't hear her, but the kids at the front of the class sure did. From the back of the room I could see their shoulders shake as they tried to muffle their laughter. "Oxnard? *Posh!*" I heard Alexandra Waterman sneer.

Of *course* Alexandra looked down her nose at Oxnard, a little beach town up the coast. She thought anyplace that wasn't Beverly Hills or, like, Paris was hopelessly lame. Alexandra was one of those girls who begged her mommy for a Fendi purse and actually got it, and wore Seven jeans before anyone else knew they were trendy. Basically, if the girl could have had a designer label tattooed on her forehead, she would have.

When my parents moved to Beverly Hills, I thought it was going to be fun, like that old TV show *Beverly Hills, 90210,* where all the kids hang out at a diner and listen to live bands. Was I wrong. Most of the kids at my school were snobby and rude, always bragging about their parents' new Ferrari or their latest hiking trip to Peru. The others were socially retarded dorks or bullies who held down kids' heads in the toilet for fun. I kept to myself and stayed quiet, and as a result I got pretty much left alone. Sure, sometimes kids would make fun of me because I'm Korean, pulling at their eyelids to make them look slanted, but if I ignored them, eventually they forgot about me.

I could already tell it wouldn't be that easy for the new girl. There were just too many things to ridicule, the least of which was the ducky sweater. But mostly it was the expression on her face. She looked so scared, even I could tell it would be easy to torture her. She'd obviously never fight back. I almost felt sorry for her.

I say almost, because when Mrs. Simpson assigned her to sit next to me in the back of the room, I wanted to crawl under my desk and die. The absolute last thing I needed was to be associated with the class punching bag.

I stared at my pencil and prayed this pathetic loser didn't catch my eye or, worse, smile at me. I didn't really have close friends at school, just a few other outsiders I could eat lunch with, but I sure didn't want a friend if she was going to be walking anthrax.

And to think I was already embarrassed to be in this chick's zip code before she puked on my shoes.

I think it was just after lunch that Taylor threw up in class, right in the space between our two desks. At first I thought she was just leaning over to pick something up. But then I heard a gurgling noise, which would have been embarrassing enough because it was plenty loud. I wasn't the only person who turned and stared at Taylor, and I'm sure that didn't help.

She puked so violently that what was left of her lunch splattered all over the floor (and, as you know, my shoes) with this awful, liquidy splash. And then I smelled the puke. It was the nastiest odor you can imagine, like some sick experiment involving rotten meat, Brussels sprouts, and battery acid. I don't know what she had to eat at lunch, but it looked like vegetable soup with little bits of corn. Just remembering it now makes me feel queasy, and to this day I still can't eat certain kinds of soup.

Then, as everyone started yelling and running across the room with their hands over their faces, Taylor lowered her head onto her desk and started to cry. I'm not even sure anyone else heard her, what with everybody freaking out and Mrs. Simpson screaming, *"In your seats, now! Students, settle down!"* But I did. It was such a sad, broken sound, it made me want to cry a little, too.

Mrs. Simpson finally had the common sense to walk Taylor down to the nurse's office, and we didn't see the new girl for the rest of the day. But I knew that as bad as her first day of school was, her second day was going to be a lot worse. Already some of the bullies were coming up with nicknames for Taylor.

"Did you get a load of Malibu Barfie?" Alexandra cackled to her friends. "Must have been that vomitous outfit of hers. Made me want to throw up, anyway. And that headgear! She looks like a hockey goalie!" Cassie, a chubby blonde who followed Alexandra everywhere like a retarded puppy, just about fell out of her chair—she was fake laughing so hard, the creep.

But it was Roger Ott, the class thug, who was really psyched about Taylor's big purge. "Hey, I think we should call the new girl Feddervomit," he screeched, pointing at the puddle as the janitor covered it with red sawdust, then mopped it up.

I think everyone in class secretly hated Roger, who was as dense as he was big. Sometimes I'd see kids roll their eyes at his lamest jokes (and they were all pretty lame), but no one dared cross him. He'd been held back at least two years, and he was huge even for a kid his age. Roger was taller than Mrs. Simpson and bulky in that football player way, kinda fat but strong, too. You knew just by looking at him, with those squinty eyes and that slash of a mouth like crooked razor wire, that he was a bully. And now he'd set his sights on Taylor.

Yeah, it was already pretty clear that Taylor's first year at West-haven Middle School was gonna suck.

"She threw up in the class?" My mother stopped setting the dinner table for a minute and her eyes went wide. "Next to where you sit?"

"Yes, Mom, right next to my chair." My mom was from South Korea, and even though her English was really pretty good, sometimes I had to repeat things.

"Did someone take her to the doctor?" It was only five o'clock, but I could already smell dinner bubbling away in the kitchen. Steamed rice, of course, and *bulgogi*, which is this really spicy beef barbeque that was possibly the best thing my mom cooked. She did some American things, like hot dogs and chicken soup, but she mostly liked to cook the kinds of food she ate back in Seoul.

"I guess so. She didn't come to class today. I'm sure she'll be back tomorrow."

"Invite her over," Mom said in a voice that was definitely not asking a question. "Make a friend."

"I have friends," I muttered. What I really wanted to say was "Are you completely insane?" but then my mom would start lecturing me about respecting my elders and how my snotty attitude would never be tolerated where she came from, blah di blah di blah.

"Make another friend. You have a lot in common."

"Like what?" I knew I sounded pissed off, but I was. What could I possibly have in common with this stupid girl with the ducky sweater and the chunks of puke stuck in her headgear? I might not have been popular, but I wasn't a total loser, either.

"You're new to the school. So is she." My mom smiled. "She could be a new best friend. You never know until you try." She always liked any opportunity to use some American catchphrase, like "Just do it" or "Never let them see you sweat." When she first came to the States my mom learned a lot of English watching bad TV, and it showed.

"Fine, whatever." I figured it was easier to go along, then never do it and hope Mom forgot about it. I just couldn't bear the thought of adding one more thing to the list of stuff my mom and I fought about, because we fought about almost everything. She picked on me about how clean my room was, what I wore, and whether or not I spent enough time playing the cello, which I hated.

She just had no clue what it was like to be a kid in America, and she had all these psycho ideas about how I was supposed to behave and dress. The biggest brawl we ever had was when we went shopping for school clothes and she wouldn't let me buy jeans because they weren't "ladylike." Can you believe that? My dad finally broke down and brought home a pair for me, just plain old Levi's from Target, and told my mom that all the guys he worked with at his aerospace company let their girls wear jeans. After that, she finally broke down. But if it weren't for my dad, my mom would have been sending me to school wearing crap like Taylor's dumb-ass ducky sweater.

Mom looked at me, hard, like she could see right into my

brain. "If you don't make plans, I will call the school and ask them to give me her mother's number and I will make plans." God, it was like she was psychic or something whenever I wanted to disobey her. I sometimes think she had some sort of superspy microchip installed in my brain so she could read my thoughts. You laugh, but if it existed, my mom would've been first in line to buy it.

"Okay! I've got homework," I said, pushing away from the dinner table and grabbing my backpack. I ran to my room, but even locking the door behind me, I couldn't block out the sick feeling I had in my gut. This rotten new girl was going to completely screw up my life.

When I walked into class, Taylor was already in her seat. Her outfit was more normal than the previous day's fashion disaster, just jeans and a T-shirt, but it didn't make any difference. Everyone was pointing and whispering about her, and it was like that the whole day.

I knew I had to talk to her at some point, but I just couldn't do it. I tried to sit near her in every class we had together, but whenever I thought about talking to her, Roger would be turning around in his seat and sticking his finger down his throat, making gagging noises. And then at lunch, when I thought I might casually talk to her in the cafeteria line, she disappeared. Poof. Just gone. Years later she told me she would eat lunch in a bathroom stall every day, her feet up on the seat so no one could see them.

Finally at 2:25 I realized I had exactly five minutes to get this playdate crap over with and I still hadn't done it. So I tore a scrap of paper out of my binder, scribbled "Want to hang out?" on it, and slid it to her.

Taylor just looked at it, folded it in half, and looked at Mr. Davis, our English teacher, at the front of the room. She didn't look at me, didn't take out her pen, nothing.

I couldn't believe it. Here was the school's biggest loser of all time, and she was blowing me off! I was just about to tear out another scrap of paper and write "My MOM made me ask because she felt SORRY for you, you dumb-ass!" but just then, she turned, looked at me, and nodded. She looked scared, like she was waiting for bad news.

Only then did the truth hit me. She probably thought I was setting her up for a practical joke, because who in their right mind would want to hang out with her, especially now?

That Saturday I pushed the buzzer to Taylor's apartment and waited while my mom watched from the car. She was a little pissed that I didn't invite Taylor over to our house, which would have been "proper manners," but I had convinced her that Taylor really wanted me to come over. The truth is, I never liked having kids over to my house. Other kids had PlayStations and their own computers and TVs, but my big sister, Victoria, and I didn't have anything like that. There was one TV in the living room, which my mom always had set to the Korean-language station or CNN, and we couldn't even touch my dad's computer except to do homework. God forbid we found ourselves in a chat room or surfing the Web for "dirty smut," as my mom liked to call it.

When we lived in San Francisco, I invited one of my friends over and thought everything was fine until the next day, when she told everyone we had stinky roots in jars all around the house like witches and that all our furniture looked like salvage from a Chinese restaurant. It was a total lie. Most of our furniture was from IKEA, and she was so dumb she didn't even realize that kimchi isn't a root at all, just this super-spicy pickled cabbage you can buy at any grocery store. And it wasn't all over the house anyway. My mom had a little refrigerator that was just for kimchi so we could keep it at the right temperature and it didn't stink up the other stuff in our regular fridge. A lot of Korean families have kimchi refrigerators, so it was no big deal. But that was the last time I invited anyone over, no matter how much my mom complained.

"Hi." It was Taylor's voice on the intercom. She still sounded kind of nervous, which came as no surprise. All week long the teasing had been getting worse. One day I had suggested to the kids I ate lunch with that we invite Taylor to sit with us. They looked at me like I'd lost my friggin' mind. "No way," said Amy, a frizzy-haired girl who sometimes helped me with my social studies homework. "Like, Roger only just stopped picking on me when she got here. It's her turn now."

I knocked on Taylor's apartment door, and a woman opened it. Her face was almost as red as her hair and she was dripping with sweat. From her goofy pink shorts and the towel around her neck, I guessed she'd been exercising. "You must be Erin," she said, waving me inside. "I'm Maryanne's mom—you can call me Sheila. Anyway, welcome to Chez Fedderbit!"

Calling the place "chez" anything seemed much too fancy, because the apartment was small and dark and smelled musty. People think you have to be rich to live in Beverly Hills, but the truth is, a lot of people rent run-down apartments in the city just so they can say they live in the 90210. Looking around, I wondered if Taylor wished she still lived in Oxnard. None of the furniture matched, and the orange shag carpeting was so ugly it was hard to look at.

Taylor popped up from the sofa. "Hi," she said, again.

"Hi."

And the conversation died right there.

Sheila looked at her daughter like she was the most pathetic person on earth. "Maryanne, why don't you show your friend around your room so I can get back to my workout tape? I swear, if I didn't know better, I'd think you were slow."

I think right about then was when I started hating Sheila.

After Taylor showed me her room, which was just as dark and small as the rest of the place, we still didn't have a lot to talk about.

"Do you like horses?" Taylor asked.

"Not really." I'd ridden one once and hated every minute. My horse kept wandering off the trail to eat stuff and it smelled awful, like hay and crap. Which makes sense, I guess. Of course, Taylor was obsessed with them, even knew the kind she wanted to get someday. A palomino.

"Do you collect anything? I collect teddy bears."

She pointed to a sad little pile of stuffed animals in the corner next to her bed, and I have to say, I thought that was the most retarded thing I'd ever seen. Teddy bears are fine, if you're six. But we were practically teenagers.

"I have a cat named Bree. And I Rollerblade," I said, trying hard to resist the urge to call my mom and beg for her to pick me up. "And I play the cello."

"Oh." Taylor looked disappointed. "Want to play cards? Or Uno?"

This was worse than visiting my great-aunt at her nursing home in Long Beach. "Is there anything else to do?" I looked at my watch, and couldn't believe that just fifteen minutes had passed. My mom said she'd pick me up at four, which was three hours and forty-five minutes from now.

Taylor looked at her hands. "Want to see my portfolio?"

"What's that?" It sounded weird, but at least it was better than Uno.

"I used to be a model," she said. She reached under the bed, pulling out a thick binder and flopping it onto the covers.

I almost started laughing, because I thought for sure she was making this up. If Taylor was a model, then I was a world-class brain surgeon. But then she opened the binder.

Taylor flipped through the photos, and there were a lot of them. Taylor as a little girl in a yellow swimsuit next to a bottle of sunscreen. Taylor as a baby gobbling up a spoonful of strained peas. Taylor modeling a goofy sweatshirt, Taylor naked next to a bottle of baby lotion.

"I did this one for Coppertone, and this was a national ad for Johnson & Johnson. I was in a commercial for them, too. Sometimes you can still see it on TV."

"Wow," I said, flipping back through the pictures. "That's really cool." And it really was.

"My mom says I made a lot of money, but we can't spend most of it until I'm eighteen," Taylor said. "I'm going to use it to go to college. I want to study drama."

Taylor smiled then, and for a minute I could see that beneath the headgear she was actually kind of pretty.

"You want to be an actress?" I could just imagine what

my mom would say if I told her that. I'd be living out of a suitcase under a freeway overpass before I could even finish the sentence. And even then, my mom would make sure I packed my cello.

"I'm already an actress, really. I did a lot of commercials."

"That sounds fun."

Taylor's eyes lit up. "Someday I'm going to win an Oscar, I know it. I was born to be an actor. My mom even says the first time she took me to an audition, everyone in the room said I was the most talented kid there. It's all about being able to draw on your life experience. You have to show people your heart, show that you know what it's like to hurt." The light in Taylor's eyes abruptly dimmed. "That's easy for me."

I nodded, not really knowing what to say. I wasn't that passionate about anything. Sure, I'd fantasized about being a famous actress, but I didn't really think about it beyond being loved by adoring fans and looking gorgeous. Taylor, though, she had it all worked out.

"Maybe later we can watch my reel," Taylor suggested. "If you want to."

"Sure, why not?" This was kind of fun. Even though I lived in Beverly Hills, I didn't actually know any real actors. They send their kids to hoity-toity private schools, so it's not like I took classes with celebrity spawn or anything. Sometimes you'd see an old star like Cher or Pierce Brosnan picking up groceries, but that wasn't very exciting. And it's weird, because most of the time, unless someone's a paparazzo or a huge fan, no one who lives in L.A. ever bothers the stars. I think it's because we all know celebrities are just trying to go about their business like the rest of us, and you're supposed to pretend you aren't really seeing them in their sweatpants with no makeup on.

But here was Taylor, with this big crazy secret and a trust fund to boot. I guess I must have looked pretty shocked by everything, because Taylor reached out and slammed her portfolio shut with this miserable look on her face. "You think it's stupid, don't you?" She said it like it wasn't a question, but a statement of fact.

"It's not that. You just seem so . . . shy. Like on the first day of class."

As soon as the words escaped my lips, I regretted them. Taylor crossed her arms over her chest, and her mouth settled into a scowl. "Even big stars get stage fright, you know," Taylor said, sounding more than a little defensive. "And I hadn't gotten a lot of sleep the night before. Sometimes that makes me feel . . . queasy."

"I'm not criticizing you," I said quickly. "I'm just saying I thought you'd be more out there, being an actress and all."

"School is different. With a camera and a director, you have a job to do. You have a script. Everything's all mapped out. Acting is a lot easier than real life." When she spoke again, she covered her mouth with her hand. She hadn't done it all day, not until just that moment. "But I'm taking a break from acting," she muttered.

"She'll work again. As soon as we straighten out those horse teeth." Sheila was leaning in the doorway, wiping sweat from her face.

Out of the corner of my eye I could see Taylor's spine stiffen. Sheila reached over her daughter's shoulder and opened the book to one of the baby pictures. "That was a cute one. Never should have let those teeth come in, should have just capped them right from the get-go and called it a day. You might have gotten a series then. But blame your father. That's from his side of the family. Maryanne, did you ask your little friend if she was hungry?"

Taylor and I both shook our heads.

"Swear to God, you have the manners of a barnyard animal. Well, if your friend gets hungry, you know where the peanut butter and crackers are. But I don't want you pigging out. Once the pounds go on, they're hell to get off," she said, laughing as she squeezed her thigh, which looked pretty skinny to me.

I watched Sheila walk out of the room. "Wow. Your mom was kind of harsh."

Taylor shrugged. "She says she just wants me to give a dose of reality. Because no one ever tells the truth in this town."

"You don't have to be mean to be honest." In what alternate reality is telling someone they have horse teeth constructive criticism?

"She says she's helping me toughen up. It's working great, huh?" Taylor made a face that told me it really, really wasn't. "Are you sure you don't want to play Uno?"

I was, but we played anyway. All I could think about was how my own mom suddenly didn't seem so horrible to me anymore. Really, when I compared my life with Taylor's, it didn't seem bad at all.

After that, Taylor and I found out we did have a few things in common, like we both loved Mexican food and 'NSync. (This was seventh grade, okay? Like you didn't love them back then.) And surprisingly, Taylor actually had a pretty good sense of humor. She could do a dead-on impersonation of Roger, right down to his walk, which was like a limping elephant's but less graceful.

That Monday at school, it was a lot harder to listen to Roger and the other cretins make fun of Taylor. So at lunch, I made my decision. I would convince her to eat lunch with me, even if no one wanted to sit with us, and my so-called friends pretended we didn't exist. When I look back now, it doesn't seem like such a big deal, but then it felt like I was walking in front of a speeding Metrolink train with my eyes closed. Like I was crazy and damn near suicidal.

"Um, okay," she said, her eyes darting in that nervous way of hers. I don't think she had completely ruled out the possibility of betrayal.

"Monday's taco day," I said in my most encouraging voice. "It practically tastes like real food. Kind of."

Almost the second we set our trays down at a table, one so far in the back of the room it was practically on the lawn outside the building, it started. I hadn't even taken a bite of my taco when I looked up to see Roger hovering over us, that nasty slit of a mouth upturned into something resembling a smile.

"Well, if it isn't Feddervomit! Are you going to be able to keep all that down, or should I eat it for you?" Roger reached onto Taylor's tray and scooped up a handful of fruit salad. Then, holding it next to his face, he pretended to puke, dropping the grapes and cantaloupe onto the floor with a sickening plop. "Ooops, looks like Feddervomit couldn't hold it!"

Taylor said nothing, but I could see tears welling up in her eyes.

"Cut it out, Roger," I muttered.

"What are you, her bodyguard? She paying you now?" Roger asked in a mocking voice. "I bet you're cheap, like everything else they make in China."

Taylor's mouth dropped open, but I wasn't surprised. Roger was the king of the cheap shot, even if it meant being a racist pig.

I figured it was time to play Taylor's one ace. "You know something? Maryanne's an actress. She's been in commercials."

It wasn't only Roger and his buddies who laughed when I said that, and I immediately regretted it.

"What commercials did you do? Pepto-Bismol? Adult diapers?" Roger cackled.

Taylor's face was so red I thought she might explode. I felt instantly awful. Why hadn't I known that Roger would find a way to make something cool sound embarrassing?

"What's going on over here?" It was Mr. Weil, the art teacher. Mondays he was also the lunch monitor, and I'd never been so glad to see him.

"Can I be excused?" Taylor said quickly, jumping up from the bench.

"Me, too," I said. I wasn't about to get left alone with Roger, even if that meant I wouldn't get to eat lunch that day.

Mr. Weil nodded, and we ran out of the cafeteria, the sound of laughter echoing off the walls behind us.

In the bathroom, I checked the stalls to make sure we were alone. "I am so sorry. I thought that telling him about your commercials would shut him up."

"It's no big deal," Taylor muttered, but I knew that it was. Her work was the one thing she felt proud of, and now, thanks to me, some nimrod was coming up with a whole goody bag of insults about it.

"God, I hate him!" I said, tearing a paper towel into shreds just to keep my hands busy. "*Hate* him!"

"Me, too." Taylor sat on the edge of the sink, looking exhausted. "I'm sorry you got pulled into this. He shouldn't have said that stuff about China. That was horrible."

"I'm not even Chinese. I'm Korean. Man, I can't believe he's so stupid he can't get his racist slurs right."

Taylor smiled, but weakly. It was a long moment before she spoke again. "I don't know what to do, Erin. I really don't. Everybody hates my guts but you."

Her voice sounded so hopeless and lost, I stopped tearing up the paper towel. I hardly knew Taylor, but I knew enough to think that if this went on, day in and day out, something really bad was going to happen. Something that couldn't be fixed. No one can be expected to get up each morning and go to school knowing that she is going to get kicked around, ridiculed, and humiliated, and there's nothing she can do about it.

"Look. We're going to come up with a plan, okay?" I said. Taylor barely nodded, looking at her shoes. "Okay? You have to help me out here. I can't do this alone." I made my voice sound as much like my mother's as I could, the one she used when I had no say in the matter. Which was the voice she used most of the time.

It seemed to work. Taylor looked me in the eye, and for once she didn't look away. "Okay. I mean, it can't get any worse anyway."

For some reason, I started thinking about Taylor's portfolio. She always looked happy and confident in her pictures, nothing like the frightened kid standing in front of me. "You're a good actress, right?"

Taylor looked kind of nervous, but nodded. "I think so."

"It's time for you to act like the person you want to be. Act like someone who isn't the least bit afraid of Roger Ott."

Taylor thought about it. "I'm not sure I'm that good. That's, like, Oscar-winning good."

One of my mom's stupid TV catchphrases, one she used when she was trying to be funny (which wasn't often, believe me), popped into my head. I paused for dramatic effect. "Whatchoo talkin' 'bout, Willis?"

At last, Taylor actually smiled. "Okay. So what are we going to do?"

We came up with a lot of lousy ideas, crazy ones, but it wasn't until right before the bell rang that we decided on a plan. We knew it could backfire; we knew it didn't make a lot of sense. But we were desperate enough to try it.

And the best part? Taylor proved to everyone, me included, that she wasn't just a good actress. She was a great one.

Tuesday was meat loaf day, and Taylor and I loaded up our trays with so much crappy cafeteria food we could barely lift them. I got two Jell-O desserts, a slice of cake, extra green beans, and two cartons of milk, plus extra gravy on my meat loaf. Taylor got pretty much the same thing, but with a chocolate pudding instead of the cake. We looked like pigs, but we didn't care.

"Well, looks like Feddervomit wants to barf up a lot! Man, everybody stand back—she's gonna blow chunks big-time!" Roger roared as he looked over our trays. It took him even less time to find us today, since we had picked a table right in the middle of the cafeteria.

Roger picked up Taylor's chocolate pudding and, once again, pretended to barf it up. Even I could tell the joke was getting old; his buddies laughed halfheartedly at best.

I felt Taylor squeeze my hand beneath the table. It was go time.

"No, no, *no*!" I yelled at Roger with the kind of voice you'd use on a naughty dog. "Don't you know *anything*?"

I don't know how long it took me to notice it, but the cafeteria had gone deadly silent. Everyone was looking at us, frozen in midchew. "Binging and purging is *very* Beverly Hills. In fact, your mama does it, right?"

Taylor stood up. "Jeez, you'd think repeating seventh grade so many times, you'd pick up a few things," she chirped while Roger stared at her in shock. "Here, let me show you how to throw up. I'm really good at it."

Taylor picked up her green beans and bent at the waist, clutching her stomach and moaning. Slowly, she let the green beans dribble to the floor as she made the most disgusting retching sounds I'd ever heard. Right away you could tell she'd be a good actress, at least in horror movies.

"What is wrong with you? You're totally stupid!" Roger said in a squeaky voice, but no one was paying attention to him. For once, Taylor and I were the center of attention, and it wasn't such a bad thing.

"See, Roger, if you knew anything, you'd know it's a slow, gradual movement," I said, making some revolting noises of my own as I let my meat loaf plop onto the floor.

Taylor and I looked at each other, and that was it. We started giggling, and when we saw the frightened looks on everyone's faces, we just laughed harder. Cackling like lunatics, we picked up the food on our trays and tossed it onto the floor. Taylor even did a little bit of her imitation of Roger, though she was laughing so hard I'm not sure anyone recognized it.

For the record, I'd like to say I wasn't the person who threw an apple at Roger's head. But when we saw it bounce off that thick skull of his, we looked at each other and just knew what we had to do without saying a word. We both reached onto our trays and grabbed up enormous fistfuls of food, green beans and gravy and God knows what else, and pelted Roger with it all, full force.

Of course, in our enthusiasm we hadn't factored in an important little detail. Roger was a big guy. Really big. And now he was really mad. And yelling his head off, he lurched forward, his long gorilla arms reaching for us.

We were running, but I could feel his hand tugging on the back of my shirt, and when I looked to the side I saw him clawing at Taylor's hair, which slipped through his fingers like silk thread. But he was already tightening his grip on my shirt, twisting it with his hand. And I knew he wasn't going to let Taylor get away so easily, either.

Luckily for us, that was the exact moment when Roger's sneakers slid into the pudding.

Boom! Roger went down hard. By this time, the food fight had started in earnest around us. Lunch bags and milk cartons whizzed through the air like grenades, and kids were screaming their heads off, so I never heard the crack. But I wasn't the only one to hear Roger scream. And I wasn't the only one to stare, in shock, when he started to cry. I don't mean the kind of quiet sniffling you see at funerals or weddings, either. I mean sobbing like a little kid who skinned his knee, snot running down his face and these wounded-animal noises coming out of the back of his throat.

"You broke my leg!" he wailed.

I almost walked over to him, but just then Mrs. Jetter, the Spanish teacher, grabbed Taylor and me by the arms to drag us to the principal's office. We never saw the rest of the food fight, or the paramedics who came to take Roger to the hospital. But everyone in the school had it in their heads that the whole mess was our fault, not Roger's or even that unknown apple thrower's. Not that we minded.

Sitting outside Principal Zinner's office, I squeezed Taylor's hand. "That was so cool," I whispered. "I mean, I feel bad about Roger, but still."

Taylor grinned back. I don't think I'd ever seen her smile, not like that, anyway. You know the look. It's the one you've seen on the cover of magazines and on movie posters. She seemed genuinely happy, but there was something else. She looked triumphant.

"Yeah, sure. I feel kinda bad about that, too. But otherwise?" she whispered back. "It was the coolest."

I was feeling pretty good until the principal called us in. I'd never been in his office before. After all, I'd always been a Goody Two-shoes, getting mostly straight As and winning awards for my science projects at the county fair. When I saw his big bald forehead wrinkled up disapprovingly, it suddenly struck me that, as much fun as we'd had, we were in trouble. Big trouble.

"Sit down, girls," Principal Zinner said, his voice rumbling and deep. Mrs. Jetter stood by his side, looking more worried than angry.

Principal Zinner started talking about things I hadn't even thought about, like how much the school would have to pay in overtime to the janitors cleaning up our mess, and how upset our parents were going to be about this. Just thinking about what my mom and dad were going to say made me want to throw up for real.

I was busy calculating how many years my parents were going to ground me for when Mrs. Jetter interrupted the principal, who seemed to be building up to some big, dramatic finale in which Taylor and I were going to be burned at the stake.

"Principal Zinner, I don't know the whole story, and what the girls did was obviously wrong," she said quietly. "But I will say they've never been a problem in my class. Roger Ott, though, he's a different story. I know he's been teasing Maryanne, and I'm certain he has something to do with this. When he gets back from the hospital, his first stop is to visit you."

Principal Zinner blinked quietly, like he'd hit his head on something and didn't know where he was. He looked at us, then at Mrs. Jetter. And sighed. Then he sent us back to class with one week of detention, which was what most kids got for skipping class and other minor stuff. I swore that from then on I was going to become Mrs. Jetter's best Spanish speaker, even better than the Mexican kid in my class whose first word was *agua*.

We got off easy, but even if we hadn't, even if we'd been suspended or forced to clean the whole cafeteria by ourselves with a single Q-tip, I think it would have been worth it. Because after that day, our whole lives changed.

Instead of being the classroom puker and the Chinese girl (why could no one remember Korean? Was it that hard?), for the rest of the year we were the girls who broke Roger Ott's leg and started a food fight in the cafeteria. We weren't pathetic losers anymore. We were, well, troublemakers. Bad girls.

It didn't make us any more popular. But no joke, I think people started respecting us. They didn't talk over me when I spoke in class, or bump into Taylor in the halls without apologizing. Roger didn't insult Taylor anymore, at least not to her face. And that was absolutely fine with us.

The funny thing was, Taylor liked being thought of as dangerous a lot more than I did. She started walking straighter, laughing louder. After a month or two, I realized I hadn't seen her eyes darting around in a long time.

"You were right, you know, about acting like the person I wanted to be," she said to me one day. "But the cool thing is, once you do, and you see that people believe it, you actually become that. And now, well"—she grinned—"I'm kinda fearless."

I wish I could have said to her that I was, too. I look back on that day in the cafeteria and think it was the one time when I really stood up for myself. Taylor walked away from our little adventure completely transformed. All I got out of it was detention.

But sometimes I wonder if that day, that pivotal triumph over Roger Ott, was the beginning of all Taylor's problems. Maybe if that food fight had never happened, she wouldn't have been crazy-brave enough to do the things she did later, when the paparazzi were watching. Then again, if Roger Ott hadn't pushed her to go a little nuts, maybe she'd never have had the guts to go as far as she's gone, and the fans wouldn't love her as much.

All I know for sure is, from then on, that shy, scared girl with the darting eyes disappeared forever. And that could never be a bad thing.

Chapter Two

People think I'm going to parties all the time, but I'm not really like that. I'd much rather spend time with my friends watching DVDs at home or bad reality TV. We order pizzas, hang out, catch up, just like anyone else. Parties are fun, sure. But my friends, they're everything to me.

—TAYLOR CHRISTENSEN in *Teen People* magazine

I hardly noticed, but by ninth grade Taylor's braces had done their dirty work. One day in November she walked onto the school grounds transformed, a butterfly sprung from her steely cocoon. No wires, no headgear, no more metal mouth. She was beautiful, and no one could deny it. And from that moment onward, everyone started treating Taylor differently.

See, beautiful people, truly beautiful people, have this thing about them that makes others want to be near them. People want to talk about them, analyze them, stare at them like they're exotic animals in the zoo. They don't have to be celebrities, either. That year, our first at Beverly Hills–Glenoaks High School (we just called it Bev Hills), was when I got a taste of what it was like to be in a star's orbit, even though no one knew she was going to be a celebrity back then. But already people were paying a lot more attention to Taylor (who, thanks to a court order her mom filed, was no longer stuck with the craptastic name Maryanne Fedderbit). Some of the attention was good, some of it bad.

The bad was that even at Bev Hills, Alexandra was still the queen bee of the popular girls. Amazingly, she and her suck-up groupies had become even cattier since middle school. Instead of hissing "retard" and "geek" in the hallways, they moved on to sneering "slut" and "whore" at Taylor. Which was stupid, because until Taylor lost the headgear, she wasn't getting a lot of attention from guys.

Personally, I'd rather just tell you about the good part. People started saying hi to us in the halls, which was a huge shock after Westhaven. Sometimes kids would save seats for us, and guys were always offering to do Taylor's homework. And then there were Kelly and Jenna.

I hadn't really noticed that Kelly and Jenna had been sitting at the same table as Taylor and I during lunch. Thanks to all the crap we used to get in middle school, Taylor and I had gotten really good at tuning people out, so much so that sometimes people would have to repeat things a couple of times before I'd realize I was being spoken to. So I was a little surprised when Jenna slid down the cafeteria bench and tapped her finger on my lunch tray.

"Hey, are you guys trying out for cheerleading?" she asked, tucking a strand of red and black hair behind one ear. Jenna was all-out goth, with black lipstick and black nails and a black leather jacket.

"No, are you?" I sneered in my most sarcastic voice. I naturally assumed she was trying to insult me. Like I looked like the cheerleading type, come on!

"Yeah, actually," she said, serious as hell.

"We want to bring down a misogynistic, frivolous institution from the inside," Kelly added. If you didn't know Kelly and Jenna, it was hard to see what they had in common, because Kelly wasn't goth at all. She was strictly a jeans and T-shirts girl—straight auburn hair, no makeup. But never trust a plain brown wrapper. If anything, Kelly was more of a rebel than Jenna.

"And there's always the bonus of making Alexandra miserable," Jenna said. I knew enough about Jenna and Kelly to know Alexandra was about as mean to them as she was to Taylor. She called them the "bull dykes" and said Jenna looked like the lead singer of My Chemical Romance.

"I like the way you think," Taylor said, smiling.

"Probably because we *do* think," Kelly said. "Unlike everyone else at this school."

Taylor and I looked at each other. These two girls were going to be fun. Trouble maybe, but fun.

After that, we all started eating lunch together, and then hanging out on weekends. When Kelly and Jenna made the cheerleading team (which predictably made Alexandra, who got on the team only after another girl dropped out, absolutely furious), we even went to see them cheer, knowing they'd sneak in some slightly obscene hand gestures or make faces at Alexandra behind her back during halftime.

Taylor and I finally had our own clique, our own gang. Even though sometimes I missed it just being Taylor and me, mostly I was thrilled to know I had these two cool girls in my corner. So when my life got turned upside down, I was so grateful Jenna had tapped on my lunch tray all those months earlier. I couldn't have known it then, but the day was coming when I'd need all the support I could get.

"I can't believe Greg Fromer has a crush on me. *Greg Fromer!*"
Taylor was combing her hair in front of her vanity mirror, angrily
pulling at a stubborn knot. For the last year we'd been fixing up
her bedroom, and I no longer minded hanging out there, even
with Sheila around. The teddy bear collection was hidden in a box
in the closet (and if you're wondering, yes, she still has it), and now
Taylor had bright pink walls and band posters instead. We'd even
bought old furniture at Goodwill and painted it black and white.
I'm sure she's thrown all of it away since then, but we loved it at
the time.

"Why is that so unbelievable?" asked Kelly, sitting cross-legged
on the floor. "He's a walking hormone."

"But this is the guy who followed me around school at West-
haven making metal-mouth jokes," Taylor said. "Is he freakin' retarded?"

"Well, yes," said Kelly. "You're just figuring that out?"

"I wish I needed braces," Jenna sighed from where she was
flipping through Taylor's CD collection. "They would go perfectly with the eyebrow piercing I want."

"You're insane," Taylor said.

"I'm not the one with a suck-ass Maroon 5 album," Jenna
shot back.

"I'm totally going out with him. Just so I can dump him,"
Taylor said.

"Make him buy you a nice dinner. And flowers," Kelly
suggested.

"Then stomp on his heart like a grape. Love that," Jenna added.

"Don't be so hard on Greg. He's sickeningly in love with you," I said, squeezing a pink-and-purple pillow to my chest.

"I know." Taylor grinned. "That's the best part."

I hated talking to Taylor about boys. Even after Westhaven, I had pretty much forgiven most of the jerks at school and could honestly say some of the guys were pretty nice. One boy in my chem class, Brandon, was even insanely cute. But did I ever get asked out? No. At best most guys treated me like one of the gang. Probably because I looked so much like a damn boy. It didn't help that my mom wouldn't let me wear makeup or anything she considered sexy. Which included sleeveless shirts.

But since she lost the braces, Taylor was knee-deep in testosterone. The thing was, she had become a heartless, malicious tease. Cruel wasn't even an overstatement. Alexandra had it all wrong when she called Taylor a slut. When it came to guys, she was pure bitch.

She'd wink at a guy in the hallway, then make fun of him mercilessly once he was out of earshot. She'd go out with guys for a few weeks, wait for them to fall madly in love with her, then dump them cold. She'd make them do stupid things to prove their love for her, like wear a bow tie and suspenders to class, then laugh at them when they tried to kiss her. As far as she was concerned, all the guys at school were worse than dirt. And she treated them that way.

I tossed the pink-and-purple pillow to Kelly, who promptly stuck it under her butt. I had no great love or anything for Greg Fromer, but I still hated hearing Taylor's date-and-dump plots. I mean, the gory details of how she blew through guys like Kleenex didn't make me feel any better about my status as the dateless wonder.

"Forget Greg. How's work?" I asked. Almost the day after Taylor got her braces off, Sheila had driven her to a modeling agency. It figured. Sheila always seemed a lot more interested in her daughter when she thought she could make a buck off her.

"I'm only doing a little catalog modeling," Taylor said, carefully putting mascara on her top lashes. She'd only done one photo shoot, but she'd picked up a ton of hints from the makeup artist there, like using blush to make her face look thinner and how a little white eye pencil makes your eyes "pop." "I told my agent I'd only work for her if she got me a theatrical agent, too, for acting. Sheila about had a fit, you know."

"Why? Doesn't she want you to be an actress?" Kelly asked, absentmindedly painting a toenail black using a felt-tip pen.

"Oh, definitely. There's a lot more money in it than modeling, so that makes Sheila happy. But she doesn't want me turning down any jobs, whether they're modeling or acting. She totally doesn't get that I need the right kind of exposure. National commercials, not just regional crap."

"Can't she see you're a star, dammit?" Jenna howled, banging her fist on the floor.

It was weird to hear Taylor talking about "the industry" (as she liked to call it). It seemed so foreign and scary to me, but she loved everything about it. Talking about "the trades" (really boring daily newspapers about the movie business) and "weekend grosses" (what a movie made over the weekend) was a lot more interesting to her than talking about the boys at school, even the ones I thought were cute.

I hopped off the bed. "I should call my mom," I said. "She wants me home for dinner."

"I wish you could stay." Taylor made a frowny face. Sometimes she still did things that made her seem like a little kid, like sulking when she was mad or making faces. It was funny, because Taylor had hit puberty (and *hard*) in the last year. She hadn't grown much taller, but she was filling out a 34C bra. Oh, like you thought the boys just liked her for her nice new teeth? Please. Sheila actually made Taylor wrap an Ace bandage around her chest when she went to the modeling agency so she'd look younger. But with a little makeup she definitely looked her age, whereas I looked like I was still twelve. I didn't even need to wear a bra, but I did anyway.

"I wish I could stay, too," I sighed. Even eating Sheila's crummy casseroles was better than going home these days. The situation between my mom and me had escalated from mild mutual irritation to full-scale warfare. After pushing me so hard to become friends with Taylor, she started griping about her plenty after the food fight. Like we were the bad guys in that scenario.

The funny thing is, Taylor really liked my mom. The few times I had her over, she followed my mom around the house, complimenting her taste in wallpaper and her cooking. At first I thought she was just being a suck-up, but even when we were alone, she went on and on about her. For whatever reason, Taylor was my mom's biggest fan.

"I know you two don't get along, but I so wish Sheila was even a little like your mom," Taylor had said as we sat in my TV-less, computerless room. "Your mom is a really positive person, you know. It's pretty impressive to think she came all this way to a foreign country where she didn't even know the language to make a life for herself." I kept waiting for the sarcasm, the punch line, but it never came.

Of course, I never had the heart to tell Taylor the things Mom said about her when she wasn't there. I mean, I was glad one of us loved my mom so much.

My mom was no fan of Sheila, either. The first time Sheila came to our house to pick up Taylor, she was wearing a pair of hip-hugger jeans and a tank top that showed her belly button. My mom hated her instantly. It didn't matter that I did, too. Mom kept saying corny things like "Apple doesn't fall far from tree, Erin." She actually thought Taylor was going to end up becoming just like her mom, a "woman of loose morals, like the 'Pretty Woman.'" And nothing I said would convince her otherwise.

When my mom came to pick me up from Taylor's, it was the same old crap. "What did you do all day with that Maryanne?" my mother said with a scowl.

"Her name's Taylor now," I sighed. She could remember every little thing she didn't like about the girl, but her name? Forget about it.

"I don't care. I don't like that girl, Erin. *Mun jei ah.*" A trouble-maker.

Sometimes, hearing Taylor talk about how she was going to tear some poor guy apart for sport, I kind of agreed with her. As much as I loved Taylor, she had started doing stuff that really bugged me. But at least I still liked her more than I liked my mom. So I just didn't say anything, and we drove most of the way home in silence. As usual.

———

"Erin, time for dinner," my sister, Victoria, yelled through my bedroom door. It was a Wednesday night, so that meant Mom was probably making something gross, like chicken cacciatore.

"In a minute!" I yelled back. Taylor had just called, and she was squealing so loud, I thought I'd never get my hearing back. Whatever had happened, it was big.

Victoria stuck her head into my room. "Mom's gonna freak. She's in a crappy mood, I'm warning you." Victoria sometimes bugged me, but ever since she got into UCLA she'd been a lot nicer. I'm sure it had something to do with her knowing she'd be moving out of the house soon, which must have been a huge relief even if it meant living in some crappy dorm. But I think even she could tell things were so bad between me and Mom that somebody had to run interference. Dad sure wasn't up to the task.

I nodded at Victoria but didn't hang up. "Make it quick, Taylor, really quick," I muttered into the receiver.

"I got an audition! For a movie!"

"Are you serious? What is it, who do you play, oh my *God*!"

Now there was a banging on the door. Mom.

"Dinner, *now!*"

"Taylor, I'll call you back, gotta go," I whispered, then stuffed the phone under my pillow and picked up a book.

Just then the door opened. "What are you doing in here?" Mom looked pissed. She worked as a real estate agent, and it had been a while since she'd made a sale, so I knew it wasn't entirely about me.

"Reading," I said.

"No, you weren't," Mom snapped back, taking the book out of my hands and turning it right side up. Oops. "You were talking on the phone. *Eom ma mal jom deul eo ra.*"

I wanted to tell my mom I'd start respecting her when she respected me, but I didn't say anything. I figured lying more would just get me into bigger trouble.

"When I say it's dinnertime, you come to dining room. No more phone for rest of week."

"Mom!" I was truly going to explode if I couldn't call Taylor back. I mean, it was one thing when we were just sitting on the phone talking about Justin Timberlake (oh, I'll admit it, big crush there), but this was serious.

"Keep sassing me, no phone for month."

You've got to understand, I was so angry I just couldn't hold it in. My words leaped out of my mouth, as if I had Tourette's syndrome and no control over myself. "God, I hate you," I hissed.

My mother just stared at me for a long, awful moment. I think she was waiting for me to apologize. And I wanted to, I really did. But I was still so mad at her. She was always on me to study more, practice the cello more, be more like my sister, and I was tired. Tired of not being what she wanted me to be, and tired of her hating my best friend, the one person in the world who actually understood me.

Basically, I was tired of being a big, stinking disappointment.

"Dinner," Mom said simply, and walked out of the room.

After dinner, during which no one talked and we all ate as fast as we could without choking to death, I tried to make a quick escape. "May I be excused?" I asked.

"*An dwue*," my mother said. So I sat and watched as Victoria and my dad drifted away to the living room, and then as my mom cleared the table, dish by dish. Finally, she sat down at the table across from me. She crossed her hands in front of her and stared at them for a long time. My mom was the kind of person who was always doing something—cleaning, cooking, making phone calls—so to see her so still and silent was strange. And I knew it was a bad, bad sign.

"You know the phone is a privilege and not a right, yes? We have talked about this?"

Actually, I thought a phone pretty much was a right. I mean, I was the only kid I knew who didn't have a cell phone, for God's sake. Giving me a landline seemed like the least my parents could do. "It was an important call," I said, crossing my arms over my chest.

"What was so important? Someone in hospital? Terrorist attack Los Angeles? What?" Mom's voice got higher and louder, but I could see she was trying to control it. I knew she must be really mad, so mad she was afraid that if she let loose, there would be no way to rein in her anger again.

I just shrugged. I couldn't help thinking she was overreacting. Fine, I hadn't rushed down to dinner willy-nilly. So what?

"Victoria never did things like this when she was your age," Mom said, and her voice sounded sad. Disappointed. "She was always very responsible."

"Well, I'm not Victoria," I said, and now it was my turn to hold back some anger. "Sorry I'm such a big letdown for you."

My mother's head spun around. "You are not a big letdown to me. You let down yourself."

"But I *don't* let myself down, Mom." Why couldn't she

understand this? "I'm a good kid. I get good grades. I want to hang out with my friends. I don't want to be a professional cello player, you know? I want to have a life like everybody else!"

My mom sighed, and she looked older all of a sudden. Worn. "I know you do," she said softly. "I just think you have potential to be much better. I want you to be all that you can be. Army of one."

Well, I didn't know what the hell to say to that. Part of me was kind of happy. I didn't know my mom even thought I had potential. But part of me still felt rotten, like the person I wanted to be would never, ever make her happy.

It was a long moment before I said anything. "Aren't you going to ground me or something? I want to get started on my homework."

Mom shook her head. "I want us to not be angry at each other, *kongju*," she said.

"Okay." I felt bad that she called me princess. It's what she used to call me when I was little, when we still got along. This wasn't what I was expecting at all, but I was hoping it meant I wasn't going to be stuck in my room for a month.

"Maybe we make a deal. You can spend time with your friends on the weekends. Sleepovers, that stuff. During the week, school. No phone calls. *Heot so ti*. All school. And cello lessons."

I didn't like the sound of "no phone calls," but I figured I could agree to it in the short term. "Okay."

My mother reached out and stroked my hair. "You know Dad and I want best for you. American dream, all that."

"Yeah, I know." I got up from my chair. My mom just stared

at me, and I felt like I should say something. Something nice. "Thanks," was all I could muster.

My mom nodded, and got up from the table. She hesitated there, as if there was something else she wanted to say before she headed back into the kitchen to do the dishes. For a second I thought about following her, helping her load the dishwasher or something, but I didn't. I wish I had. Maybe she'd have told me what it was she wanted to say.

But the moment passed, and we retreated to our own separate worlds, me doing homework in my room, her washing dishes in the kitchen.

And whatever my mom was holding back, I'll never know.

The next day at school, Taylor got Jenna, Kelly, and me filled in on all the details about her audition. She had a shot at playing Tom Hanks's daughter in a spy movie. It wasn't a big part, because she'd get killed in the first half hour, but it was still pretty enormous to think that she might make her movie debut opposite Tom freakin' Hanks. There was something funny about thinking that Taylor, who used to be the class punching bag, could be a major movie star in a year or two. And I'd be able to say that I was her best friend.

"Hey, do you think you'll meet Tom Hanks at the audition?" Jenna asked.

"Oh, if you do, you should totally pants him or something," Kelly blurted. "He seems so nice all the time, it would be funny to see him lose his shit."

"I don't think he'll be there," Taylor said. "And I wouldn't pants him, anyway."

"You're no fun!" Jenna said, punching Taylor in the arm. "Hey, when you're a big movie star, do you think you'll be able to get us into Hollywood parties?"

Taylor rolled her eyes. "You guys are so lame," she sighed, but I could tell she liked the idea of sneaking the gang of us into some fancy club and drinking mojitos with Jake Gyllenhaal or something. I liked that idea, too.

Later, Taylor pulled me aside. "I go in today at four p.m. Apparently they've looked at a ton of girls, and nobody's been right for it. I guess that's why they're willing to talk to a newbie like me," Taylor explained. "I really need you to come along. Sheila's just going to make me neurotic."

"There's no way my mom will let me." I had already filled Taylor in on the big fight the night before. When I had told her what I'd said, Taylor's eyes went wide.

"I've never even said that to Sheila." Taylor's voice was so quiet and serious, it just made me feel more awful about the whole thing.

But now she was tugging on my arm, her voice whiny and high. "You have to go! Sheila will pick me apart, and I'll go in there and bomb, and it will be all her fault!"

It sounded like Taylor was being a baby, but I knew what she said was dead-on. Sheila would criticize every little thing about her before she even got in the door, and by the time she finally met the director or casting agent or whoever, she'd be so beaten down she'd barely be able to read the script. Taylor needed a buffer. But did it have to be me?

"Take Jenna. Or Kelly."

Taylor sighed. "Come on. You know as well as I do that

they'll do something crazy. Like find Tom Hanks and pull down his pants."

I laughed. She was right. But that didn't solve the little problem of what to tell my mom. I felt like she and I had finally, amazingly come to some sort of truce, so for me to blow it now just seemed stupid. "Let me think about it. Maybe I can figure something out."

Taylor let go of my arm and stared at me. "What does that mean, figure something out?"

"It means I have to come up with a really great lie." I was already trying to decide if I had the guts to break my own arm or give myself a concussion.

Taylor started shaking her head. "No way. You've got to ask her. Ask her nice."

As much as Taylor liked my mom, she still didn't really get her. I knew from our whole sit-down chat that my mom already felt like she'd softened up too much. Just my asking permission to go would be a huge disappointment to her, solid proof I hadn't really heard a word she'd said. I was better off with the concussion. "Do you want me to go with you or not?" I asked Taylor, knowing I sounded annoyed.

Taylor didn't hesitate. "Absolutely."

Now that I've been on so many of the lots around town—Paramount, Warner Brothers, Sony, yada yada yada—it's funny to look back at that first time and remember how impressed I was. But I have to admit, even now, that Disney is a pretty cool place to visit. And I'm not talking about the theme park. Anybody can go to Disneyland. You have to have connections to get onto the Disney lot.

Sheila exited off the 134 freeway, and I saw the gates almost immediately. The words THE WALT DISNEY COMPANY were printed in graceful lettering on a low stucco wall, and an iron gate surrounded the parking lot. But it wasn't just any iron gate. At the top of each post were artfully sculpted Mickey Mouse ears. So cute!

We drove up to the gate, and Sheila smiled at the security guard in his little kiosk. He smiled back. Maybe this really *was* the happiest place on earth.

"We're here for the *Spy on You* casting call?" Sheila said in this super-fake, saccharine-sweet voice.

"Just give him my name," Taylor said in an exasperated voice. Lately, she'd been mouthing off to Sheila a lot more than she ever used to, and Sheila was putting up with it. I guess the prospect of Taylor becoming a rich movie star made it easier for her to put up with her kid's crap.

Sheila ended up having to give the guy not only Taylor's name, but her own name, her driver's license, and a contact person to boot. We even had to pop the trunk of the car for the guard to make sure we weren't driving a bomb into the place. It was harder getting onto the lot than clearing airport security at LAX.

But once we were inside, I forgot all about the intense security check. The lot was adorable, with perfect green lawns and little street signs for Dopey Drive and Mickey Avenue. The coolest thing was that one building had these enormous—and I mean enormous like twenty feet high—stone gargoyles holding up the roof that were carved to look like Snow White's seven dwarfs. It wasn't like going to Disneyland or anything, but it was plenty more fun than most places you could work at.

We walked into the Animation Building, which seemed like a

weird name for it because I didn't see anyone animating anything, just lots of offices with secretaries and desks. We finally found the one office we were looking for, and stepped inside.

"We're here for the auditions," Sheila said to the reception-ist in that buggy plastic voice of hers, telling her Taylor's name and then complimenting the lady on her ugly pink blouse. The receptionist nodded, then said, "If you'll have a seat, we're running a bit behind," and pointed to the waiting area. I'm guessing she completely saw through Sheila, the ultimate pushy stage mom.

And there in the waiting area, sitting in a handful of chairs with their middle-aged moms, were five other girls who could have been Taylor's clones. They all had long, blond hair. Blue eyes, perfect skin, ditto. They were all just as pretty as Taylor.

And each one of them gave her a cool, appraising once-over, then looked away.

It sent a shiver through me, the way you feel when you see the psycho killer in a movie zero in on his next victim. Everyone there was competing for the same thing, but no one was speaking to anyone else, just staring ahead or examining her fingernails. I still can't quite explain why it creeped me out so bad. I think I knew that even though these girls were politely sitting next to one another, they were all quietly wishing the others would drop dead.

Taylor sat down in a chair and leaned back. "Sit up straight," Sheila whispered.

Taylor gave me her "I'm so gonna kill her" look, then nudged her mom. "Scoot over so Erin can sit next to me."

Sheila stared daggers at her, but she did it.

So there I was, in a deathly quiet room full of angry beautiful girls, their moms, and Sheila. I was trying really hard to remember why I agreed to do this, and why it was worth getting my mom all pissed off, when Taylor squeezed my hand.

"I owe you so, so much for this," she whispered, and that's when I remembered.

When they called Taylor's name, Sheila stood up, too, even though none of the other moms had gone in with their daughters. Taylor gave her a dirty look, but it didn't stop good ol' Sheila. The controlling bitch was determined to go in.

But when Sheila got to the door, the casting assistant stepped in front of her, blocking the way. "I'm sorry, but we'd really prefer to see Taylor on her own," she said sweetly.

Sheila's face flushed bright red. "That is not acceptable. I need to be with my daughter."

Taylor looked like she wanted to die right there. *"Mom!"* she hissed. "I'm fine!"

The casting assistant just smiled as if this weren't totally horrifying. "She'll just be a few minutes, so if you don't mind having a seat—"

"I do mind," Sheila snapped. "Why do you have to see her alone, anyway? Is there nudity in this film?"

The casting assistant stopped smiling. "Mrs. Christensen, please take a seat." The way she said it, even Sheila understood that if she didn't obey, a security guard was probably going to drag her, me, and Taylor back to our car and pistol-whip us.

Sheila went back over to her seat, but she couldn't shut up. "I think it's criminal to separate a mother from her child. Criminal," she muttered.

The casting assistant rolled her eyes, but thank God, she let Taylor go into the audition.

It seemed like Taylor was in there forever, and sometimes I could hear laughter through the walls. That hadn't happened with any of the other girls who'd already auditioned, and none of them had stayed inside as long as Taylor. I had to think that was a good sign.

But most of the time I was sitting there, I was thinking about my mom and how angry she was going to be. I should have already been home for a few hours by then, and I knew she was worried. I thought about asking Sheila if I could borrow her cell phone, but I didn't. I still had to come up with an excuse, a really good one.

By the time Taylor walked out of the room, I was so absorbed by plotting how I could break a bone or voluntarily throw up blood, I jumped a little.

"Want to meet someone?" she said, smiling.

I shrugged, until I saw Tom Hanks standing in the doorway. Yeah, I know. Tom Hanks.

I know everyone always says movie stars look shorter in real life, and usually they do, but he was really tall, like, over six feet. And he didn't look much different than he does in the movies, except for his blue polo shirt and dorky khaki pants. Okay, I did notice he had kind of a gut. Like, he wasn't at his *Cast Away* weight or anything.

I don't think I even understood what he was saying to me for a minute, because I couldn't get over the fact that Tom Hanks was talking to me and shaking my hand. "I guess you're the quiet one. Your friend here"—he gestured towards Taylor—"she talks enough for the two of you, I think."

Taylor punched Tom Hanks in the arm, grinning like he was just some regular guy and not a big stinking movie star. "Oh, come on, I don't talk that much!"

Tom Hanks laughed and shook hands with Sheila, who had the same awed look on her face that I probably did. "It's so nice to meet you, Mr. Hanks. I'm a really big fan," she stuttered, blushing. It struck me that he must get really tired of hearing that every time he meets someone. Now that Taylor's who she is, I know it doesn't even register after you've been a star for a while, like when people say "bless you" after you sneeze.

But Sheila didn't stop with simple gushing. Oh, no. She had to go and stick her foot in her mouth. "I didn't realize how handsome you were in real life," she whispered, fluttering her eyelashes. I wanted to die. She was flirting with Tom Hanks! Everyone knew the guy was married. And his wife was a hell of a lot hotter than Sheila was on her best day.

Tom Hanks just smiled like he wanted to be polite even though he'd eaten something that tasted bad. But Sheila wasn't stopping there, oh, no. "You know, I was just sitting here thinking how much I missed that series of yours *Bosom Buddies*. And boom, I came up with a great idea for a reunion movie. If you ever have a chance, I'd love to talk to you about it over lunch." She leaned forward a little and winked. "You'd have a much bigger role than that other guy, the blond one."

Sheila, in her completely delusional state, must have been thinking that, now that Taylor and Tom were such good buddies, she had an in to pitch him a script idea. How crazy is that? Everyone knows you don't pitch people you don't know, especially stars. Why? Because if they ever make a movie anything like your lame-o half-baked idea, you won't be their "biggest fan" anymore. You'll try to make a quick buck by suing them. Sad, but you know it's true.

And yet Tom Hanks just patted Sheila on the arm. "Now, I'm never one to be a screen hog," he said, in a much nicer tone than I would have used. Then he looked at his watch. I bet he was wondering how quickly he could get away from Sheila without coming across as a jerk. "Boy, we were in there for a long time," he said.

He turned to a woman with glasses, probably the casting director, and smiled. "You think we should get a TV in here, Rebecca? So people don't lose their minds waiting? Maybe some HGTV would make everyone more relaxed. Or one of those aquarium videos. What do you think, Erin?"

I couldn't believe Tom Hanks was asking me a question, like he actually cared what I had to say. "I think that would be great," I mumbled. "You'd want to keep the volume way down low, so people who didn't want to watch weren't distracted."

"You heard the woman," Tom Hanks said, looking at his pink-shirted receptionist. She smiled at him. "And hey, you could watch your soaps, Jennie. Everybody wins!"

I was just grasping that Tom Hanks had made a decision, even a little decision like this one, with my input, when he shook our hands again. "Nice meeting you," he said before disappearing back through the door with Rebecca, the casting director, a step behind him.

I was so freaked-out, I couldn't think of anything to say on the way back to the car, but Sheila couldn't shut up. "Whatever you did, you must have done it right, honey," she said, stroking Taylor's hair. "I could tell he thought of you like his own daughter."

Taylor jerked her head away from Sheila and rolled her eyes. I couldn't get over how calm she seemed, as if this sort of thing happened to her every day. "I don't have the part yet. Don't get carried away."

Sheila ignored her and kept talking. "We should celebrate. We could get ice cream, the full-fat stuff at Baskin-Robbins. How does that sound?"

Taylor looked at me and shook her head. "We need to get Erin home, Sheila. Like, pronto."

And here's the reason why I will never, ever stop hating Sheila. "No, we're getting ice cream," she said, driving down Buena Vista towards a Baskin-Robbins.

"*Sheila,*" Taylor yelled, her face turning red. "We have to get Erin home!"

"I really do need to get home," I said, suddenly feeling super lactose intolerant.

"It'll only take a minute," she said, putting the car into park and opening the door. "What do you kids want?"

"Nothing!" Taylor said, but Sheila ignored her.

Taylor and I just sat there, staring at Sheila through the glass doors. All I could think about was my mom. I pictured her sitting at the dining room table, staring at her hands. Losing all faith in me, forever.

After what seemed like an hour Sheila came back and handed both of us cups of mint chocolate-chip ice cream, which I don't even like. Then Sheila sat in the front seat and daintily nibbled at hers, as if she had all the time in the world.

"Go ahead, eat!" she said, smiling.

"If we eat, can we leave?" Taylor asked, glaring at Sheila.

"Of course we can leave. I just don't want ice cream melting all over the car seats."

Taylor literally took her cup of ice cream, tilted it up, and let the whole mushy mess slide into her mouth. "Let's go," she said, wiping soupy dribbles off the sides of her mouth.

I did the same, and Sheila looked at us with total disgust. "You're supposed to savor a treat," she said in a prissy tone. "I can tell you're both going to be as big as houses by the time you're twenty, eating like that."

But finally Sheila put the car into drive, and we headed for home. And so far, my only excuse for being late was an ice-cream headache.

By the time I flew through the door of my house, I'd come up with a stupid story I was desperately hoping my mom would buy. It was something about being nauseous, so nauseous I couldn't get on the bus, and then somehow getting a ride from Sheila. The particulars don't really matter, because I never had to tell the story to anyone.

When I walked inside, Victoria was in the kitchen nuking a frozen dinner, and Dad was in the office paying bills. They didn't seem particularly concerned about my showing up three hours late. That was always Mom's problem, I guess.

"Where's Mom?" I asked Victoria.

"I don't know," she said. "I'm guessing she's running late or something. She hasn't called."

Score! Somehow I had been lucky enough to dodge this bullet, and I swore I would never disappoint Mom again. I went right to my room and started doing homework, even though I was still feeling a little gross from the ice cream. I even wrote a list of things I was going to do to impress my mom. No TV, not even *American Idol*. I'd play cello at old folks' homes. All sorts of crazy stuff.

I was so caught up in feeling grateful that I didn't have the sense to feel worried. But I don't think any of us really felt worried. Not until we got the phone call from the police.

My dad went to identify Mom at the morgue, and Victoria and I stayed at home. We cried some, like when we called people with the bad news, but mostly we just stared at each other, totally in shock. It didn't feel real at all. I kept thinking that she had to be alive, because I'd just seen her that morning. I know it sounds stupid, but at one point I picked up the DVD remote control, thinking if I could rewind my life, just by a few hours, I could fix everything. It seemed so simple, and yet not simple at all.

After we'd contacted all the aunts and cousins and even Mom's family in Korea, which Victoria had to do since she spoke the language better than I did, I called Taylor.

I wasn't able to say much more than "My mom died in a car accident" before I burst into tears. It would be a month before I was able to tell Taylor the whole story without crying, how some stupid punk-ass thug who'd stolen a Mercedes was going seventy-five miles an hour down Wilshire Boulevard (in a thirty-five-miles-per-hour zone, I should point out), whizzing in and out of traffic, when my mom pulled out of the Pavilion's grocery store parking lot and got broadsided by this jerk. She died before the paramedics came.

She died before I could tell her I loved her. Or that I was sorry.

Taylor didn't hesitate. "I'm coming over," she said. "I'll be right there, I promise." And then she hung up the phone.

And she was right there, before Jenna and Kelly or even the rest of our family, who arrived at our doorstep with envelopes of *jo eui geum*, or "condolence money," to help pay for the funeral. Taylor hadn't even bothered to change out of her grungy cutoffs and T-shirt, and Sheila was still sweaty in her pink workout gear.

Taylor didn't say anything when I opened the door. She just hugged me. And for some reason the look on her face, serious and sad at the same time, made everything real, and I started sobbing so hard it made my chest hurt. It had finally hit me that my mom was gone forever. And there was nothing I could do to change it.

The weeks after my mother died are a blur to me. A lot of it I blocked out, though sometimes even now I remember things at weird times for no reason, like when I'm at a premiere or visiting Victoria or just doing nothing.

I'll remember the moment I saw my father cry at the funeral, or how Victoria and I had to look for a nice dress for my mother to wear in her casket. I'll remember opening the kimchi refrigerator and sobbing over a jar of the stuff, something that had once seemed so embarrassing but now reminded me of Mom. To this day a lot of things remind me of Mom.

I didn't go to school much, but no one expected me to. It was only a little over a month until the end of the school year, so it wasn't like I missed a lot. Taylor, Jenna, or Kelly would bring me homework from school, and sometimes the teachers would call and check in with my dad, but that was about it. Sometimes I would do my homework because I thought it would make my mom happy if she was looking down on me from heaven, but most of the time I was too depressed.

A friend of my dad's was a psychologist, and Victoria dragged me to see him after she realized I had been stumbling around the house without showering for a week. He wrote a note on official-looking paper that Victoria took to my principal, and I think whatever it said was dramatic enough that no one wanted to push me too hard after that. My teachers all got together and decided that, instead of making me take finals, they'd just come up with the average for my test scores up to that point and make that my grade for the year. The principal said they wouldn't have done it if I hadn't been such a good student. I guess having my mom harp on me to study all the time paid off, which made me even more bummed out just thinking about it.

The doctor gave me a prescription for Serzone, some stupid antidepressant, and told me he wanted me to come in every week for "talk therapy." I said I would, but I never did. He wasn't exactly creepy, but there was something about the way he looked at me that made me feel like he was trying to crawl inside my brain and camp out there. And once I realized the Serzone made my mouth feel like a cotton-ball factory without improving my mood at all, I tossed the pills down the john.

The truth was, I was scared in a way I had never been before. I know it's weird, because the worst had already gone down. But it seemed to me that if this could happen without any warning, there was nothing to stop the rest of my world from crumbling. It was like I was in the middle of a frozen lake, and all around me the ice was shifting and cracking. At any second, I could fall through and disappear.

I know Jenna and Kelly came to visit every few days, and Taylor was around a lot, though I don't remember if we really talked very much. She didn't try to cheer me up, which is good because I would have slugged her if she had. She understood that I was going to feel bad, period. There was no "Keep your sunny side up" angle here.

It was funny. I had always felt like I was the stable, steady one in our friendship, the one with normal parents and no big dramas, while Taylor's life was a pure chaos theory. And now, just like everything else, our relationship was turned upside down. When we met, Taylor was the fragile, broken one. She was the loser. And now she was this strong, beautiful almost movie star, and me? I was on the verge of shattering into a million pieces.

Towards the end of the month, I started feeling like I needed to get out of the house, or at least out of the dark places in my head. I still cried a lot, though sometimes I would turn on the television and channel surf until I found a dumb old sitcom, like a rerun of *Friends* or something random on Nick at Nite, and for a little while I could laugh. And forget.

Taylor must have sensed that I needed some fresh air, so one day she and Sheila came over and told me to get dressed. We were going to get burgers at In-N-Out and eat them at the beach.

Sheila was trying extra hard to be nice to me, urging me to order more food than I thought I could ever possibly eat. ("You've lost weight, little girl, so if there was ever a time to order a chocolate shake, it's now.") She was right, though; I really had dwindled down to a stick figure. I remember one time Victoria walked in on me when I was changing clothes in my bedroom, and she let out this little scream that caught in her throat. And when I turned my head and looked in the mirror, I got it. I was so thin I looked like an end-stage anorexic, each rib jutting through my skin so hard it looked like I might split wide open. Even for our big trip to the beach I couldn't wear my bathing suit because it had gotten too big, and I had to roll down the waistband of my shorts to keep them from falling off.

After seeing my super skinniness, Victoria had been making dinner and buying frozen meals at the grocery store, but none of us were ever very hungry and it was depressing to sit down at the dining room table, just the three of us, with no one having anything to say.

But I was still surprised when I found myself licking the last piece of cheese off the burger wrapper before we'd even left the drive-through. Sheila and Taylor were quietly watching me, so I guess I had really hoovered my food. Without a word, Sheila got back into the drive-through lane and ordered another complete meal for me with extra fries to boot. I finished that, too, but only after we'd gotten to the beach.

It was a beautiful day, all bright blue sky and puffy white clouds. Not too cold, not too hot. But even that depressed me, because the day we buried Mom was exactly the same, and I re-membered thinking then that it wasn't right. How could it be so nice out when something so bad was happening? In the movies, it always rains at funerals. But life, I was figuring out, was nothing like the movies.

Of course, I kept that to myself, and when Sheila suggested Taylor and I play Frisbee on the beach, I tried to enjoy every little detail, from the wet sand between my toes to the damp Pacific air against my face. It felt good to move.

Still, it didn't take long for me to start feeling a little sick. The combination of not eating much for a long time and then gulping down two hamburgers with fries and shakes probably did it. I belly flopped onto the sand, and Taylor joined me. She propped herself up on one elbow and looked at me. "How are things at home, anyway?"

For a minute, I thought about lying. I was so tired of being the world's biggest bummer. But this was Taylor, and I couldn't. "Not so great. Victoria is leaving for school in a few months, and I don't think my dad can handle it."

"What about you?"

"I don't know. I guess I'll have to."

"What's your dad say about it?"

"Who knows? I think I could tell my dad I was getting full-body tattoos and dealing meth out of the garage, and he'd just grunt and leave the room."

Taylor didn't laugh. "You know, I'm kind of worried about you."

I sat up, brushing sand off my arms. "Don't be. We're at the beach. Let's not get all bummed out. Hey, did you get the movie with Tom Hanks?"

"Oh my God, that's not even interesting compared to school right now," Taylor said. I couldn't imagine that was true, but she was already steamrollering ahead with her story.

Taylor started telling me about her new favorite hobby,

which was joining Kelly and Jenna in torturing Alexandra and her bitchy friends. Now that Taylor was modeling, sometimes the stylists would let her keep an item that they couldn't return, like a purse that got smudged or a designer blouse with a tiny rip in the sleeve. So Taylor had started wearing these fabulous things to school, then having Kelly and Jenna loudly coo over them. When Alexandra and her stupid friends stared at her Prada bag or Dolce & Gabbana pants, she'd look at them, smile sweetly, and say, "Oh yeah, it's spectacular, and it's real."

"But get this. Now they're copying me. I'm totally serious. Alexandra came to school the other day with a Fendi purse just like mine. Same color and everything."

"Isn't that, like, eight hundred bucks?"

Taylor snorted. "I know! She's such an idiot. Like, you know what I would do with eight hundred bucks?"

"What?"

"Get acting lessons. Put it towards a car. Anything but buy a stupid purse."

I tried to think of something I would do with that kind of money, and I couldn't. There was only one thing I wanted, and I couldn't have it. I wanted to go back in time. I wanted my mom back. And that's when I started sobbing.

"What's wrong?" Taylor asked, but I couldn't answer her. I was so tired of crying, but it just seemed like I couldn't get all the tears out.

It wasn't long before Sheila stopped doing yoga on the sand and walked over. "What happened? Did you tell her?" Sheila whispered to Taylor.

I wiped my arm across my face. My nose had started running,

and I knew it was gross, but you try to find tissues on a beach. "Tell me what?"

Taylor and Sheila looked at each other. It was like they knew something I didn't, which is an awful feeling, if it's ever happened to you. After a long moment, Taylor turned to me. I could tell she was thinking something over, but I had no idea what.

"I'm turning down the Tom Hanks movie," she said firmly.

"*What?*" Sheila screeched. Apparently, this wasn't the announcement she was expecting.

Taylor turned to face Sheila, a wall of blond hair cascading over her shoulders like something out of a shampoo commercial. "It's not a good time," she snapped.

"I already told your agent you were packing your bags!" Sheila yelled. "*You are going!*" A couple on a towel behind us started picking up their stuff to move away from the crazy screaming lady.

"You can't make me," Taylor said, not raising her voice. "Erin needs me."

I did, but I snuffled, "No, no, don't stay for me."

"You heard her," Sheila barked. "She doesn't even want you to!"

"But I want to," Taylor said, crossing her arms over her chest.

I grabbed Taylor's hand. "This is a big opportunity for you, Taylor. You should take it. I'll be fine."

"*See! See!*" Sheila was as red and sweaty as I'd ever seen her. She looked like a crazed Oompa-Loompa, waving her arms in all directions and stomping her feet.

"I said no, and that's final," Taylor said simply. I remembered how I'd always been a little scared of crossing my mom, but Taylor didn't seem the least bit concerned about back-talking Sheila. It was as if they were warriors on opposite sides of a battleground instead of mother and daughter.

"Since you think you can make all your own decisions, you just get home on your own," Sheila barked. "Because I'm leaving." We watched as Sheila packed up all our stuff and headed out to the car.

"Is she really leaving without us?" I asked.

"Looks that way," Taylor said. She didn't look surprised, either. "I took a couple twenties out of her wallet when she wasn't looking, so we can get a taxi later. It's not like she hasn't done this before."

I picked up a handful of sand and tried to start a castle, but no matter how hard I tried, it kept crumbling apart. Kind of like my life, just on a smaller scale. "Seriously, don't pass up this job on my account. I'm going to be fine," I said. "I can hang out with Jenna and Kelly."

Taylor put an arm around my shoulder. "I know. But I also know if I were in your shoes, I'd want you to do it for me. Plus I really, really don't want to spend two months dangling out of a helicopter somewhere in Kansas."

"Dangling out of a helicopter?"

"It turns out almost all of my scenes are me and a kidnapper fighting for control of this chopper, and you know I don't like heights."

I should point out that I think Taylor made this up for my benefit. For one thing, she couldn't look me in the eye as she said it, and when I did see the movie, there was just one scene in a helicopter and it wasn't that scary. So when you read in the tabloids that Taylor's a spoiled brat who doesn't care about anyone but herself, just know that you're not getting the whole picture. Because sometimes she can be a really amazing person, even when there are no movie cameras around to prove it.

After that, I wasn't completely back to normal, but I think knowing Taylor had made such a huge sacrifice to back me up kind of motivated me to start taking care of myself, eating and showering and occasionally running a comb through my hair. Knowing I didn't have to go through finals didn't hurt, either. The weird thing was knowing that this was going to be the first time I wouldn't have to spend summer vacation taking some intensive cello seminar or Korean-language tutoring or a History of Ancient Roman Nose-Picking Methods class or God knew what else. My mom always wanted me to be improving myself, plotting the next move in the big game plan of my future. And now, well, Victoria was busy getting ready for UCLA and Dad didn't seem to remember he had any kids, honestly. It made me miss my mom a lot. Even though she forced me to work my ass off all summer, at least it showed she cared.

But I have to admit, I was glad in one respect that I didn't have to do any of that college prep stuff, because it meant I got to hang out with Taylor on the set.

Even though she hadn't taken the movie offer, she was still getting lots of little jobs in national commercials and on TV shows. With the minimizing bra Sheila bought to replace the Ace bandage, Taylor could still pass for twelve if you squinted. And that's the secret of being a successful child star, passing for younger. The younger a kid is, the more rules there are about how many hours they can work in a day. So, as much as Taylor hated it, she did her best to pass for a little kid.

But she didn't take all these jobs because she wanted to work. After she passed up that Tom Hanks movie, Taylor came home from school one day to find her room stripped bare. No bed, no clothes, no posters on the wall. There was just a pillow and a sleeping bag on the floor, and a change of underwear folded up in one corner. And that was it.

"You want your things back, you have to earn them, one by one," Sheila said. Taylor cried and screamed and even threatened to call Child Protective Services, but Sheila just ignored her. So Taylor had no choice but to take every little job that came her way, just so she didn't have to wear dirty underwear to school. It took a good six months for her to earn back her bed, and to this day I still don't know if she got all her stuff back. Think that's bad? Get this: Sheila charged Taylor crazy prices for stuff, like two hundred dollars for a ratty T-shirt, just to make sure she kept working.

Taylor still hates looking at the commercials she did back then. It just reminds her of how uncomfortable she was, all bundled up in that stupid bra that pulled so hard it made her back hurt. But worse, it reminds her of when she first realized her mother wasn't only a bitch, but cruel right down to the core.

Taylor might have hated those jobs, but every time one came up, I always jumped at the chance to tag along. I was happy to get away from the house, which was so dark and depressing, even though it meant spending a whole day with Sheila. I could tell the woman hated me with a passion now. I had, of course, ruined Taylor's career, and she had a hard time keeping her opinion to herself.

"I can't believe I'm driving you to a cereal commercial when you could be on the set with Tom Hanks," she'd sigh as we pulled up to a soundstage, and Taylor would silently mimic her until I couldn't help giggling, which only made Sheila shoot me a look that seemed to say, "If I wasn't driving, I swear I'd reach into the backseat and beat you to death with my bare hands." Yeah, good times.

But I didn't care about Sheila, because even though she thought a commercial set was no big deal, it was pretty fascinating to me. Sets are kind of exciting, because there are all these people, lighting guys and sound guys and set decorators and on and on, and they're all running around like crazy to make everything come together. And it's not easy, because everything, and I mean everything, is fake. That's why they call it Hollywood magic.

For example, the commercial you see on TV may look to you like it shows an average mom standing at a plain old kitchen counter, but in reality the "mom" is an actress who's never had kids, the kitchen is a set in a dark warehouse, and the sunlight coming in through the window is a big light aimed through a fake window attached to a wall made out of wallpaper and plywood. Not so simple now, is it?

On the first few commercial sets I went to with Taylor, I ate this stuff up. I loved watching the cinematographer make everyone "block the scene," and hearing the first AD order the actors to find their "marks." It was like learning a new language, or being invited to join a club with a secret handshake.

The thing that really blew me away was how long it took. They'd shoot a little bit of the commercial, then have to move the lights around and tinker and fuss for, like, an hour just to shoot a little bit more. You see only thirty seconds or a minute on TV, but in truth it takes all day. And it didn't help speed up the schedule when, during those last few weeks of school, Taylor had to work with a tutor every time she turned around.

There's some law in California that says child actors have to get in three hours of class time during each workday, except during school vacations. But it's not like Taylor got a lot out of it, even though she really needed to cram for finals. It seemed like every single time she'd open her book, she'd get called back to the set. And if you're wondering, her grades that year were thoroughly mediocre, mostly Bs and Cs. If you ever wonder why someone who used to be a child actor doesn't seem particularly well educated, well, there you go.

On the set of this one orange-juice commercial, Taylor's tutor was this woman named Margo. Each time Taylor would have to be dragged away, either for wardrobe or a rehearsal or to actually shoot some of the commercial, Margo and I would talk.

"So, why aren't you in school, Erin?" she asked, but not in an accusing way or anything. I told her about Mom's accident, and she agreed that stressing over exams probably wasn't the best thing for me.

"Just as long as you go back next year, you're fine. You don't want to miss your junior and senior years. That's the thing I feel so bad about with child actors. They're so ambitious, but I think when they get older, they really regret not having had all the regular kid experiences, you know?"

I nodded, but I didn't know. I thought Taylor's earning a living and being almost sort of famous was a lot cooler than going to school with cretins like Alexandra every day.

"Do yourself a favor and stay out of the business," Margo said in a whisper, even though we were alone in the room. I guess she was worried Sheila might barge in, which she seemed to do every five minutes. "I see so many kids. . . . Let's just say the business changes them. And not for the better."

"If Taylor can survive her mom, I don't think Hollywood is going to be a big problem for her," I said. I was joking, but Margo looked at me like she didn't think that was particularly funny.

"Why do you say that?"

I didn't really mean to, but I started telling Margo all about Sheila. How she dragged Taylor to auditions and how she freaked out when she didn't take that Tom Hanks movie and how she stole all of Taylor's stuff to punish her. Once I got started it was hard to stop bitching about Sheila. I mean, it didn't hurt that I really hated her.

Margo, I have to say, was a great listener. Most adults just kind of half listen to you, but she hung on every word I said like it was really important.

"Let me ask you something." As she spoke, she walked over to the door and leaned against it. She did it casually, but I knew what it meant. Sheila wasn't coming in even if she wanted to, at least for a few minutes. "Has she thought about emancipating herself?" Margo asked in a low voice.

Emancipation. I knew what that meant from history class, the freeing of the slaves and all that, but I wasn't sure what she meant here.

Margo explained that once they turn fourteen, actors can file for emancipation from their parents, which allows them to work the same hours as adults. There were some rules, like you couldn't live at home and you had to handle your own money and stuff, but it sounded like a pretty good deal to me. No more Sheila.

"I usually think it's an awful idea," Margo said. "I hate to even mention it. But if Sheila is really doing the things you say she is . . ." Margo hesitated then, taking a deep breath as if she had to brace herself just to finish the sentence. "I'm worried for Taylor."

When she said that, it made me feel weak and frightened at the same time. Because I was worried, too. I'd been wondering for a long time if Sheila wasn't more trouble than she was worth to Taylor. I could tell on the set that the director didn't like her mom very much. Sheila asked a lot of questions that didn't matter, like whether or not he was getting Taylor's "best side." And even if Taylor didn't want to do something, like wear hot pants at a modeling shoot, Sheila always cut her off and said she'd do it, no problem. I swear if someone asked Taylor to juggle chain saws, Sheila would help him gas up the machines.

I didn't have a lot of time to think about what Margo had said, though, because pretty soon Taylor was back in the room, Sheila right on her heels. "Because it's against the *law*, Mom!" Taylor hissed. When Margo heard the word "law," her head swiveled around fast, as if she'd gotten an electric shock.

"What's against the law, Taylor?" she asked in a cool, steady voice that was pure steel.

Taylor put on a sulky face, and for a minute I could have sworn she really was as young as she looked. "They want me to work until six, and I'm supposed to go at five."

Margo quickly got out of her chair and walked to the door.

"I'll take care of it," she said, and I had no doubt she would. Damn, why couldn't she be Taylor's mom?

After she left, Sheila lit into Taylor as if she were the one who'd done something wrong instead of the film crew. "What were you thinking? They'll never want to work with you again!"

"Who cares? This is a stupid orange-juice commercial." Taylor shrugged, plopping onto a dirty sofa in the corner of the room.

Sheila moved so fast I didn't even see it coming when she slapped Taylor across the face, hard. Then she did it again, and again. "I keep telling you, you be polite and nice and maybe, just maybe, you keep working," she hissed. "First Tom Hanks, now this! I didn't put you through five thousand dollars' worth of braces for you to ruin it all acting like a spoiled brat!"

Taylor's hand went up to her cheek, and her eyes were watering. But she didn't cry. "You just ruined my makeup," she said flatly.

Sheila glared at her, and Taylor glared right back. They both had such hatred written on their faces, it was the only time I ever saw a real family resemblance.

Margo came back in a few minutes later, after Sheila had stomped off to God knows where. Margo told us that she'd talked to the director, and Taylor would be leaving at five, period. And then I pleaded with her to tell Taylor what she had told me, about emancipation. Taylor didn't say much, but I could tell she was absorbing all the details like a sponge.

It wasn't until late that night, after I'd suffered through a painful, silent dinner of lukewarm frozen meat loaf with my dad, that the phone rang.

"Hey." It was Taylor. She sounded like she'd been crying.

"Something wrong? Did you and Sheila fight again?"

"Kind of. Not exactly. We talked, I guess."

"Talking's good," I said, hoping it was.

"I don't know if I can do it," she whispered.

"What?"

"Get emancipated. It would kill Sheila."

"I would think that's a bonus."

"Yeah, I know. Sometimes I really hate her. And I know she does stuff that's probably illegal. Like, I don't even have a bed to sleep in."

"But?" I couldn't imagine why there'd be a "but."

"But she's still my mom. And I don't have anyone else."

I thought about that. I had really hated my mom, too. Hell, I'd said it right to her face. But I knew, at heart, she had wanted what was best for me, even if she didn't go about it in the best way.

Taylor kept talking. "I don't know my dad, and the way my mom talks about him, he sounds worse than her. If I got emancipated, I'd be totally alone. Totally."

"Oh, snap. That's pretty intense."

"I'd have to rent my own apartment, pay all the bills. I don't know how to do that stuff, not on my own at least."

"You'd learn, right?"

"I guess." There was a long, long pause. "I'm just not ready yet. I'm still a kid, you know?" Another pause. "You must think I'm totally stupid."

Taylor's voice sounded small and worried. Maybe she really did need Sheila more than I'd realized. I didn't think Sheila was a very good mother, but she was the grown-up who managed the money, put dinner on the table, did all the stuff my mother had done that I had taken for granted. It hit me that sometimes any mom is better than none at all, even one as abusive as Sheila.

"No, Taylor," I whispered back, even though there was no one around to hear me. "I don't think you're stupid at all."

Chapter Three

I think everything happens for a reason. Everything. Even things you think are disasters, like losing the part you really want or getting dumped by the guy you think is perfect for you. It just means there's something better right around the corner, something that wouldn't happen otherwise. You just can't see it yet.

—TAYLOR CHRISTENSEN in *Vanity Fair* magazine

I should have been more excited to go back to school for my sophomore year. But everything just bummed me out. Victoria offered to shop for school clothes with me, but she kept wandering off to the shoe section, so I was on my own. I couldn't get very much anyway, because money was really tight since my mom had died. Dad would talk about selling the house, and Victoria said he should do it to save money. She told me once that he was going into debt each month making the house payments, and it made me worry. I hated the idea of moving, but I didn't want Dad to go broke. I almost thought it would be a good thing to sell the house, to live someplace that wasn't so full of memories.

At school, it was good to see Jenna and Kelly on a daily basis again. They got me completely back up to speed on all the gossip, and they made sure no one gave me crap about anything.

Now that Jenna and Kelly weren't newbie cheerleaders anymore, they had a lot more status at school. Some of the popular girls who weren't such close friends with Alexandra were friendly with them, and all of the stoner and rocker kids thought Jenna was cool for being the subversive goth chick on the squad. I know Jenna's hair and makeup made their coach, Mrs. Metrino, crazy, but once she saw that kids who never, ever went to the school's basketball games started showing up just for Jenna, she stopped bugging her about it. Once I even heard her bragging about her "stylistically diverse" cheerleading squad to another teacher in the hallway. Like she had planned it that way. Please!

No one other than Jenna and Kelly really talked to me much, which was okay. I think death freaks people out, and the truth was, I didn't want to talk. It was like I had lost the skill of conversation. It had been different hanging out on Taylor's sets. There no one knew me. More importantly, the people there didn't know what had happened to me. But at school, my story was like an artificial leg or a humpback, some deformity everyone could see and I couldn't escape. I was a little scared about talking to people anyway, no joke. I worried that if someone asked me how I was, I might say something too honest and burst into tears. Luckily, when anyone talked to me, it was mostly about Taylor.

Sometimes kids would tell me they'd seen her in a commercial. Depending on the person, that was either a good or bad thing. Alexandra and her friends would sneer about it when the commercials were for dumb stuff like Lunchables, but I think they were secretly jealous. Most of the other kids thought it was cool, anyway. Brandon, who had just gotten cuter since I'd been away, was always really nice about it. But in addition to getting cuter, he'd also gotten a girlfriend, that hell-spawn Alexandra. What he saw in her, I'll never know.

I didn't see Taylor much. She was working almost nonstop, and I think her agent was just trying to get as many little-kid gigs for her as she could, because Taylor was in the middle of a growth spurt. It was pretty clear she wasn't going to look twelve for long as she got taller. By the end of the year, she was almost five feet ten, a full five inches taller than me, and three inches taller than Sheila. "I don't know where you got that from, because your father was a shrimp," Sheila would say. That was about all I ever heard about Taylor's father, that and how his family had bad teeth and he never paid his child support on time. I think that's all Taylor ever heard, too.

Anyway, Taylor would phone almost every day to tell me these hysterical stories about wherever she was working. Like there was the day when a little boy she was working with had to be strung up in a harness so it looked like he was flying, and he wet his pants, peeing on the director and about three other people below him. Taylor thought he did it on purpose, because the director was a jerk and kept him in the harness for a lot longer than he was supposed to.

She'd tell me about the gross old extras who snarfed down all the food at the craft services table (that's the place where you can get snacks on the set), and the producer who actually threw a director's chair at a grip (a lighting guy) and cussed him out, even though he knew kids were around.

And then she'd tell me about the famous people she'd seen. The Rock had walked past her on the lot at Sony Pictures, and she'd seen Angelina Jolie and her kids at Paramount. She'd tell me who looked good in person, and who didn't. She said Cameron Diaz was super nice, but her skin? Worse than a pizza delivery boy's.

Listening to Taylor made me hate going to school. Her life was so much more interesting to me than picking extracurriculars and worrying about geometry. And, surprise, surprise, my grades started slipping. Not a lot, but enough for Victoria to notice.

"Don't you want to get into a good college?" she asked, looking at my Bs and B minuses while we ate cold pizza for breakfast one Saturday morning.

"I'm only a sophomore."

"It doesn't matter. You have to think about this now, before it's too late." Victoria was into college in an almost creepy way. She'd pledged a sorority, so now she had all these stupid sweatshirts that said "Tri-Delts Rule!" and crap like that.

"Maybe I don't want to go to college," I said. It so wasn't cool for Victoria to play mom whenever it was convenient for her, popping in for a weekend and lecturing me before disappearing back to college for a month.

Victoria looked at me like I'd said I wanted to date a serial killer or eat snails. "You've got to go to college," she said, her voice rising. "Why wouldn't you?"

"Maybe I'll work in the film industry," I shot back.

"Then go to film school," she said, crossing her arms.

"What for? I already know all about the industry from Taylor."

Victoria shook her head. "Why are you so content to follow that girl around like a trained dog, Erin? Jesus. You need to get your own life."

Boy, that pissed me off. "What life?" I screamed, looking

around the room. "This one? The one where Dad doesn't talk to me? The one where you only come by to yell and pretend you're Mom? Is that it? Is that what I should be spending my time doing?"

Victoria sighed in that tired, old-woman way she'd picked up since Mom died. "I know it hasn't been easy. It hasn't been easy for any of us. But you've got to start making your own way."

"Well, maybe the way I want is working on a movie set," I said, heading for the front door. I let it slam behind me and sat on the steps.

I'd never really thought of working on a movie set. I'd always assumed I'd go to college like everyone else in my family, become a lawyer or a doctor or something. The things my mom wanted for me. But now that she was gone, I didn't see the point so much anymore.

So, you can kind of tell what my frame of mind was when Taylor called me and said, "Want to be my assistant?"

"What are you talking about?"

"I just got a part on a TV show. A big part. Like, this is so much better than that Tom Hanks movie, I shit you not."

"No way!" I screamed.

"I know!" Taylor screamed back. "I'm going to be an actress, a real one, on TV! No more selling orange juice or Lunchables or any of that crap. I'm going to have a character and everything!" She stopped for a moment. "God, Erin, the pilot has to get picked up. Has to. I want this so bad, you have no idea!"

Taylor had been cast as the daughter on the new (so new it didn't have a name yet) Julia Hanson television series, a kind of

Desperate Housewives with only one housewife. Apparently it was a huge deal that Julia agreed to sign on for a network TV show, because she was a big Oscar-winning actress, and major movie stars don't usually do TV. I couldn't imagine the pilot not getting picked up for a full season.

"I've always been such a big fan of hers," Taylor sighed. "When I was a little kid, I would rent her movies, the romantic ones, and just pretend I would be her when I grew up. This really nice, really sweet girl who gets the guy. And now she's going to be my mom. She's, like, the most perfect person in the world to be my mom. You know?"

I didn't say anything, because I never really liked Julia Hanson. That big toothy smile of hers that everyone talked about as being so charming just struck me as fierce, like she wanted to take a bite out of someone. I wasn't even thinking about my own mom until Taylor started tripping all over herself to apologize.

"Oh my God, Erin, I'm sorry. I shouldn't be talking about moms—"

"Taylor, seriously. That wasn't even what I was thinking about." Not until right then, anyway.

"Anyway, blathering on and on about Julia isn't even why I called. I want to celebrate. I want to celebrate Hollywood-style."

Taylor's big plan was to take Jenna, Kelly, Sheila, and me to the Ivy on the Shore, this restaurant on the beach where celebrities sometimes go. It was really, really expensive, like, almost thirty dollars for steak tacos and seventeen dollars for a make-your-own sundae, which was crazy. But it was nice to sit on the patio and look out at the beach, or at least the little sliver of the sea you could spot past Ocean Avenue.

"The show creator said Taylor was the best audition he'd seen since Hilary Duff," Sheila said while we looked over the menus. She was in a good mood, so I guess she hated me a little less than usual. "Hilary Duff!" she said, too loudly.

Jenna mouthed "Hilary *Duff*!" to Kelly from behind her menu, and then made a goofy, I'm-so-excited face. It was all we could do not to start rolling on the floor laughing, so we just hid our faces in our menus.

"Mom, you're embarrassing me," Taylor whispered. I don't think she was talking just about Sheila's volume, either. Sheila had a good body for a mom, I guess, but she was wearing this skimpy miniskirt and tube top I swear she stole from Taylor's closet. When we left the car with the valet, they gave her that up-and-down look guys sometimes do, but with smirks on their faces.

Amazingly, Jenna's making fun of her, and Taylor's request to take it down a notch, had no impact on Sheila. The crazy bitch just kept running her stupid mouth. "And guess who plays the father on the show? That actor from *Sex and the City*. He's very, very good. A real quality name. The network is very, very excited about this show."

Taylor nodded. "I think we've got a really good chance of getting picked up," she said.

"God, I hope so. I can't wait to get out of that rotten apartment."

"You're moving?" I asked, but from the look on Taylor's face I could tell that this was news to her, too.

"Well, it's Taylor's decision, but I would guess she'd want to buy a house for us after she started working a regular job."

"Well, maybe," Taylor said. "I don't want to rush into anything."

Sheila leaned over, her boobs almost popping out of her top and onto the table. Taylor had told me that the old bag had recently gotten implants by appropriating some of Taylor's commercial income for "medical expenses." It was so wrong for so many reasons. Not only was it borderline theft, but now that I'd gotten a closer look, I could tell that besides looking fake, they were kind of crooked.

"Honey, we've lived in that pit of an apartment for three years. I wouldn't call it rushing," Sheila said. She leaned back in her chair, like a well-fed cat about to purr. "I've even talked to a few real estate agents. You know, for the Hollywood Hills, Bel-Air. Or maybe you like Santa Monica, dear? What do you girls think?"

"Bel-Air sucks," Kelly said. "The Hollywood Hills are much cooler."

"Lots of artists live there," Jenna agreed. "Like, I think Trent Reznor has a house there. Only old, nasty people live in Bel-Air."

"Like my grandma," Kelly said. "Definitely old and nasty."

While Sheila debated the best neighborhoods with Jenna and Kelly, I noticed Taylor had this weird look on her face, as if she'd never seen her mother before. Or, at least, never like this. "We can talk about it later, Sheila," she said, before asking everyone what they were ordering to change the subject.

The rest of the evening was actually really fun, because Taylor told us all about the show. She hadn't gotten a chance to meet Julia yet because she was finishing work on a movie in Berlin. But she said everyone else was really nice, even the kid who played her brainy little brother. He was actually older than Taylor but had some sort of kidney problem that had kept him short. The best part, though, was that Taylor was playing exactly her age. Her character's name was even cool, Brianna.

It all sounded perfect. And I knew that, somehow, I wanted to be a part of it. Just figuring out how to make that happen was the hard part.

You've got to understand, I didn't mean to do this more than once or anything. And my dad's handwriting is really basic, so that didn't take long for Kelly, who can draw almost anything, to figure out. But you can see why my forging an excuse so I could hang out with Taylor on the pilot just didn't seem like a big deal.

"You're going to have so much fun," Kelly said, practicing my dad's *p*'s over and over again. "If I thought I had half a chance of snowing my parents, I'd go with you."

"Me, too. I don't know why I ever thought you were a Goody Two-Shoes," Jenna said, messing up my hair. "We've got to get you a new badass look. Like, lots of leather."

"Ignore her," Kelly said. "She just wants to go shopping."

Where I probably screwed up was telling my dad I was going on an extra-credit field trip to Washington, D.C., one funded by the crummy bake sales my school really did seem to hold every other day. I only did it so I could stay at Taylor's. I didn't want to take the chance of coming home late from the set one night and having him completely freak out. I never thought it would come back to bite me on the ass. I mean, I even brought my homework with me to the set, so it's not like I was trying to slack off or anything.

Asking my dad was the worst part. When I talked to him, he was sitting in front of the TV watching the Korean news. He smiled a little when I told him about the trip. It wasn't much, but it was the first time I'd seen him look even remotely happy since Mom died, and it made me want the stupid imaginary field trip to be real. "You have fun there," he said. "Learn about politics."

"And visit the big statue of Abe Lincoln," I added, hating myself.

"Maybe we go to Woo Lae Oak after, when you come back," my dad said. It's this really nice Korean restaurant in Beverly Hills, and I almost said, "How can we afford it?" but I just nodded and said, "That would be nice."

I told him how long I'd be gone, and after that, there wasn't a lot to say. My dad's attention sort of drifted back to the television. He looked so tired. I knew all of us—Victoria, me, Dad—didn't look so good since Mom died. We didn't eat enough, didn't sleep enough. Didn't talk enough, either. Just lost in our own little worlds, lonely planets orbiting one another and never connecting.

I started walking away, then stopped. "*Sa rang hae*," I said under my breath. I love you. But of course my dad didn't hear me, and we both just floated off into space, as usual.

"Are you sure your dad is okay with this?" Sheila asked as I piled into the car on the way to the studio.

"It's like a field trip," I fibbed. "I'm thinking of going to film school for college." God, could I lie more?

Even knowing what I know now, I can't completely regret skipping that week of school. I had thought I'd gotten a taste of

Hollywood by crashing the commercials Taylor worked on. But I had no idea. The TV pilot, well, that made all those commercial sets look like my fifth-grade production of *Winnie-the-Pooh*.

There was no denying it. Taylor had made the big time.

The minute we walked on the set, everyone seemed to know who Taylor was, even people who'd never met her. "So nice to finally meet you, Taylor!" gushed one middle-aged woman with black-framed cat-eye glasses. We later found out she worked for the network, though I still don't know what her actual job was.

The set was huge, like a whole house built in the middle of a soundstage. There was a living room, a kitchen, and two bedrooms. One of the bedrooms was for Taylor's character, Brianna, so the set designer asked her which bands she liked and who her favorite actors were, so he could decorate her "room" with posters she'd actually pick out herself. The bed had this amazing quilt on it, little scraps of red and orange and purple. I almost hoped Taylor's show didn't get picked up, just so I would be able to ask the set designer for it.

But the coolest part was Taylor's trailer. I know what you're thinking, that a trailer is some cramped little RV with a miniature bathroom and no room to turn around. But this trailer was, swear to God, bigger than Taylor and Sheila's apartment. It had a sunken bathtub, a sofa, and a big kitchen area with a full-size refrigerator that someone had stocked with sodas and bottled water and snacks. And, oh yeah, it had a king-size bed and its very own patio. Once we got inside, I didn't even care about going back to the set. I just wanted to crank up the television (a plasma, of course) and veg out.

"Taylor's trailer," I said. "We should call it the Trayler. With a *y*."

"Yeah, the Trayler," Taylor said, nodding. Taylor tried not to act too impressed, but I could tell what she was thinking. She was getting the star treatment, and that could mean only one thing. She was, finally, a star.

Sheila was clearly coming to the same realization. She rubbed her greedy little fingers over every surface, her eyes glistening with desire. "When the show gets picked up, we're definitely requesting one of these trailers for me. I think that's only fair, seeing as I'm your legal guardian." The lunatic bitch was so absorbed in examining the trailer she never saw the looks of disgust on our faces.

After we found the trailer (or Trayler), things started moving really quickly. There was a knock on the door, and this scary-thin middle-aged guy who introduced himself as Sammy walked in. Later, Taylor told me he was the creator of the show. He seemed nice, like he could be someone's dad, which he probably was. He told Taylor that he wanted to do a read-through of the script, but first she needed to meet Julia.

Taylor, Sheila, and I followed Sammy through the lot, walking past a lot more trailers that looked like Taylor's. But when we got to Julia's, I could tell from the outside it was bigger than the Trayler. I think it might even have been bigger than my house.

Sammy hadn't even knocked at the door before Julia popped her head out.

"Well, if it isn't my new daughter!" she squealed, pulling Taylor into a hug.

I swear, I've never seen Taylor look so happy. And I've never seen Sheila look more pissed off.

"And I guess you're my new mom," Taylor replied, beaming.

That was it for Sheila, who muscled her way in between the

two of them to shake Julia's hand. "I'm Taylor's mom, Sheila," she said in her sugary-sweet, fake-nice voice. "I'll be here on the set. Every day. As Taylor's guardian."

Julia didn't seem to notice the edge to Sheila's words. She just smiled that big smile of hers and pulled her into a hug, too. "It's so nice to meet you! You have such a talented daughter!" she trilled. Then she looked at me. "And who are you?"

Taylor put an arm around me. "She's my best friend, Erin," she said. "She wants to go to film school when we graduate, so she's here to observe."

Julia shook my hand and nodded. "Excellent idea," she said. "You're so smart to get started early. If you have any questions, just ask. We need more female directors and producers."

I couldn't really see myself popping into Julia's trailer to ask her for tips on becoming a producer or anything, but I was impressed that she offered. She seemed so down-to-earth, like she was just anyone, not a huge star who couldn't even walk out of her house without paparazzi dogging her. So yeah, I felt a little bad for ever thinking she was this big-toothed monster with people-eating tendencies.

Julia took both of Taylor's hands in hers and looked her dead in the eye, suddenly serious. "I really want you and me to spend some time together doing mother-daughter stuff. It's going to make such a difference in what you see on the screen. Have you got time for some girl chat, just the two of us?"

I could see from the look on Sheila's face that she was about to veto that idea, but Sammy must have sensed this and spoke quickly. "She absolutely has time to spend with you," he said, giving Sheila a "Don't you *even*" look in the process. "We can do the read-through around two. Does that work?"

Sheila put both her hands on Taylor's shoulders, spinning her around to face her. "Are you sure, honey? You don't have to if you don't want to." God, she was acting like she was sending Taylor off with a child molester or something.

You should have seen the look on Taylor's face, which was somewhere between mortified and furious. "It's okay, Sheila," she said, her voice dripping with sarcasm. "I want to."

Then Taylor and Julia both smiled at each other, and for a moment I could see the resemblance. Taylor, with her perfectly straight post-headgear teeth, had Julia's exact same smile. They looked more like sisters than mother and daughter, though. Julia was probably Sheila's age, but she looked so much younger and happier, I would have guessed Sheila was twenty years older at least.

I walked back to the Trayler with Sheila, who suddenly decided I was her new confidant, which bugged the crap out of me. I just wanted some alone time in Taylor's fantastic new trailer, but instead it looked like I was going to have to listen to her mom's incessant bitching.

"You would think I didn't exist," she fumed. "Her new mother? I'm standing right there and she says that?"

I just nodded, because I seriously doubted Sheila wanted me to say anything. I think if I hadn't been there, she would have been perfectly happy to walk around the set talking to herself like a lunatic.

"It wasn't like this when Taylor was little," she said. "When we worked on those lotion commercials, they made sure I was taken care of."

Hello, delusional much? "Wasn't that only because you were the one taking care of Taylor?"

Sheila shot me a look that suggested I might not be coming back tomorrow if she had anything to say about it. "Why don't you find something to do? I have to make some phone calls."

And just like that, I was kicked out of the Trayler. Without Taylor, I didn't feel so at home on the set. And I really shouldn't have, because honestly there was no reason for me to be there. All I had learned about making TV shows was there were a lot of people you had to meet, and stars got some really nice digs.

I realized I was getting hungry, and since I didn't have access to the snacks in the trailer, I figured I should look for the nearest vending machine.

"Where can I get something to eat around here?" I asked a big, burly guy walking by with a coffee table under one arm.

He stopped and looked around. "There's a Subway place across the street. Why, not up for the catering truck?"

I'd totally forgotten about catering. The best perk when you work in TV and movies is you never have to go out for lunch. "I guess I should check that out first," I said, hoping he didn't catch on that I was a total fraud. "Where is it?"

He pointed me towards a little truck that looked like one of those places that sells Mexican food out on the street. But when I walked up, it smelled a lot better than a taco truck. A woman stuck her head out of the window and said, "Today it's chicken Florentine with mashed garlic potatoes, grilled salmon with sautéed broccoli, or filet mignon with tomato risotto." Clearly, not a taco truck at all.

When she handed me the plate, not a paper plate but a real one, the filet mignon looked really good, like something you'd find in a fancy restaurant. The problem was where to eat it. Everyone else who walked by seemed to have something to do, and here I was, eating lunch at eleven o'clock in the morning. I was hungry, but feeling so stupid and useless was killing my appetite.

I finally saw a few other people pick up plates from the truck and head into a separate soundstage. I followed them and saw rows of people eating at cafeteria tables. I felt like I was at school all over again, but worse. I didn't recognize anyone, and I had no idea where I should sit. What if a table was just for stars of the show or electricians or something? Would they make me leave?

I finally sat down at a table where a man and a woman were so engrossed in conversation, I don't think they even noticed I was there. I polished off my steak and was just starting to work my way through my tomato risotto (which I thought sounded pretty fancy, but tasted like mushy rice to me) when someone sat down next to me.

"So, what are you doing on the pilot?" The man was wearing one of those artfully torn band T-shirts, this one for Sonic Youth. Tattoos of Japanese writing crawled up one muscular arm, and his dirty-blond hair, short and messy, looked like something out of a magazine ad. He was, in a word, incredibly hot. Okay, that's two words, but you know what I mean. I swear tomato risotto almost dribbled down my chin—I was so close to drooling over this guy.

I almost blurted out, "Nothing," but stopped myself. "I'm sort of Taylor Christensen's personal assistant," I said, impressed with myself for covering so quickly. And really, I was helping Taylor, even if I was only running interference with her mom.

Incredibly Hot Guy nodded seriously. "Cool. I'm Dax. I'm sort of a production assistant, technically."

"I'm Erin," I said, shaking his hand. I couldn't take my eyes off his tattoos. I don't usually like guys with a lot of body art, but in this case I was willing to make an exception. Wait, who am I kidding? On him, the tats were sexy as hell. "What do you mean, technically?"

"My dad is a producer on the show, so here I am." Dax grinned. "It's just an excuse to keep me busy for a while." He leaned forward. "Keep me out of trouble," he whispered, grinning wider.

He was close enough to kiss me, and I almost wanted him to. And yet in my head I could hear a million sirens going off, and the voice of my mom. "Boys want one thing," she'd say. "They lie. Nothing but trouble. You focus on schoolwork, worry about boys later."

But I'd finished my schoolwork, and I didn't have a mom, not anymore. I felt myself blushing, and looked down at the risotto growing cold on the plate.

"What kind of trouble?" I finally asked.

"Oh, nothing serious. I just partied way too much, and it was either work here and get back on track for a semester or three or go on some freaking spiritual retreat. My dad's one of those guys who likes to pay other people a lot of money to fix his problems."

"That's terrible," I said, even though I was thinking that it must be nice to grow up that rich. And at least his dad cared enough to fix his problems. Not that my dad didn't care, not exactly—he was just so lost. If I had a problem, he wouldn't even know about it, much less fix it.

"Sometimes it is, sometimes it isn't. And most of the year I'm at Columbia, so what he doesn't know won't hurt him."

Columbia University, I guessed. So he was in college. That meant he wasn't too much older than me. Not that it mattered, since I didn't have a lot of hope that a guy already in college would be interested in me. Especially not a guy who spent a lot of time on movie sets, surrounded by girls who looked like Taylor.

"So, how did you end up being Taylor's assistant? That sounds like a pretty tough job."

"Why would it be tough?"

"You know, actresses. They're all insecure and whiny. 'Get my Diet Coke. Do I look fat in this? Where's my nonfat, no-sugar iced mocha?' That shit would drive me crazy." Dax looked at my plate. "Hey, check it out. You actually eat like a real person."

"Taylor isn't obsessive like that," I said. "She'd eat this, too." But the little part of my brain that was louder than the warning sirens in my head was jumping up and down. He thought it was cool that I was pigging out! And more importantly, he didn't seem to like actresses very much.

We talked about a bunch of other stuff during lunch. I told Dax my mom had died not so long ago, and that I was taking time off from school. I didn't say high school, and he might have just assumed I meant college. After all, since my mom died I'd started wearing makeup, which my dad never seemed to notice, but I was pretty sure I didn't look like I was twelve anymore. Even so, college seemed like a stretch, but I was getting more and more comfortable with twisting the truth. That's what everyone does in Hollywood anyway, right?

Dax, it turned out, was a super-interesting guy. He'd been all over the world because of his dad being a producer. Sometimes he'd spend the whole summer wherever his dad was shooting his latest movie, like Italy or France. But that all depended on which wife his dad was living with at the time and whether she thought Dax was a cool kid or a spoiled brat. Dax's dad was on his sixth marriage, and he was thinking about getting divorced again.

"So, do you have to go cater to the whims of Miss Taylor?" Dax asked me as I carefully scooped up the last bit of my risotto. It had gotten cold and tasted disgusting, but I was determined to clean my plate so I could drag out our lunch as long as possible. "Or can you hang out? I can show you around if you want."

Walking around the lot, I barely noticed any of the landmarks Dax pointed out. I kept thinking that I couldn't wait to tell Taylor that I'd met this amazing guy. And then I wondered what it would be like to be his girlfriend and maybe live in some big house in the Pacific Palisades with him. And when I wasn't thinking about that, I was just looking at how cute he was. Blue eyes, tan skin, the body of a swimmer or a surfer (and it turned out he was both). So I didn't really notice when we stopped outside a small bungalow.

"This is my dad's production company," he said. "I gotta check in, you know. Pretend like I'm working."

I stood there and stared at him. It was crazy, but I was sort of hoping he would kiss me, or ask for my number. It felt like we'd been on this really great first date, and I didn't want it to end.

Instead, Dax ran his hand along my arm so gently it gave me goose bumps. "I'll catch you later, I hope."

And then he looked at me with those eyes, those ocean-colored eyes, and walked through the door. I'm glad he didn't turn around to look at me again because I was just standing there, frozen in place like a big idiot. That look he gave me, I had no doubt about what it meant. It wasn't the way you'd look at someone if you thought she was some underdeveloped high school kid. He looked at me like I was a woman, all grown up and then some.

I was so wound up thinking about Dax, I got completely lost trying to find my way back to the Trayler, but I didn't mind. I actually liked having some time to think about what I wanted to wear tomorrow in case I bumped into Dax. God, I wanted him to make a move on me. Just the idea of kissing him made me feel light-headed. Except for a few games of Seven Minutes in Heaven in grade school, I hadn't really kissed a boy. Not seriously, at least.

When I finally found the trailer, I hesitated at the door. I didn't really want to be stuck alone with Sheila, so I pressed my ear against the door, hoping to hear Taylor's voice. And boy, did I. She and Sheila were clearly in the middle of a fight.

"She's not your mother!" Sheila screeched.

"Oh, like you're Supermom or something!" Taylor screeched back.

For a minute I thought about leaving, but I felt too guilty to go through with it. Taylor didn't need Sheila's crap right now when so much was at stake. Getting all rattled and freaked-out because of her mom when she was supposed to be learning lines and rehearsing? Not good. You'd think someone who was already plotting how to spend Taylor's money would be more thoughtful, but Sheila, well, she just isn't that bright.

I opened the door of the trailer a crack, and I saw both of their heads turn in my direction. Taylor instantly broke into a smile.

"You guys busy?" I asked in my nicest voice, for Sheila's benefit.

"Get your butt in here! Where have you been?" Taylor said, patting a spot next to her on the sofa.

Shockingly enough, Sheila didn't seem as excited to see me. "We were in the middle of a conversation, Taylor," she said, ignoring me.

"Well, I'm done. So why don't you get something to eat?" Taylor said.

Sheila stared hard at her daughter, who stared right back. Finally, Sheila picked up her purse, an ugly gold lamé thing, and stalked out.

Taylor sighed heavily and turned to me. "Oh my God, I am so glad you're here! It has been the wildest day ever. Swear to God."

And then, before I could even mention Dax, Taylor started talking. And talking. It turned out that she and Julia were now the best of friends. They'd eaten lunch together in Julia's trailer, and not the craft services mushy rice I ate but grilled salmon salads shipped in from this restaurant called Axe (pronounced *Ash-ay*), specially made. Julia had told her all about her childhood, how she was a big geek and kids made fun of her. "She was just like us!" Taylor said, bouncing up and down on the sofa. I almost wanted to say, "Just like you, maybe," but Taylor was talking so fast I didn't have the chance.

"We are, like, almost the same person," Taylor said, shaking her head with amazement. "It's scary, you know?"

A few hours ago, I'd have been so impressed by the major breaking-news story that Taylor had become Julia Hanson's new best buddy. But right at this minute, I wanted to tell Taylor my news, because for once in my life I actually had some. I'd just met a guy, a real, smoking-hot, interested-in-me guy, and if Taylor had had a shotgun marriage to Keanu Reeves, I don't think I'd have given a crap.

"Hey, I have something to tell you, too," I said, but Taylor just kept yapping. The first read-through had gone "perfectly," and everyone, even the network people, had laughed when Taylor read her lines. And then, right after the read-through, the writers changed the script and made Taylor's part even bigger.

"They loved me, Erin. The director told me I'm going to be a really big star."

I guess I didn't look appropriately excited about this, because Taylor gave me a funny look. "What's wrong with you?" she said, in a way that suggested there was definitely something wrong with me.

"Nothing," I said. "It's just that I met a guy on the lot, this incredibly cute guy—"

"Everyone here is incredibly cute, Erin," Taylor said to me, as if I were a little stupid. "Like, I just told you I'm going to be a big star, and you're talking about some guy?"

Maybe it was just the tone of Taylor's voice, but I don't think I'd ever been angrier at her than I was right then. It would be one thing if this had been Taylor's first day in the spotlight, but lately I felt like I was trapped in some all-Taylor, all-the-time basic-cable channel. Usually, it was exciting. It wasn't like I ever had anything interesting going on in my life. But today, I finally did.

I thought about telling Taylor to shove it. I thought about telling Taylor she was becoming a big brat. But then I thought about how she kicked Sheila out of her trailer. I didn't want to fight. But more importantly, I didn't want to get sent home, never to return. Especially after meeting Dax.

"Sorry," I said. "I'm just distracted."

Taylor sighed. "Fine, what did you want to tell me about this guy?"

"Forget it," I said, deflated. All of a sudden, I realized that even if Taylor suddenly turned around and begged me to tell her about Dax, she didn't really want to know. She was so wrapped up in all this Hollywood stuff, there wasn't any room for me. I knew it wasn't that she didn't care, exactly. It was that there was so much going on, so many thoughts in her head, that somehow I'd gotten crowded out. "I just . . . sometimes I think you think of me as your sidekick. That's all."

Taylor stared at me. "If you were just my sidekick, would I have turned down that Tom Hanks movie after your mom died?" she said.

My face felt hot. It was true; Taylor had sacrificed a lot for me. But that felt like a lifetime ago. So much had changed, so fast. "I'm sorry, I just . . . I've got to get some air."

I heard Taylor behind me as I walked onto the set—"Wait," she called—but I didn't turn around. I wasn't sure what to think anymore, but I knew, in some weird way, I couldn't go back again.

I don't know how long I walked around the set, maybe a few hours, maybe more. It was only when it started getting dark that I thought I should head back. After all, I needed a ride home.

Back at the trailer, I saw Sheila pacing outside, listening intently to her cell phone. When she saw me, she hung up fast. "Erin, where have you been?" she said in a worried voice I'd never heard from her before.

I didn't even get a chance to tell her before she ran up to me and grabbed my arm. "When I couldn't find you I called your father to tell him he may have to pick you up, and now he's hysterical. He thought you were in Washington. What the hell is going on?"

All of a sudden I felt like *I* was going to become Malibu Barfie. I couldn't believe it. Sheila, the world's lousiest mom, had gotten interested in what I was doing at the worst possible time. Great.

"I need to get you home, right away. He's worried sick," Sheila said, dragging me towards the parking lot.

"What about Taylor?"

"One of the production assistants will drive her home," Sheila said. "I want you to get in that car and start talking, you got me?"

I nodded. This was going to be an even worse ride than the one coming here.

When I got home, my dad and my sister were both sitting in the living room. Apparently my dad was mad enough to pull Victoria away from UCLA, and she was in total pit bull mode. Sheila must have sensed that I was desperate to bolt for my bedroom, because she put a hand against my back and steered me to the sofa. And the second my butt touched the upholstery, the screaming started.

"What the hell were you thinking, lying to Dad and playing hooky for a week?" Victoria shrieked. "What's next, Erin? Drugs? Stealing?"

"You told me your dad was okay with you being on the set, Erin," Sheila said in a stern voice. "You shouldn't have done that."

Victoria started yelling about a bunch of other stuff, like how worried my dad had been, and how the last thing anyone needs right now is a troubled teen, and how if something seriously wrong had happened, they wouldn't have been able to get in touch with me, and after Mom had died the way she did, you'd think I'd know better, yada yada yada. I knew Victoria was right, but after a while all the screaming just started to sound like an ambulance siren, droning on and on and on, all meaning lost.

The thing that was weird, though, was that my dad just sat there. Didn't say a thing. Hardly looked at me. Victoria kept talking about how angry he was, and how worried. But he sure didn't seem to be either of those things. He just looked drained and out of it.

Eventually Victoria ran out of steam and moved on to the punishment phase of the evening. She told me I couldn't go to the set again, and that I was grounded for at least a month. I wasn't particularly worried about any of that, because I seriously doubted that Victoria would be around to play enforcer. But then Sheila told me that whenever I wanted to see Taylor, even on the weekends, she'd want to talk to my dad first. So much for sneaking onto the set anytime soon. But even that would've been okay if I hadn't started thinking about Dax. I realized I might never see him again. And suddenly my punishment seemed a whole lot harsher.

I was trying to figure out how I could sneak a note to him through his dad's production company when I heard a choking sound. It was my dad. He was crying, his shoulders shaking up and down as he covered his face with his hands. Victoria put an arm around his shoulder, which just made him cry harder. Even Sheila seemed worried about Dad, hopping up to run into the kitchen and get him a glass of water.

Somehow this was so much worse than the yelling. As weird as it sounds, I felt like I'd broken him, ripped out some essential part of his soul and ground it under my heel without even meaning to do it. And the worst part was that I knew that no matter what I said or did, I couldn't fix the damage I'd done.

My dad drank some of the water, and then, finally, looked at me. His eyes were bloodshot and swollen. He didn't seem to care that tears were running down his face, something he would have been too proud to let me see in the past. But things were different now. *"Eo teok kae nahan tae geu reol su it ni?"* He kept repeating "How could you do this to me?" in Korean, over and over, even though it was hard to tell through his sobs. But I heard it, each and every time.

Then, so softly I almost didn't hear it, I heard him say, "How could you leave me like this?"

That didn't make a lot of sense to me at first, but when I saw Victoria's face had turned ashy gray I got it. He wasn't talking to me. He was talking to Mom.

I decided it was time for me to say something, just so he might get distracted and stop his crazy muttering. I would have promised anything, like a kidney or my CD collection, just to make my dad start acting normal again. I don't think I was the only person in the room who felt as if she was seeing something really terrible, something much worse than just a guy freaking out over his teenage daughter's disobedience. "I'm really sorry," I stuttered. "I'll never do it again, I swear. It was just a stupid mistake."

My dad didn't respond. Instead, he just got up and walked out of the room. It was so quiet I could hear his bedroom door shut. The whole scene was so awful it even stunned Sheila and Victoria into silence, which is saying something.

Sheila got up to leave, and when she looked at me, she didn't seem angry anymore. Just sad, the way she had looked the day my mother died. Nothing that bad had happened this time, thank God, but I think she already knew what I was going to find out. That even though my dad had tried to act like everything was going to be okay since Mom died, it wasn't. And it might never be okay again.

Chapter Four

Hollywood is like high school. It is! It's like a big popularity contest, and everyone wants to hang out with the cool kids. And there's a lot of competition. Everyone acts nice to your face, but the truth is, Scarlett Johansson and I would claw each other's eyes out for the right role. That's just the way it is.

—TAYLOR CHRISTENSEN in *Cosmopolitan*

For the next few months, things were pretty rough. I'd come home from school and the house would be dead quiet, even if my dad was there. It was like living with a ghost, one that would occasionally make the floor creak or slam the refrigerator door, never speaking and just leaving a spooky vibe in the room. He wasn't there much, though. I guessed he was at the office working late, even though I never tried calling him there or anything. I felt ashamed of myself whenever I saw him, and I never knew what to say. I think he might have felt the same way.

As I'd guessed, Victoria pretty much disappeared after her big tough-love act, so I wasn't actually grounded. But I felt guilty about going out, so I might as well have been. And thanks to Sheila playing the good parent, there was no way to hang out with Taylor on the set during the rest of the pilot shoot without my dad getting a "check-in" phone call. I had no idea if he would enforce Victoria's stupid rules, but I figured that I should play the dutiful daughter, at least for a little while.

The only good thing was that after the pilot Taylor came back to school for a while. Her agent didn't want her to work on any long-term projects until they knew whether or not the TV show was getting picked up, which was going to take months. Plus, now that Taylor had finally played a real teenager, she wasn't so eager to do commercials where she had to strap her boobs against her chest to look like a twelve-year-old, even if that meant she never bought back her old T-shirts from Sheila.

It was a pretty big deal when Taylor came back to class, because it didn't take long for news to get around that she'd filmed a pilot with Julia Hanson. All of a sudden it was like Taylor was visiting royalty. Kids she'd never met before waved at her in the hallway. Teachers congratulated her, and Mrs. Metrino even asked if Taylor might be able to get her an autograph for her niece. The topper was when the principal mentioned Taylor in a school assembly, saying that she was a "star achiever" in the dramatic arts.

It was crazy, because it wasn't like there had never been a famous kid at our school before. Like, in the nineties some kid from *Home Improvement* skated by for a semester or something. But this was different. I don't know why, but I think everyone sensed that Taylor was going to be big, not just some disposable child star that gets chewed up and spit out by Hollywood. Or hell, maybe everyone was secretly hoping Taylor would invite Julia Hanson to tag along to English comp—I don't know.

The first day Taylor came back to school, the table Jenna, Kelly, and I sat at was like the 405 freeway at rush hour. People kept coming over to say hi or ask questions.

"Julia's really sweet," Taylor told a timid-looking girl I'd never seen before. "She's so normal, not like a movie star at all."

"Can you please scoot over?" Kelly asked a dorky guy who was practically climbing on top of her to get to Taylor. "Your breath is disgusting. Did you have tuna for lunch?"

"You should totally run for class president," I whispered to Taylor. "I think they'd let you burn the place to the ground if you wanted to."

"Nah, I don't have the time for a political career," Taylor said with a smirk. "Maybe after I win an Emmy, though. You never know." Yeah, the attention wasn't going to her head or anything.

At first I was really psyched that Taylor was back in class, even if she was the number one reason why I wasn't pulling up my grades. For a few weeks after Dad's big meltdown, I was totally motivated to study. I didn't think anything could really make him happy, but I figured a perfect report card wouldn't hurt. Still, it was hard to keep my eyes on the prize when Taylor wanted to pass notes in class, or hang out in the bathroom with me and Jenna and Kelly all through poli-sci.

But after a while, I wasn't so excited that Taylor was back. It's hard to explain, but she was different.

Suddenly it wasn't enough for Taylor to taunt Alexandra and her friends with designer labels. It wasn't enough that we knew we were a hundred times cooler than her and her stupid friends. Now, Taylor wanted something more. She wanted to bring Alexandra down. And then grind her heel into the girl's neck, kick her in the gut, and leave her for dead on the side of the road. And I think she wanted to do it just to see if she could.

The funny thing was, once Alexandra heard about Taylor's

TV show, she actually started being nice to her. Not "Let's be best friends" nice, exactly, but she started making little gestures. She'd nod at Taylor in the hallways instead of insulting her. One time she actually complimented Taylor on a T-shirt she was wearing and asked her where she got it. And for some reason, this only bothered Taylor more.

"She's so fake I want to wring her neck," Taylor hissed to me during lunch. "She thinks she can suck up to me and what, meet Julia? Like, I'll just magically forget all the crap she's pulled on me?"

"Being a TV star means people are going to suck up to you and be fake all the time, Taylor," I said.

"Well, she's not the only one who can act fake," Taylor snapped back. "I'm the actress, after all."

I shrugged. That didn't make a lot of sense to me then. But pretty soon it did. Because, even as Taylor started acting sugary sweet to Alexandra's face, she was mounting a campaign to drive the girl ape-shit crazy.

First was the tarantula she sneaked into Alexandra's locker, which made the girl so hysterical she missed school for the next two days. Then, Taylor posted Alexandra's cell phone number in some creepy chat room for guys who liked to be spanked by transsexuals. She must have gotten a lot of phone calls, because Kelly said that during cheerleading practice Alexandra was complaining about having to change her number.

Then every few days Taylor began slipping evil notes into Alexandra's books and her purse when she wasn't looking, awful stuff about how pathetic she was and how everyone in school knew it. Taylor even started talking about snagging some of

Sheila's hard-core prescription painkillers and planting them in Alexandra's locker on a day when the principal had one of his random inspections.

Okay, yeah, it was kind of funny, but only talking about it, not doing it. By this point I was starting to think Taylor was losing it. I tried to talk to Jenna and Kelly about it, but they shrugged it off.

"Alexandra's such a bitch, who cares?" Kelly shrugged. "I mean, Taylor's just screwing around."

"But don't you think she's crossing the line?" I asked. "She's being totally vicious, and Alexandra isn't even mean to her anymore. Taylor didn't used to be like this, you know?"

"Eh, she's probably doing Alexandra a favor," Jenna suggested. "Like, that girl's a rich kid who gets everything she wants. Time for a reality check."

Kelly patted me on the arm. "You're so nice, Erin," she said, smiling. "Sometimes I'm surprised you're any fun at all."

"What can we do to Alexandra?" Taylor asked Kelly, Jenna, and me, furiously sucking on her Diet Coke. The four of us were sitting at the mall food court on one of my rare unsupervised outings. It had been a few weeks, and Sheila had started to figure out that my dad wasn't going to lose his tenuous grip on sanity if I hung out with Taylor and the girls during the weekend.

When everyone just shrugged, Taylor scowled. "Come on, you guys! I can't stomach the idea of her showing up at the Spring Fling like Cinderella at the ball."

"Get used to it. Wild horses couldn't keep that girl from an opportunity to play dress-up," I said. Spring Fling was what our school had instead of a prom, and everyone was invited. We all knew it was a little lame, but it was still a very, very big deal. The rich kids rented limos and hotel rooms, and snagged their parents' tuxedos and Versace gowns. Considering my current financial situation, I'd be lucky if I could pay for a ticket, much less a dress.

But Taylor, well, she was determined to spoil Alexandra's fun. Not that the rest of us took her very seriously. Even if they weren't interested in stopping Taylor, I was starting to sense that Jenna and Kelly were getting just as sick of Taylor's anti-Alexandra rants as I was. "Maybe you could push her down some stairs. That would be very dramatic," Jenna joked.

Kelly shook her head. "A car bomb. Fiery and painful. And disfiguring."

"Not if Brandon's driving, please," I said. Honestly, that was the only thing I really held against Alexandra. She had the nerve to steal the cutest guy in our grade who had not only his license but his own car. Not that I was still crushing on him. I mean, yes, Dax was still my number one fantasy, but a girl needs a little masculine distraction during chem class, okay?

Taylor's eyes suddenly went wide. "Oh my God, I have a much . . . better . . . plan," she said, drawing out the words as if they were delicious candies melting on her tongue. I don't know why I knew exactly what she was going to say, but I did. And I hated it.

"Are you sure that's a good idea?" I asked after Taylor had spelled it out.

"Absolutely," Taylor responded, her eyes practically sparkling with malevolent glee. "You have to go along with it, Erin. The plan doesn't work without you. No one else has an afternoon class with him."

I, of course, was completely outnumbered. Jenna and Kelly

didn't much care about Alexandra or Brandon, but they were dedicated troublemakers and this was too tempting to resist. Taylor had concocted the ultimate prank, one that would live on in Bev Hills history.

Even though I went along with their plan, even though I tried to convince myself it was a good idea, I knew in my heart of hearts that it wasn't. It was mean and petty and simply a shitty thing to do to someone, even someone like Alexandra. But with Taylor, when she really wanted something, there was no stopping her. You either got on board or got out of the way.

I got on board.

It took a few days to plot out all the little details, like finding the ideal time to steal Brandon's car keys without him noticing, and the window of opportunity for planting our evidence. When I didn't think too much about what we were doing, it was actually fun, like being secret agents or something. Taylor would sidle up to the rest of us at my locker, scanning the hall for potential tattletales.

"Got the underwear," she'd whisper.

"Got the keys," Kelly whispered back.

"I'll catch you in fifth period," I added.

"I want something to do!" whined Jenna.

Taylor shrugged. "Keep your fingers crossed or something. Don't be a pain in the ass."

Everything went flawlessly. Brandon, who had a bad habit of throwing his keys on his desk during chem lab, never even noticed they were gone after Kelly's diversion. She poured two of the wrong chemicals together for her class experiment and created a small inferno, one that required two fire extinguishers to put out. The next period, I just slipped the keys into his backpack, the damage already done. He never suspected a thing.

The next day, we heard the fight between Alexandra and Brandon before we saw it. *"I didn't do anything!"* he pleaded in the hallway as she slammed her locker shut.

Alexandra hissed, "Shut . . . *up!*"

That was the point when Brandon did something stupid. As Alexandra began walking away from him, he grabbed her arm to pull her towards him. Bad, bad idea. I don't think he even saw the first slap coming, but that was okay because there were a lot more to watch out for after that. *"Don't touch me!"* Alexandra shrieked, flailing at Brandon like a freakin' lunatic. Let me just say that this hissy fit topped her tarantula reaction by a mile. The girl had completely and utterly lost her cool.

Everyone in the hallway froze, watching as Brandon covered his head with his hands and Alexandra kept swatting at him and yelling. I couldn't even really understand what she was saying because she was crying and screaming at the same time. By this time Brandon wasn't saying much, either, other than "Ow!" and *"Shit!"* and "Please, Alexandra, listen!"

I think it was Jenna who was the first to start giggling, but it was hard to tell. Because after a few seconds of shocked silence, everyone in the hallway was laughing. We couldn't help it. Alexandra—flawless, übercool Alexandra—was melting down right in front of us, and I don't think we were the only people there who were a little thrilled to see it happen.

After a minute, Alexandra finally stopped hitting Brandon and turned on the rest of us. *"Shut up! Shut up! Shut up!"* she shrieked.

And when that only made everyone laugh harder, her face turned bright red with rage, redder even than her trashy designer lipstick. *"Screw you all!"* she yelled before stomping away, Brandon trailing behind her at a safe distance.

By second period, the whole school was buzzing about Alexandra's fit. The details of our prank, which no one else knew was a prank, were out. When Brandon was driving Alexandra to school that morning, she'd found a thong stuffed in between the cushions of her seat. And nothing Brandon said could convince her he hadn't been with some other girl. Some other girl who wore a lacy pink thong.

As great as it was to see Alexandra completely disintegrate, the truth was I couldn't stop thinking about Brandon. He hadn't done anything to deserve getting slapped around, and the worst part was, I think he really liked the crazy bitch. Just watching him trying to talk some sense into Alexandra as she pummeled him, I could see how desperately he wanted her to believe him.

Taylor tried to make me feel less guilty. "Look, we're doing him a favor," she said when she saw me gloomily picking over my tuna salad at lunch. "In a week or two, he'll realize what a she-beast she is. I mean, even if he had cheated on her, that doesn't give her the right to use him as a punching bag."

I had to agree with her on that point. And pretty soon I stopped feeling so guilty every time I saw Brandon in the hall. It wasn't that I'd accepted what had happened or anything. I was just distracted. Spring Fling was coming up.

Already banners were up in the hallways at school screaming SPRING FLING! DANCE THE NIGHT AWAY! and teachers were bugging us to get our parents to sign up as chaperones. I fantasized about going with Dax, even though I knew that was never going to happen.

In the past few years I've been to a lot of parties, fancy parties, ones with celebrities and fifteen-foot-high champagne fountains with diamond-encrusted glasses and sashimi served on naked women, crazy stuff you couldn't imagine if you've never seen it. But my little high school Spring Fling still sticks in my memory. For a whole lot of reasons.

The Wednesday before the dance, Taylor came running up to me outside study hall.

"It's happening!" she squealed, jumping up and down while nearly ripping my arm from its socket. "It's really happening!"

The untitled Julia Hanson show, which was now called *Family Style*, had been picked up for a full-season order. That meant Taylor was going back to work, and come this fall we'd be able to watch her Monday nights at eight thirty, right after that sitcom about a bunch of doctors.

"My agent just called. I can't believe this. I'm going to series!"

"Oh my *God*!" I couldn't think of anything else to say. This was so surreal, the idea that my best friend was about to become a television star.

"It gets better, though," Taylor said after both of us had stopped freaking out. "I told my agent I was going to Spring Fling this weekend, and she called the show publicist, and she thought it would be a good opportunity to promote the show. Get a magazine to cover it, maybe some TV crews."

"Like, *Entertainment Tonight* is coming to our Spring Fling?"

"Maybe, but wait—that's not even the best part. Get this. They're getting us a limo. They'll pay for our tickets. They'll even decorate the gym. And"—Taylor lowered her voice—"the publicist said she might be able to get Rooney to play."

"At our dance?" I'd heard Rooney on the radio, so I couldn't imagine the band coming to our stupid high school.

"Yeah. It all depends on whether they can get *Teen People* to write an article about me. So don't tell anyone, not yet, okay?"

"This is amazing!" I said, trying to keep my voice down. This was like the Oscars of school dances, I swear.

"Oh, and I almost forgot," Taylor added. "I have a date."

"Greg Fromer?" The guy followed Taylor around like a lapdog, so it seemed like a logical conclusion.

But Taylor just rolled her eyes. "No, silly. Brandon."

She must have seen my face twitch. It wasn't so much that I still liked Brandon. But he had been my crush. Mine. And Taylor knew it.

"I know, I'm sorry, but don't you see? This will kill Alexandra. Kill her!"

I nodded, but I didn't see. Who cared about Alexandra? Taylor was starring in her own friggin' TV show. Plus I hated the idea of Brandon getting hurt again. I knew Taylor was going to toss him aside like every other guy she went out with.

"Did he ask you?"

"More or less. I dropped a really, really big hint," Taylor said, winking at me. "Do you want me to get you a date? Greg Fromer would totally go with you if you want."

Ewww. I didn't have a date, but I was so not interested in going out with some twerp from Taylor's reject pile. "I'm fine, really. I'll hang out with Jenna and Kelly." Even though Jenna had been asked to the dance by some dorky guy in her science class, she decided it would be more fun to go stag than be stuck with some guy she didn't really like. Kelly and I, well, we didn't even get invites from losers.

"We'll all hang out," Taylor said. "Erin, someday we're going to look back on this night as the moment our lives started getting good. Really good. And we will never, ever forget it."

Taylor was right. Everything about that night was insane.

When the limo pulled up outside my house, my dad came out on the porch to look at it. "TV people pay for this?" he asked.

"Yes," I said, hoping Victoria's hand-me-down dress didn't look too shabby. I should have asked Taylor if the network would get me a new dress, but I didn't want to be pushy. "Nice, huh?"

My dad looked at me and smiled. "You look pretty. You have fun," he said. *"Jo sim hae ra. Sul ma si ji mal go. Jip ae jal deul eo wa ra, kongju nim,"* he added before walking back inside. *Be careful. Don't drink. Come home safe, Princess.* Right. Still, he forgot to give me a curfew. That used to be Mom's job.

The driver of the limo opened the door for me, which was already pretty cool. Inside the limo, Taylor and Brandon were sitting snuggled up side by side. I felt a prickle of jealousy, but let it go. Taylor looked beautiful in a wispy blue green dress and sparkly gold shoes. And Brandon, well, he was as cute as ever, maybe more so in his penguin suit.

Across from them, Jenna and Kelly were just as dressed up, and I started thinking Victoria's little pink prom gown from Ross

Dress for Less wasn't going to cut it. Just then a flashbulb popped in my face. "Ow!" I yelled, covering my eyes.

"Sorry," a voice said. "I'm Patrick." A skinny guy with glasses reached over and shook my hand as I sat down.

"He's the photographer from *Teen People*," Taylor explained. "He's going to follow us around for a little while." This was back when it was an actual magazine, even. Suddenly I really wished I'd gotten another dress.

"They said they wanted a pictorial," Patrick explained as he reached into his bag to change lenses on his camera. "So that includes you."

I was just about to ask him if he could do me a favor and fix my dress in Photoshop, when Jenna yelled, "Hey, let's open the moonroof!" Pushing a button, she promptly stood up in her seat. Under her poufy black and purple ball gown she was wearing her beloved combat boots. "You can taste the smog!" she bellowed.

I popped up right next to her, in part so I didn't have to see Taylor stroking Brandon's hand. The city looked so beautiful at night. Outside a movie theater on Wilshire a bunch of people standing in line waved, and we waved back. "Jude Law gets killed in the end!" Jenna screamed as we passed.

"Is that really how the movie ends?" I asked her.

"I don't know. But if he doesn't, they'll be pleasantly surprised."

If the evening had ended with the limo ride, I would have been perfectly happy. We convinced the limo driver to blast KROQ on the radio, and we even had him make an extra loop through the school driveway just to make sure there were enough kids in the parking lot to see us climb out of a limo with our own personal photographer.

That was pretty cool. But that was just the beginning.

As soon as we piled out of the limo, a woman in a suit came running up to us.

"Hey, Andi!" Taylor said, giving the show publicist a hug.

"I got E! News here and the TV Guide Channel," Andi said, gesturing towards two camera crews behind her. "You need to spend some time with both of them. They're banking the pieces, just in case the show becomes a hit."

"What does that mean?" Jenna asked.

Andi looked at Jenna as if she were a space alien. "Um, do I know you?"

Taylor turned to Jenna. "They're recording it now, but they may not air it for a while. That's all."

But we didn't have time to talk about banking, because pretty soon Andi was pulling Taylor towards the cameras. "What about my friends?" she asked.

Andi looked at the rest of us and shrugged. "We can put them in the background. No stupid hand gestures or waving at Mom, though."

"Darn, I had it all planned out," Brandon said to me. "I was going to do the Macarena."

I laughed, probably a little too loud. Brandon was no Dax, but he was still pretty adorable. Of course, I'd been too shy to say one word to him all night. Yeah, I know, I suck.

We all tromped over to the camera crews, Taylor leading the way. In her shoes, I would've been entirely intimidated by the cameras and the lights, but Taylor just grinned and gave the reporter, a pretty woman I'd actually seen on TV, a hug.

Once word got around that actual TV crews were at our dance, a crowd started piling up behind us, trying to see what was going on. I ended up getting squeezed right next to Taylor, who put an arm around me and smiled.

"Who's this?" the reporter asked.

"This is my best friend, Erin," Taylor said.

I couldn't believe it. I was actually going to be on TV. And, of course, all I could do was nod mutely like I had brain damage.

"Tell me a little something we don't know about Taylor, Erin," the reporter said to me. The cameraman swung his camera over in my direction. "What's she really like?"

I froze for a split second. I wasn't expecting to have to talk on camera, so that kind of threw me. But more than that, I wasn't sure how to answer. What was Taylor really like?

I did the rundown in my head. Lately, she'd been kind of mean, but not to me. And she'd been pretty self-obsessed. But what she'd said about giving up that Tom Hanks movie stuck with me. When I'd needed her, she'd been there. And clearly, I hadn't really appreciated it. "She's the best friend you could ever ask for," I said, meaning it. "She deserves to be a huge star, and she's worked so hard to get here. I'm just really proud of her."

I looked at Taylor. I couldn't believe it. She was just staring at me with this surprised look on her face, her eyes tearing up. I actually thought the girl was going to cry. She looked back at the reporter and dabbed at her eyes with her pinkie finger.

"Great, my mascara's running," she said. "But with friends like Erin, who needs publicists, right?"

I didn't hear much of the rest of the interview, because at that moment I saw Alexandra and her girls in the distance, climbing out of a limo of their own.

Just then I heard the reporter say, "And where's your date tonight, Taylor?"

Taylor grabbed Brandon, who was standing slightly behind her, and pulled him forward. He looked nervous, but I think he was psyched to be on TV, too.

I'm pretty sure it was right then that Taylor spotted Alexandra, and I'm damn certain Alexandra had spotted us.

So Taylor did what any good actress would do. She pulled Brandon into a big, wet kiss.

Alexandra was still plenty far away, but not so far away I couldn't hear her scream, *"Brandon! You bastard!"*

But Brandon, well, he was plenty distracted with the kissing, so I don't think he even heard her. But I bet Taylor did, because she just started kissing Brandon harder. A big *"Whoooooooo!"* went up from the crowd. Kelly, who was standing on the other side of me, started clapping. "Man, if this doesn't give Alexandra an embolism, nothing will," she said.

I was going to say hell yeah, but suddenly everyone was moving. Taylor was heading for the gym, arm in arm with a swooning Brandon, and the camera people were right behind them, filming the whole thing. And the rest of us just followed along.

I expected the gym to be decorated in paper streamers and other lame birthday party decor, but the network people had gone all out fixing the place up. There was a disco ball, and the walls were covered in billowing red fabric, so it looked more like a big nightclub than a stinky gym. I couldn't even tell where the basketball hoop had gone; that's how slick this makeover was.

Just as we were all standing around and staring slack-jawed at the place, I heard a guitar chord. There was a curtain over the stage, so there was no way of knowing who the band was, but I was betting it was Rooney.

Unfortunately, Rooney would have to wait. Principal Stein was walking onto the stage, nervously clutching a cordless microphone.

"Is this thing on?" she asked. Why do people always say that? If it isn't, we can't hear you, can we?

"All right," she continued. "I'd like to welcome all of you to Spring Fling. We have a very special treat for you tonight, thanks to one of our very own students, Taylor Christensen."

There was polite applause, except from Jenna and Kelly, who screamed their heads off. *"Go Taylor!"* Jenna yelled. "Shake what yo mama gave you!"

"She has kindly arranged for a very exciting band to come play for us tonight. Taylor?"

Taylor wafted out from the wings, her dress fluttering against her legs. She looked like a beauty pageant winner but so much cooler. This time, there were a few cheers from the audience, and not just from Jenna and Kelly. I think there was something about seeing Taylor up there, looking so perfectly at home dressed up like a real celebrity onstage while the rest of us were wobbling on our high heels or tugging on our bow ties, that made it really sink in. Taylor wasn't just the girl we sat next to in class. She was going to be, was meant to be, a star.

"Thanks, Ms. Stein," Taylor said, grabbing the microphone. Patrick the photographer, who'd somehow ended up in the front row, snapped a bunch of pictures. "And now I'd like to introduce a band that's very special to me. They perform the opening theme to my new television show with Julia Hanson, *Family Style*. And I've just found out it will be airing this fall, so watch for it! Everyone give a big Bev High welcome to Rooney!"

The curtain was pulled back, and an electric guitar roared to life. Rooney ripped into "I'm Shakin'" and everyone hit the dance floor. I could see Taylor rocking out with Brandon just offstage in the wings. It made my heart hurt a little, but it made me wonder, too.

Had Taylor's mission to destroy Alexandra just been about revenge? Or was it about stealing something, or someone, who belonged to her? And let's face it—that someone was a guy I had crushed on so hard it hurt. I started spinning out worst-case scenarios at lightning speed. What if this was the guy Taylor didn't throw away? What if they fell madly in love, and I was alone for the rest of my life, a dateless old spinster that nobody wanted, not even disgusting Greg Fromer? I was getting a little pissed off, too. If Taylor actually liked Brandon, why hadn't she ever said anything when I spent all those hours swooning over him in her bedroom? I kept turning all the possibilities over and over in my head until my stomach started to hurt.

I shouldn't have worried. As I was sulking by the drink table, Taylor came flying up to me, her cheeks flushed. "Oh my God, I'm having so much fun!"

"With Brandon?" I asked, hoping there wasn't too much of an edge to my voice.

Taylor looked around, like she'd forgotten him somewhere. "Brandon? Oh, he's fine, sure. Okay kisser. But I heard Alexandra is totally freaking out. Do you see her anywhere? I don't want her talking to the camera crews."

I looked around. Alexandra was nowhere in sight. "I haven't seen her since we got in."

"Good. Is this not the best band ever? I am so buying their CD. Hell, maybe I'll ask them for a copy. They can autograph it for me." She leaned over to whisper in my ear. "The drummer is cuuuuute."

The band started playing another song, some eighties cover I couldn't quite place, and Taylor was off again. "I've gotta talk to TV Guide Channel," she said. "We'll catch up later!"

Just then Jenna and Kelly appeared, each grabbing one of my hands and dragging me to the dance floor. "This is the *best* song," they screamed, almost in unison. And it really was.

We danced until we were soaked through with sweat, song after song after song. I was pretty sure Victoria's pink dress had had its last wearing.

Eventually Brandon and Taylor joined us on the floor. Brandon, it turned out, was a really good dancer, and I told him so.

"You're not so bad yourself," he said with a wink. Okay, I know he was on a date with my best friend, but I'm telling you, we totally had a moment.

Rooney started playing a slow song, and Brandon and Taylor paired off. "Let's get some air," Kelly said to Jenna and me.

We walked outside of the gym and sat down in the cool grass outside. We were quiet for a while, listening to the music wafting out of the gym's windows.

"Things are gonna be different now," Jenna said quietly, plucking a handful of grass from the lawn.

I knew what she meant. After this, Taylor was going to be acting full-time. It would definitely be different from when she was doing commercials. This time, she wasn't just some kid popping up in a random TV spot. She was going to be a name. A star.

"I know," I said. "But she'll always be friends with us."

"You really think so?" Kelly seemed skeptical.

"Yeah," I said. I knew Taylor had changed a lot, and she did things I didn't always like. But seeing her get all choked up when I said I was proud of her, well, that told me a lot. It told me that even if she became a great big celebrity, I was someone she trusted. And that had to count for something.

Jenna grinned and shoved me. "Taylor will always be friends with us, because she knows we can blackmail her hard."

"Why wait? I want a plasma TV or I'll sell her bad yearbook pictures," Kelly yelled.

"Oh, I'm going to demand a Mini Cooper or else I'll tell *Entertainment Tonight* about the time she blew cranberry juice out her nose," Jenna joked.

We went back and forth for a while, thinking of stupid things Taylor had done and how much it would be worth to her to keep them out of the press. After a while, Kelly stood up, smoothing her sweaty hair off her forehead.

"Let's go to the bathroom," Kelly said. "I need a towel. Or twenty."

When we got there, one of Kelly's cheerleading buddies, Monica, was walking out. "Don't go in there," she said, shaking her head. "It's a bad scene."

I looked through the door as it was swinging closed. There was Alexandra, sobbing outside the bathroom stalls, her stupid friends all gathered around her.

Kelly and Jenna had seen the pity party, too. "Has she been in there all night?" Kelly asked.

"Think so," Monica said. "And don't let the boohoo crap fool you. I heard she's ready to claw Taylor's eyes out, hard-core."

We backed away from the door and headed towards the gym, just as Rooney was finishing up their encore. "Should we tell Taylor?" I asked.

"If we can find her," Jenna said, scanning the crowd. "God, does this mean I have to pee in the bushes?"

I looked around the gym. Rooney was ambling off the stage, the camera crews were breaking down, and kids were slowly wandering towards the door. It was time for the after-parties to start, or at least the postparty making out in the back of the limo, one or the other.

I felt someone tap me on the shoulder. I turned around and saw Andi standing beside me. "Have you seen Taylor? I wanted to say good-bye before I left," she said, looking at her watch.

I shook my head, but then I spotted a sparkling gold sandal stage left. There was Taylor, sitting on an amp, her arms wrapped around Rooney's drummer.

Andi must have seen this, too, because she took off towards the stage as fast as she could without actually running.

"Hey, is Taylor getting it on with the drummer?" Kelly asked, squinting to see better.

"Good for her!" Jenna crowed. "Drummers are hot. All that upper-body strength."

But it didn't look like Taylor was going to get it on with the drummer if Andi had anything to say about it. Pretty soon Andi was escorting Taylor back in our direction, and I could just overhear her whispering to Taylor, "I know it's hard, but you have to think about Brianna's image, at least for a little while. Brianna would not make out with a drummer, Taylor. Especially if she came to the dance with someone else."

Taylor was pouting a little, but I could tell she was trying hard not to smile. As for me, I was wondering how Taylor managed to distract Brandon long enough to cuddle up to the randy Roonster.

I didn't have to wonder for long, because Brandon came running up to Taylor, completely out of breath. "It took me forever to find the limo driver, but he's here," he gasped. "But the parking lot is pretty jammed."

"No problem, we'll just hang in the limo," Taylor said, pressing herself against Brandon and giving him a kiss on the cheek. That made Andi smile, and she gave Taylor a thumbs-up sign as she headed for the door.

As we walked out into the parking lot, Taylor linked her arm through mine, too. "Was this not the best night of our lives? Seriously," she said, looking at all of us.

"Absolutely," Jenna said. "Like, our party was hot. So, SO hot."

I had to admit, it had been an awesome evening. I didn't even care that I hadn't had a date. At least I did get to spend a little time with Brandon, even if he came with Taylor.

Suddenly, Taylor let out a scream, as if she was being torn apart. And technically, she was.

Alexandra was right behind her, yanking her hair so hard Taylor fell to her knees.

"You bitch!" she screamed, abruptly letting go of Taylor. Taylor fell forward onto her hands.

"What is wrong with you?" Brandon shouted. Alexandra looked at him, her eyes red from crying.

This wasn't good. I nudged Jenna. "Run, get one of the chaperones, the principal, anyone," I whispered. It took a second to sink in, but Jenna finally took off. I could already see everyone else in the parking lot gathering around to watch the catfight.

"Were they her panties? Were they?" Alexandra pushed Brandon so hard he stumbled.

Alexandra went back to where Taylor was picking herself up off the cement. "They were, weren't they? You slut. You disgusting little slut! You may think you're a big-shot actress, but you're just trailer trash from Oxnard!"

Taylor didn't say anything. Alexandra tried to kick her, but Taylor reached out and grabbed her foot before she could. It threw Alexandra off-balance, and she fell back onto her butt, hard. But that didn't stop her. She just paused, slipped her left shoe back on, and lunged, claws out.

Brandon was the one who pulled her back before she could scratch out Taylor's eyes. *"Stop it!"* he yelled. Alexandra just flailed and kicked and screamed as he held her by the waist. *"What is wrong with you?"*

I could see Principal Stein and Jenna running towards us. Taylor was standing now. And she was smiling. I'm sure she could see Principal Stein over Alexandra's shoulder, too.

"Let her go," Taylor said to Brandon. She was almost frighteningly calm. "Come on, Alexandra. I'm not afraid of you."

That was all it took. Alexandra broke free, and went wheeling towards Taylor, who put up her arms, bracing for the worst. That was when we all heard Principal Stein's whistle.

"Don't move another muscle," she screamed. Amazingly, Alexandra didn't, even though she was standing there with a fistful of Taylor's hair. She must have been frozen in place by the brutal realization that her academic career was entirely smoked. You see, Bev Hills had a zero-tolerance policy when it came to fighting. And there were a lot of witnesses, including the principal herself, who could say Alexandra had attacked Taylor. And Taylor never did anything except protect herself.

Principal Stein said a lot of things about shameful behavior on a special night, and ordered most of us to come to her office on Monday to tell her what we'd seen. There would be consequences, she warned, and our parents would be called. But after that, she sent us on our way. It was, as she said, a special night, and I'm guessing Principal Stein was probably up past her bedtime anyway.

"Wow," Brandon said once we were safely back in the limo. He looked shaken. "She just lost it. Totally, completely lost it. I don't get any of this."

"She's got anger-management issues, dude," Jenna sighed. "She's clearly off her nut and delusional. I mean, she smacked the crap out of you at school, remember? You are well rid of the bitch, my friend."

Brandon was quiet for a while. "Yeah, you're right. You're absolutely right. Jesus. What did I ever see in her?"

Taylor looked at him for a minute, then pulled him into a kiss. "You have completely made my night," she said.

Brandon looked a little confused, but he smiled and kissed her again.

Jenna clapped her hands together. "I am starved! Do you think the driver can squeeze this thing through a drive-through?"

"Nachos, I need nachos," Taylor yelled.

"Do those go with rum?" Kelly said, reaching into her purse and pulling out a flask. "Now that the photographer's gone, I say we get our party on! Yo, ho, ho, and all that."

And pretty soon we had convinced the driver to turn up the radio, and we were taking turns sticking our heads out the moon-roof, and we discovered that, though it's a tight squeeze, you can get a limo through the drive-through of the Beverly Boulevard Taco Bell. And rum goes pretty well with Pepsi.

Like I said. It was insane. In a very, very good way.

The next weekend, the four of us flopped around Taylor's pink, half-empty room and thought about our lives. Or, more specifically, Taylor's life. Really, it was Taylor's world. We were just living in it.

"How did you break it off with Brandon?" Kelly asked.

"I told him he had too many unresolved issues about Alexandra," Taylor said. "Which he agreed with, actually. I think he really appreciated my honesty."

"Even though you were lying?" Jenna said.

"Totally. I've been e-mailing that drummer. He's so cute," Taylor sighed. "But a terrible speller."

"Will you see him on the set?" I asked.

"Nah." Taylor shrugged. "Not unless he comes to visit me. Which I'm not ruling out."

"God, it's going to be so dull next week. You'll be gone, Alexandra's gone, no drama at all," Jenna said. Alexandra, of course, had been expelled. Even though her suck-up friends tried to convince the principal that Taylor had started the fight, she didn't buy it.

Not that it mattered, since Taylor was starting work full-time on Monday.

"So, Taylor, now that you're not coming back to school, are we ever going to see you again?" Jenna asked, one leg dangling off the side of the bed. "Like, you'll wave to us as you walk into Koi with Lindsay Lohan?"

Taylor gave Jenna a good shove, and she almost slid onto the floor headfirst. "Oh, I wouldn't dream of waving at riffraff like you, sweetheart. That would tarnish my image."

"You have to promise to get us jobs on the set once we graduate," I said. "Or Kelly will sell you out to the tabloids, right, Kelly?"

"Damn skippy," Kelly shot back, one eyebrow raised to let us know she was serious.

Taylor suddenly bolted up from where she'd been lying on the floor. "They do need extras on the set," she said, looking at us.

Jenna, Kelly, and I looked at one another. "I so want to be an extra," Jenna said. "I can be the goth girl in the back of the class. I could do my own makeup and everything."

"They do your makeup for you," Taylor said. "TV makeup is totally different from what you'd want to wear in public, anyway."

"So when do you want us?" Kelly asked.

Taylor shrugged. "I have no idea. I'd have to ask. It's not like I can make an executive decision or anything."

"I don't think my mom would let me do it," Jenna said, already sounding defeated. "Like, she wants me to start going to a shrink."

From what I knew about Jenna's mom, that seemed typical. Jenna was an only child, and her mom just couldn't leave her alone. In some respects it seemed okay, because Jenna got almost anything she ever asked for, but her mom worried about her all the time, too. Ever since Jenna started dressing goth, her mom had been freaking out about it. I was surprised she hadn't sent Jenna to rehab yet, just to be on the safe side.

"And you know my dad," I said. Actually, I wasn't sure what my dad might do about anything lately. When I brought home my last report card, which was amazingly better than I thought it would be, he barely looked at it. It was so depressing. I felt like Victoria and I were sincerely trying to get back to normal after Mom's death, but Dad was stuck. He was never getting over it, not even a little bit.

"I can still look into it," Taylor said. She sounded surprisingly desperate. "Wouldn't it be cool if we could all hang out on the set together?"

I had been so wrapped up in worrying about Taylor leaving, I hadn't realized she was probably worried we'd forget about her. She wouldn't have time to watch Jenna and Kelly fight the power with subversive cheerleading. She'd miss the goofy school field trips (real ones, not fake ones to Washington, DC). She wouldn't hear the gossip about who was slutty, who was flunking, who was feuding and why. It wasn't glamorous, but it was the world we lived in, the world Taylor knew. And now she was leaving it behind for good.

Sheila burst into the room, the real estate section of the newspaper tucked under one arm. "I'm going out," she said.

"Where are you going?" Taylor asked. I could tell she was

reading the word REAL in bold capitals across the side of the newspaper.

"Just out. Don't get into trouble," Sheila said quickly, shutting the door behind her.

"Don't you get into trouble, either," Taylor said to the closed door.

Chapter Five

It's hard to know who to trust in Hollywood, because people are fake. And I'm not just talking about their boob jobs. I've gotten burned, of course. You have to be careful who you talk to, careful who you trust. It's hard, but you get used to it.

—TAYLOR CHRISTENSEN in *Elle* magazine

It's funny, but you know how when you're in high school you can't wait to graduate, and your parents always sigh and tell you that being an adult isn't that much fun? I kind of feel that way about Hollywood.

It's not that Hollywood isn't a hell of a lot more fun than homeroom at Bev Hills. I never would have had a shot at doing so many things if not for being able to ride Taylor's coattails. I've been able to hike Machu Picchu in Peru, ski the Italian Alps, fly to Paris on John Travolta's jet (yes, Kelly Preston was there—don't be gross), even chat with Francis Ford Coppola and the Olsen twins in the buffet line at Diddy's birthday party. I mean, I've lived the good life in so many ways. But sometimes I look back on the time when Taylor and Jenna and Kelly and I would hang out, and really miss it.

It's not that I can't hang out at the mall or go to the movies anymore. Of course, Taylor really can't, not without getting mobbed or seeing her picture in the tabloids or on the Internet the next day. It's just that all those years ago we were able to relax and live completely in the moment. Have fun, be irresponsible and wild. We had so little to stress over back then. Only we didn't know it.

When we were kids, as much as we thought we had to worry about, none of it was really a big deal. You got a C on a test; you studied harder for the next one. You pissed off your parents; you apologized. The consequences of most of our mistakes were so minor, really, it was as if we could erase the past and start over. But once you're in Hollywood, nothing is ever minor, and absolutely nothing is erasable. Nothing.

Every bad movie, every stupid quote, every drunken party, can come back to haunt a celebrity. It's a lot of pressure to be pretty and perfect every time you leave the house. Don't believe me? You try it for a week.

As tough as it was for Taylor, that leap from faceless child actress to monster A-list star, it was hard for me, too. The stakes were crazy high, and everything was so much more complicated. The good life was expensive in ways I never expected. Sometimes when I talk to people my age who aren't in the industry, people with normal jobs and lives, I realize how much older I am in some ways, how jaded. I'm harder around the edges. That's what Hollywood does to you, whether you like it or not.

So yeah, I know it sounds nuts, but sometimes, when I think of all the things that happened after Taylor got her TV show, rolling back the clock to be a teenager in homeroom starts sounding good. Honest.

After Taylor started working, I didn't hear from her for a full week. I had started to get kind of bummed out, thinking she had made so many Hollywood friends, there wouldn't be time for me and the girls anymore. Then my cell phone rang one day between fifth and sixth periods, which freaked me out. Since my phone was pay-as-you-go, a little gift from Victoria after the whole field trip incident for emergencies only, I assumed something had happened to my dad. Since Mom died, I tended to think of worst-case scenarios every time the phone rang.

"You're coming," Taylor said simply. "I don't want to use up your minutes, so call me the second you get home. But don't tell Jenna or Kelly, okay?"

It was so hard to keep my mouth shut, especially when Jenna and Kelly started talking about how Taylor had disappeared off the face of the earth.

"I'm telling you, I'm calling the cops if I don't hear from her soon. Just to file a missing-person report," Kelly griped.

"Maybe we just *think* she's going to be on TV," Jenna said. "Maybe she's really been sold to a white slavery ring, and she's been shipped off to be the sex slave of some toothless guy in Wyoming."

"Eww!" Kelly and I groaned in unison.

"I'm just saying." Jenna shrugged. "It makes sense if you think about it."

Once I got home, I went into my bedroom. My dad wasn't home, as usual, but I wanted some privacy just in case.

I grabbed the phone and dialed. "So what's going on?" I asked Taylor the second she picked up.

"They recast the guy who plays my brother and he is the cutest thing I've ever seen! He's older instead of younger, and his name is Clive. Clive Sutton. Isn't that the best name ever? It's like he should be European, but he's a total surfer dude. Which is not to say he isn't smart. He's totally smart."

"And?"

"Oh, and I got you a job. Not full-time or anything, just a couple days a week, probably. They want you to come in as soon as you can."

I was glad I was already sitting down, because I seriously thought I might pass out. And not over Clive, as great as he sounded.

"Doing what?"

"Being an extra, like I told you."

I suddenly thought of Jenna and Kelly. "Like you told all of us."

There was a long pause before Taylor spoke. "Yeah, eventually I'll get Jenna and Kelly on the list. But I chatted you up to the casting director and she thought, because you're Asian, they could probably use you regularly for the high school scenes as a featured extra."

"Because I'm Asian? Are you serious?"

Taylor didn't skip a beat. "Featured extra is better than just a regular extra because you're more in the foreground. They may even give you a line here or there if they think you can handle it. Last year the network got a lot of complaints about not being diversified enough."

It seemed kind of insulting, sticking a Korean chick in the scene to meet some sort of quota, but for once, being a minority could actually pay off for me. Maybe. "Don't I need a guardian on the set?"

"Yeah, but if your dad agrees to it, Sheila can be your guardian. I'll make her do it whether she likes it or not."

"I don't know if my dad will go for it. And I don't know how to act."

"Didn't your dad tell you he was having money problems?"

"Yeah, but—"

"Yeah, *but* you'll get paid a hundred twenty bucks a day, plus meals and tutoring. And you don't need to know how to act. You just have to stand there. And if they give you a line, I'll help you with it. Come on, at least ask."

She paused. "What?" I asked.

"You know, this may sound weird, but since your mom died . . . it just made me think a lot. About life, about how fast things can change," Taylor said in a quiet voice. "Like, if we get a chance at something we want, we need to grab it. Because everything can be taken away in a minute."

"You sound like a motivational speaker," I joked, but what Taylor was saying stuck with me. I thought of all the plans my mom had made. My whole life she had talked about traveling the world with my dad when they both retired. She never would.

"Big things are going to happen, Erin. I am getting on this roller coaster, and I'm trying to save you a seat. Please. I really need you to be there."

I wanted to be there, too. "Okay, I'll try."

"Good! You won't regret it. You can help me practice my lines and stuff. And you'll get to meet Cliiiiive," she added in a singsong voice, then sighed.

Talking to my dad was honestly the only thing that scared me a little. But it turned out I had nothing to worry about. Even though it took me a full day to work up the nerve and I spent hours in my room practicing all my bullet points (I would get free tutoring *and* I'd be able to help with the mortgage *and* I'd get valuable work experience), I barely got the words out of my mouth before my dad cut me off.

"How much would you make?" he asked, picking at a bowl of nasty instant ramen he was eating (or not eating) for dinner.

"One hundred twenty a day."

My dad didn't hesitate. "*Nae.* But you have to keep your grades up." Yes, he said yes!

I don't know what came over me, but I gave my dad a hug, something I almost never do. When I wrapped my arms around him, I was shocked. He felt so skinny, it was like grabbing an Olsen twin. I thought I might break his ribs, no joke.

Before I could say anything, he interrupted again. "Your mother wanted you to have every opportunity. Good schooling. Good job."

I hadn't thought about Mom in a few days, and I felt instantly guilty. "I know."

"Things are different now. I do what I can." He looked like he might cry, but he just took a deep breath and kept talking. "Maybe this is good. You work with tutor. That's good."

And that was it. End of discussion. Even that weekend, when Victoria waltzed in for one of her monthly appearances, her end-less yapping about her slacker little sister had no effect.

That night when they thought I was reading in my room, I heard Victoria and Dad in the kitchen screaming at each other in Korean (actually, Victoria did most of the screaming, but what-ever). My grasp of Korean isn't so great, but I made out enough to get the gist of their argument. Victoria went on and on about how I was ruining my life, and then Dad finally spoke, using the low, angry voice he saved for when my sister and I had done something really bad. He told her she would get a say in how the household was run when she started contributing a paycheck. But until then, she should just take her spoiled-little-girl *ongdong-i* back to college and shut up.

And that, as they say, was that.

Applying for my first job in Hollywood was easier than I thought it would be. I dropped by the set one afternoon and Taylor introduced me to the casting director of her show. She was this really nice older woman who dressed like a teenager, but in a cool way, not like Sheila. Everyone in Hollywood wears jeans no matter how old they are. And most of the time, it looks good.

Anyway, then I had to fill out a bunch of forms for school and stuff. I would still take all my regular courses, but I'd have to work with the on-set tutor to fill in the gaps. My dad and Sheila had to work out some details, and there were more forms. The last thing I had to do, finally, was fess up to Jenna and Kelly. I'd been carrying around this secret for a whole week, and the Friday before I was supposed to report to the set, I spilled it, just before we walked into study hall.

After they stopped jumping up and down and screaming *"Oh my God,"* I realized that they seemed genuinely happy for me, not jealous at all. "This is great. Now I have another reason to TiVo the show," Kelly said, hugging me. "And I'll totally buy the DVD when it comes out, just to slo-mo through your parts over and over again. I'll go, 'Hey, that little blur in the corner, that's my pal Erin!' "

"You know, she said she should be able to get work for you, too," I said. I really hoped she would, because Jenna and Kelly were so crazy electric in person, I bet that TV viewers would sense it, even if they were only in the background with boring old me. "They only hired me because I'm Asian."

"So what?" Jenna shrugged. "You're doing your part for diversity. One small step for Korean-Americans, one big paycheck for Erin Kim."

"Like, you WILL invite us to the set, of course, even if Taylor won't," Kelly said, that one eyebrow of hers arched to let me know she wasn't kidding around.

"Do you think Orlando Bloom ever goes to your set?" Jenna asked. "I totally want to make out with him. Or at least get some of his hair."

The image I had of Jenna chasing Orlando Bloom around the lot with a pair of scissors struck me as both totally hilarious and something that could actually happen. Maybe it was a good thing Taylor couldn't get us all on the show. I mean, it was only a matter of time before Jenna or Kelly got arrested.

Going to class for the rest of the day, I was psyched, but a little nostalgic, too. Sure, I was coming back to Bev Hills, possibly two or three days a week, but it was going to be different. Back when Taylor was doing commercials all the time, I kind of got a sense from her that being a part-time student wasn't so great. It's like when you come back from school after having the flu or the chicken pox, except you feel that way all the time. You're always a little out of the loop.

So yeah, I was feeling a little sentimental. But it didn't last long. Because from the first day I stepped onto the set of *Family Style*, I didn't have a lot of time to think about anything else. I was getting on the roller coaster, and just like Taylor promised, it was one hell of a ride.

Let me just say for the record that being a regular old extra, not so glamorous. You wait, you wait, you wait some more, you eat some lunch, and then maybe they put you in a scene. And it's not like you can watch the scene, either. You're supposed to be walking down the hall, pretending to talk to another extra, or pretending to read, or pretending to do whatever the director wants you to. And this I love—when you see people dancing on TV or in a movie? There's no music playing. So if you're an extra, you have to stand there like a doofus and pretend to rock out to . . . nothing.

Now, I said it wasn't so glamorous for a regular old extra. But let's face it—I wasn't a regular old extra. Instead of having to hang out at Stage 14 (this big old warehouse, not really a stage at all) with the rest of the extras, I got to hang out with Taylor. To make sure I didn't miss a call, Taylor asked the first AD (assistant director) to let her know whenever the extras were needed, and then I just had to hustle over to the set, do my pretend dancing or walking or talking thing, and then hustle back.

The first day, my call time was really early, six a.m. I have a hard time even thinking about waking up at such an ungodly hour, much less being somewhere by then, so I gathered up every alarm I could get my hands on and set them at ten-minute intervals all around my bedroom so I couldn't snooze past five. It turned out I didn't even need them. I woke up at quarter to four, completely wired. I mean, I'd been to the set before, so no big deal. But this was the first time I was actually going to be working.

I heard a knock at the door at five, which was really weird. I'd thought Sheila would just honk from the curb, but whatever. When I opened the door, there was a man in a black suit, and in the darkness I could just make out the big black Lincoln Town Car with tinted windows parked in the driveway. "Erin Kim?" the man asked. I kind of stared at him dumbly, I guess, because he took my garment bag (extras have to bring two outfits of their own for work, no wardrobe department goodies for me) and silently carried it out to the car.

When I climbed into the backseat of the Lincoln, there were Sheila and Taylor, sprawled on the leather seats. Taylor grinned at me. "Nice ride, huh?"

"Hell, yeah! I can't believe you have your own driver!" I said. "Oh, hi, Sheila."

Sheila gave me a quick, tight-lipped grin that looked like it hurt. I'm sure she wasn't thrilled about being my guardian on the set, given my previous tendency to wander off at the wrong time.

I don't remember much else about the ride, because the minute we hit the freeway I conked out. I'm sure it had something to do with the fact I'd been up until midnight trying to pick two perfect outfits. I didn't want the nice casting director to be disappointed, or think I was a geek. But the truth was, I didn't have many cool clothes, just a few designer hand-me-downs Taylor had passed along. Still, after driving myself crazy for a while and wondering if any malls were open after eleven p.m., I resigned myself to a plaid miniskirt–oxford shirt combo and a T-shirt with jeans. After all, extras aren't supposed to stand out anyway.

I woke up just as the driver was opening the door. We were parked right outside Taylor's trailer, believe it or not. Talk about door-to-door service! I could already tell things were going to be different now that Taylor was the star of her very own show. Or I should say, Julia Hanson's very own show.

"I gotta go to hair and makeup," Taylor groaned, grabbing my arm. "Come with me. I get so bored. The makeup ladies are nice, but . . . you know."

I didn't know, having been banned from the set during the pilot, but I followed Taylor. I was kind of excited to go to an actual makeup trailer. Before, Taylor had always been made up on the fly wherever the artists could set up, and I bet this would be a lot nicer.

You could see the makeup trailer from a mile off because the door was open. I know that sounds weird, but let me tell you, a makeup trailer has the best lighting you can imagine. In the early-morning darkness, it almost hurt to look at it.

Taylor waltzed right in, while I staggered behind her. It was so bright I completely woke up, which probably wasn't a bad thing.

A pretty woman with her hair swept back in a bandanna walked up to Taylor and kissed her on both cheeks. "Sweetie pie, you always look so good in the morning! I would kill for your skin, you know."

Taylor laughed and patted the woman's arm. "Wait until you touch up this massive blackhead I've got. Mira, this is my friend Erin."

Mira shook my hand and patted a folding chair against the wall, gesturing for me to sit down. "Taylor's told me all about you! Sounds like you're a pair of little troublemakers," she said, laughing.

Taylor piled into a big barber chair that faced a wall of mirrors, and Mira immediately began combing out her hair. "Girlfriend, what did I tell you about conditioner?" she asked Taylor, disapproval in her voice. "Did we not discuss the Kiehl's coconut conditioner? Do you want to have split ends?"

Taylor pouted. "No, Mom." Taylor spun the chair a little to look at me. "Mira knows everything about hair. She gave me this great conditioner you have to try."

Mira squinted at me, then went back to focusing on Taylor's hair. "No, her hair isn't as fine, and it looks a little frizzy. She needs the Aveda Sap Moss detangler," she said to me. "But real nice hair, honey."

I was a little freaked that she could tell by just glancing at me that my hair was frizzy, but she wasn't wrong. I made a mental note to save some of my earnings for new hair products.

As Mira started putting Taylor's hair up in soft curlers, other people filtered into the trailer, hairstylists and makeup artists, from what I could tell. Everyone had take-out coffee, but none of them seemed like they needed the jolt. There was lots of kissing and joking around. It seemed to me that the makeup trailer was a pretty fun place to hang out, whether or not you were getting made up.

Then a man with a stubbly beard and messed-up hair came in and plopped down in the barber chair next to Taylor's like a big deadweight. "Nobody talk to me," he muttered, his eyes half-closed. "Not awake."

Just like that, the trailer got quiet. Another woman started putting gel in the guy's hair, and Mira rolled her eyes. She mouthed the word "diva" to the gel woman, who smirked back.

Taylor turned back towards me. "That's Peter," she whispered. Peter, I remembered, was the guy playing her dad on the show.

Mira steered the chair back towards the mirror. "Don't do that, sweetie. I don't want to mess up your bangs."

I wanted to tell Taylor I thought her "dad" was kind of a jerk, but just then a really cute guy came bounding into the trailer, grabbed Peter by the shoulders, and spun his chair around. I thought for sure Peter would reach out and slug him, but he just opened his eyes and sighed, as if he expected to get woken up this way.

"Who's my DADDY!" the cute surfer dude yelled.

"Clive, Clive, Clive. Always good to see you," Peter said in a way that implied that wasn't entirely true.

Clive just grinned and ran over to Taylor's chair, giving her a big hug.

"You're going to ruin her hair!" Mira squealed, but I could tell she was trying not to laugh.

"How is my perfect baby sister?" Clive said, kissing Taylor's hand.

That girl blushed so red I thought we might need to call a paramedic. "Not as good as you," Taylor said, shyly covering her mouth to hide braces that were no longer there. I couldn't believe it. Taylor, who flirted shamelessly with everything in pants, was getting all awkward and dorky over a guy!

One of the other hairstylists, an older woman dressed all in black, grabbed Clive around the waist and pulled him towards her. "Are you going to sit down for a minute, or do I need to get your Ritalin?" she joked.

"If you must, it's in my trailer, next to the horse tranquilizers," he said, reaching back to tickle her.

Although my heart belonged to Dax, I had to admit, Clive seemed like really fun boyfriend material. Taylor had chosen well, but then I thought how creepy it could seem if they started dating. I mean, they were playing brother and sister, after all.

By this time someone had started working on Taylor's make-up, and the older woman had Clive settled down in another chair. I was getting a little restless. Okay, that's not exactly accurate. I was wondering if Dax might be on the set today, and how I could find him.

Actually, I'd been thinking about him a lot ever since Taylor got me the job on the set. I had been worrying that he might have a girlfriend by now, or worse, that he might not even re-member me. Even though the day we met was something I'd memorized like balancing equations (backward, forward, and sideways), I had no reason to believe that was true for him. I might have been stuck with the little boys at Bev Hills, but he met cute girls, really cute girls, every day. Even if he didn't like actresses (so he said), the studio lot was crawling with plenty of other attractive women.

I tapped Taylor on the shoulder. "How long until you think they're going to need me?" I asked.

"Why?" Taylor was looking at her reflection in the mirror. Already the makeup artist had made her look even prettier, using a tiny little brush to attach individual fake eyelashes to her upper lids. They were so small you could hardly see them, but they made her eyes look like Bambi's.

"I want to go for a walk," I lied. Already I was trying to remember exactly how to find the production office where Dax's dad worked.

"Oh, fine, just go. But keep your cell phone with you, okay?"

By the time Taylor finished her sentence, I was already flying out the door, waving good-bye over my shoulder. I knew I didn't have much time, but I didn't care. If Dax was on the lot, I had to find him, even if I got to stare into those perfect blue eyes for only one stinking minute.

After loitering outside the production office for half an hour, trying hard not to look like a stalker, I started getting antsy. And depressed. Maybe he'd gone back to college. Maybe he'd gotten another job. Maybe I'd never see him again.

I finally decided I'd better head back to Taylor's trailer. There, lucky me, I found Sheila sitting just outside, yakking on her cell phone. I'd been too groggy to notice her outfit when the car picked me up in the morning, but I sure noticed it now. It looked like she'd robbed Rodeo Drive at gunpoint. She was wearing sequined high heels, a short skirt decorated with elaborate gold embroidery, and a matching jacket. The sunglasses on the top of her head had a G for Gucci, and her purse? It was a big, black Fendi, kind of like the one Taylor used to joke about being eight hundred dollars not worth spending.

I knew she wasn't wearing Taylor's modeling leftovers, because everything looked too new. Sheila must have sensed me staring at her, because she shot me a dirty look and walked away from me. But I still heard some of the conversation she was having.

"Is that the best they can do? I'm preapproved for the mortgage—that shouldn't be a problem. . . . She'll sign, of course she'll sign. It's going to be her house, you know. . . ."

I opened the door to the trailer, thinking I should give Taylor the heads-up that Sheila was plotting something, and it didn't look good. But I forgot all about it, because Taylor wasn't alone. She was sitting on her enormous sofa with a pretty girl whose long hair was so blond it looked almost white. The two of them were doubled over laughing. Like old friends.

Taylor finally saw me out of the corner of her eye. "Oh my God, Nikki, this is my friend Erin," she said, trying to catch her breath.

Nikki looked at me, but she kept breaking out into a new attack of giggles every time she tried to speak. I couldn't help feeling like I'd crashed somebody's party. "Hey, Erin," Nikki said, finally.

"What was the joke?" I asked, smiling but feeling stupid.

"Oh, nothing. It's too long to explain. But check this out. Nikki plays my best friend on the show. And you are my best friend, so how cool is that?"

"Are you visiting the set today?" Nikki asked. She was perfectly nice, so I felt a little bad that I couldn't stop staring at her. You see, Nikki was skinny. Really, really skinny. Well, except for her obviously fake boobs, which looked like two tennis balls that had gotten stuck on her scrawny chest. Her head seemed enormous, like a bowling ball that could go rolling off her shoulders at any second. I found out later that in Hollywood people like her are called lollipops. A lot of actresses try to be lollipops, because TV cameras add ten pounds. But Nikki must have thought TV adds fifty, because she was that skinny.

"I'm working, actually," I said, perching on the edge of the couch.

"She's an extra," Taylor said, and I sort of felt ashamed. This morning I had thought being an extra was the coolest thing in the world, but right this minute, when I was sitting with two real actresses, it felt lame as hell.

"That's cool," Nikki said, and I felt a little better. She reached over and tapped me on the knee. "Hey, maybe we'll have a scene together!"

Suddenly Nikki hopped off the sofa. She was wearing a mini-skirt, and her legs were so scrawny they were smaller above the knee than below it. "Erin, want to come with us to a party to-night?"

Taylor nodded. "You should definitely come, Erin. There's going to be tons of celebrities. It's up at a mansion in the Hollywood Hills."

"What time does it start?"

Nikki smiled. "Girl, things don't even get rolling until midnight, and unless the cops shut it down, it could be going on for days. This isn't the first Hollywood party for you two, is it?"

Taylor shrugged, trying to play it cool. "I guess so," she said, as if it was no big deal.

Nikki squealed, her tiny little arms flying up over her head. "Oh my *God*, you guys so can't not go to this! I feel a personal responsibility to break you in. You're, like, party virgins!"

I looked at Taylor, and was surprised to see that she seemed, well, nervous. But she covered it up quickly. "You know, I have an early call time tomorrow," she said in her most mature tone of voice.

"And so do I. But that just means we have your car pick us up at the party instead of your house. Simple." Nikki looked back and forth between Taylor and me. "Come on, you guys. Don't be such grandmas. You can sleep when you're dead." She pointed at Taylor. "You need to go for your career. You network. You meet people. How do you think I got this far? Talent? Ha!"

I didn't care about networking, but it did occur to me that if I managed to track Dax down, I could invite him without it seeming like a date. "Do you think Sheila will go for it?" I asked Taylor.

At the mention of her mom, Taylor stiffened. "She doesn't have a say," she snapped. "Nikki, count us in."

Winding through the Hollywood Hills in the Town Car, I was beginning to wonder if we'd ever make it to the top. But Taylor's driver didn't seem the least bit lost, just turning left, then right, then left again without ever hesitating.

I was wearing my plaid miniskirt and a sexy black camisole Nikki had loaned to me. Actually, Nikki had dressed both of us from top to bottom, taking our regular old clothes and making them look seriously hot just by rolling up a cuff here or slapping on a designer belt there. I thought I had an okay sense of style, but I knew nothing compared with Nikki. She even took a pair of scissors to Taylor's T-shirt and turned it into, swear to God, a backless halter top.

After watching her hack up that shirt in Taylor's trailer like she was cutting a paper snowflake, I asked her, "Have you ever thought about doing this for a living?"

Nikki shrugged. She had two safety pins between her lips and was trying to fasten a third to the back of my camisole. "If the acting gigs ever dry up, sure. And they will. I mean, no one works forever in this business unless they're, like, Jack Nicholson."

I was thinking about that in the car when Taylor pointed out the window. A bunch of superslick rides, Porsches and Jaguars and Hummers, were pulling up at one driveway, where a fleet of red-jacketed valets were frantically running around. Behind them all was an enormous house that had lights on in every room. Dozens of people were trudging up the driveway, which didn't look easy considering how many of the women were in tight skirts and high heels.

"This is the place," Nikki barked at the driver.

Getting out of the car, I swallowed hard. I was excited, but I was nervous and a little scared, too. I probably wouldn't know anybody except her and Nikki, and I guessed everyone was going to be older. Besides that, I was guessing things might get a little, well, wild. You know what I mean. Sex, drugs, and rock and roll, but without the rock and roll. I'd only been to a few parties at Bev Hills High, and except for Spring Fling they weren't exactly the cool ones like you see on TV. Like, if someone brought a joint and a six-pack, it was a big deal, you know?

Plus, even though I'd walked every square inch of the lot that day until my feet had blisters, I'd never found Dax, which had been kind of my point of going at all.

We followed the wall of people pushing towards the front door of the house. The bouncer standing there took one look at Nikki and just waved her through like he knew her. We trailed behind her like a flock of baby ducks.

I wish I had taken a deep breath before we walked through the door, because the second we entered, I was blown away.

It's almost like I need to show you a picture of what it was like inside, because it was so overwhelming, so extreme, it's hard to find the words. The air was thick with smoke, and not just cigarette smoke. I saw a bunch of laughing people sitting around a hookah, or maybe it was a bong—I don't know. I don't think I wanted to know.

People, beautiful people, were everywhere, even sitting on the mantel above the fireplace and on top of the dining room table. Some of them were kissing, some of them had their shirts off (guys and girls), and, I swear to God, I think this one couple were having sex standing up in front of the fireplace. I mean, it was dark, but you could see her skirt was up and he was, well, you get the idea.

A lot of people were dancing to the music, which was this super-loud mix of hip-hop and old disco. Some Missy Elliott remix was thumpa-thumping as we walked in. Everyone had a drink in their hand, and almost the second we arrived, a waiter in a black shirt and black pants approached us with a tray full of reddish yellow drinks in martini glasses. Even if he thought we were underage, he didn't seem to care.

We all took one. Nikki sipped hers and made a face. "Oh, Cosmos, who the hell drinks these anymore?" she asked, then took another big gulp, like it was medicine she had to force down.

I took a sip of mine. It was fruity but tasted like a lot more alcohol than fruit. Considering how little sleep I'd gotten, I started feeling woozy by the time I'd drunk half of it.

Nikki grabbed Taylor's hand, and we started pressing our way into the crowd. There were gorgeous girls who looked like models, sexy guys with perfect biceps, all of them almost too perfect to be real. Every few feet we'd have to stop, because Nikki knew everyone.

"Yo, Nikki, my girl!" a white guy with an Afro screamed. It turned out he was a music-video director who had hired Nikki for one of his student films.

"The party can begin. Nikki's here!" said a tall, good-looking guy with eyes so green they had to be contact lenses as he gave Nikki a hug. He was a big-deal player at ICM, a talent agency in town. He told Taylor and Nikki to call him, so he could take them out to lunch.

Because we were with Nikki, everyone was nice to us, or at least they were nice to Taylor. When I was introduced as "Taylor's friend," no one seemed very interested in talking to me. Not that I minded. Honestly, I barely understood what people were yakking about. Everyone at the party talked like Taylor, swapping gossip about "first-look deals" and "options" and mergers. It was hard to follow, and I was getting pretty sleepy. Funny thing was, Taylor didn't look like she was having much fun, either. Sure, it was a wild party and all, but after you've watched people making out for a while, it starts to be kind of gross. Really, you just start wishing you were having that much fun. And we so weren't. It wasn't even like we could watch celebrities, because Taylor was the biggest star there.

Another hand reached out from the crowd to grab Nikki. "Billy, baby, how are you?" she cooed to a guy with long sideburns and a Jimi Hendrix T-shirt under his jacket. "You didn't cast me in your last movie and I will never, ever forgive you, you know."

Billy put a hand on Nikki's butt and pulled her to him. He didn't pay any attention to Taylor or me at all, so we just stood there and watched this guy grind his belt buckle into Nikki. It was kind of gross if you asked me, but Nikki just tossed that white blond hair back and licked her lips. "I know how I can make it up to you," he growled in Nikki's ear.

"Maybe later, cowboy," she chirped before breaking away. "I'm here with my girlfriends. This is Taylor and Erin. Taylor's on Julia's show with me."

Billy looked at Taylor with the same hungry eyes he'd used with Nikki. "I saw your reel. You're good. Funny," he said. "And sexy."

Billy brushed Taylor's hair out of her eyes, letting his hand fall onto her shoulder. I couldn't believe it. He'd practically dry humped Nikki just ten seconds earlier, and here he was hitting on Taylor.

Nikki didn't seem to mind, just grinning and drinking her Cosmo, but Taylor sure did. I could tell, even though she never once stopped smiling. With a little jerk of her shoulder, she knocked Billy's hand off.

"Nice to meet you, Billy," Taylor said sweetly, even though her eyes were like death rays.

Billy looked at Nikki, who shrugged and began leading us farther into the crowd. "Hey, catch you later, babe!" she yelled back to him.

Once we were out of Billy's earshot, Nikki pulled Taylor towards her. "Dude, that was Billy Furman," she said, looking nervously over her shoulder. "He directs huge action movies. Like, it pays to be nice to him."

"What, I have to let him screw me in the middle of a crowded room to be nice to him?" Taylor shot back. I could tell she was pissed.

Nikki looked at her like she was stupid. "It's called working it, sister. How much of a prude *are* you?"

Taylor looked a little shaken by that. All the guys at Bev Hills treated her like a goddess, doing whatever she asked them to do. She was always, always in control. But here it was different. Taylor wasn't in control with Billy Furman, and she didn't like that one bit.

"I'm not a prude," Taylor said. "I just don't like some skeevy guy pawing me. That's all."

Nikki sighed. "Well, you better get used to it. That's what this whole goddamn town is about. I can't believe you haven't realized that by now."

If they said anything else, I didn't hear it. The combination of the noise, the crowd, and my Cosmo was making me feel down-right sick. "I gotta sit down," I said as I felt my legs buckle.

Taylor grabbed me before I could hit the floor. Looking up, I could see Nikki making the same disgusted expression she had made when she got her Cosmo. "She is *so* not doing this in front of everyone, is she?" she muttered through clenched teeth.

"Oh my God, we've gotta get her out of here," Taylor said, and the next thing I knew we were standing outside, waiting for Taylor's driver to pull up.

We must have dropped Nikki off at some point, because all I remember after that was Taylor nudging me to wake up and get out of the car.

As I walked into Taylor's apartment, all I really wanted to do was go back to sleep. But when I saw Sheila flick on the kitchen light the second we got through the door, I knew that wasn't going to happen. No way in hell.

"So who was there, at the party? Anyone interesting?" Sheila snapped. This was not the grueling "Do you know what time it is and how much I worried?" cross-examination I was expecting, but I could tell from her tone she wasn't happy.

"Not really," Taylor said. It was three in the morning, and Taylor looked exhausted. "I've got to be up in two hours, Sheila."

"You know I'm supposed to be your chaperone," Sheila said, ignoring her. "I don't mind if you go to parties. That is part of your job. But I do mind if you don't take me with you."

I think Taylor and I stared at her, slack-jawed, for a full minute. Sheila wasn't pissed that Taylor had only left a message about the party on Sheila's cell phone without asking permission to go. She wasn't concerned that we probably stank of liquor and smoke and could have gotten totally loaded on Cosmos and no one would have cared. She was just angry that we didn't invite her to come with us. Just thinking about it now still gives me the creeps.

"Mom, I've gotta go to bed," Taylor said finally. It was the first time I think I ever heard her call Sheila her mom.

"It's important you meet the right people at these parties, Taylor, and I can tell you who the right people are," Sheila said, steamrollering ahead. "Unlike you, I spend hours every day reading the trades. Hours. And there were probably important people there that you just passed by because you didn't know any better."

Taylor just ignored Sheila, and started walking towards her bedroom.

"Don't forget," Sheila called after us, "after work tomorrow I've made an appointment with a Realtor."

"Cancel it," Taylor muttered under her breath.

As tired as we were, after we got settled in Taylor's room neither of us could sleep. "What is going on with her?" I grumbled.

"You don't even know how bad it's been lately. She may be reading the trades, but I think she's doing it at Fred Segal."

"Um, you can't afford clothes from Fred Segal on a secretary's salary." Fred Segal is this tony store on Melrose where a pair of jeans can set you back five hundred dollars.

"No kidding. She's spending my paychecks, Erin. She only has to save, like, fifteen percent of what I earn. That's it. The rest can be spent on living expenses. As in, she can't *live* without a pair of Jimmy Choos."

"I can't believe she'd do that to you."

"She quit her job to be my chaperone, by the way. And now she says she wants me to fire my manager and hire her instead. She gets another fifteen percent of my money that way."

"Don't do it, Taylor."

"I won't."

I could hear Taylor sigh in the dark. "You're supposed to be able to trust your mom, you know? Like, even when you didn't get along with your mom, you always trusted her, right?"

I might have loathed her rules and even hated her a little bit, but now that she was gone, it was a lot easier to see the good things about my mom. She never tried to hurt me, not intentionally. Unlike Sheila. "Always," I said.

"I can learn how to pay my own bills and rent my own apartment. I don't need her. I don't need anyone. I can take care of myself."

We didn't say anything else for a long time, and I started to think Taylor had fallen asleep.

"I called my agent the other day," she said softly. "She's getting me a lawyer. I'm going to get emancipated."

Chapter Six

I try to eat right and exercise, but I'm a junk food junkie. The thing is, when I hit McDonald's, my personal trainer makes me suffer for it, believe me. And that's cool. Because the thing is, once you let yourself go, no one hires you; no designers want to dress you; no one wants to date you. The tabloids may say you're too thin, but the truth is, you can't be too thin, not in this city.

—TAYLOR CHRISTENSEN in *Jane* magazine

The next day I had to do a lot of background scenes, so I didn't see Taylor or Sheila very much. Occasionally I'd see Julia or Peter walking around the lot, but they didn't seem to remember me, so I never said hi. Clive, of course, was another story.

"You're my baby sister's best friend!" he yelled, swooping me up in his arms and swinging me around like a rag doll. "What is it, Erica?"

"Erin," I replied, thrilled he remembered me at all.

He put me down and smiled. "Erin. I'll remember that next time. I am starving. Want to eat?"

I wasn't hungry, but I loved hanging out with Clive. He never seemed like a star, just a great, fun guy. "Absolutely."

We'd just put our plates down at a table near the catering

truck when I heard a familiar voice behind me. "Hey, Clive, what's happening!"

I turned around. It was Dax.

Clive and Dax shook hands and clapped each other on the back. "What's up, my man!" Clive said. "Where you been?"

"Here, there, everywhere." Dax finally looked down and saw me. I swear to you, I hadn't taken one breath since I heard his voice, and I bet I was starting to turn blue. Did he remember me?

"Hey, Erin," he said with a wide smile. "Long time no see."

"Hi, Dax." That's all I could muster. I was still trying to remember how to breathe. In, out, something like that.

"Well, I gotta run, but I'll see you two around," Dax said, patting me on the shoulder. When his hand touched me, I swear, I felt it all the way down to my shoes, like an electric shock.

Dax was long gone before I noticed Clive looking at me funny. "How do you know Dax?" he asked.

"Just met him around the set. Why?"

Clive looked like he wanted to say something, but then changed his mind. "No reason."

I know Clive and I talked about a ton of things over lunch. I told him about the awful Hollywood party, and he laughed and promised to take Taylor and me to a really good one in the next week or two. We talked about music, and our favorite places to hang out in the city, and where you can get the best Mexican food on the Westside (Garden of Taxco, for sure). But the details are fuzzy, because the whole time I was thinking about just one thing. Dax.

———

Going back to school after being on the set was really hard the first time. Jenna and Kelly were desperate for stories, which was fun, but school in general just seemed so . . . well, small. Nothing much had changed, at least not for the better. Nothing much had changed except for me.

When I got home, I called Taylor on the set. "You missed the best day," she said. "Julia's back in town."

Julia had been finishing up a movie in Canada for the first few weeks of filming, so the production had been working around her. Taylor explained how Julia had had everyone on the set hold hands in a circle and send good thoughts into the universe for the show.

"Please," I said, expecting Taylor to crack a joke about her nutty-twiggy "mom." But I hadn't understood how attached she'd become to Julia.

"It was so moving," Taylor explained, sounding choked up. "I think she actually cried a little."

Julia had been monster busy, it being her first day back, but she'd made time to sit down with Taylor one-on-one anyway. "She wants us to do it every single day," Taylor said. "It's part of our mother-daughter ritual."

"Sheila must love that."

"She's too busy trying to force me to buy a McMansion to care what I do."

"Force you? Isn't that illegal?"

"Technically, yeah. But, you know. . . ." She lowered her voice. "The wheels are in motion." I knew what she was hinting at. The emancipation. Apparently there was a lot of paperwork, and her agent wanted to make sure the show was a hit before they started proceedings. No reason to leap out of the nest if you can't afford to pay your own rent, after all.

"Oh, but I told Julia all about that suckass party," Taylor added. "She said I was totally right to shine Billy on. She says he's a hack."

"How are things with Nikki, anyway?" Considering I had basically passed out in the car on the way home, I had no idea if she and Taylor were even on speaking terms.

"Oh, fine. We talked. I mean, she's just more comfortable with the Hollywood scene than I am. I'll adjust."

I have to admit, I was a little disappointed Nikki and Taylor were still getting along. The honest truth was, I felt a little jealous. They seemed to have so much in common, and as for me, well, I still felt like Taylor's boring pal from high school. The extra in the background, as usual.

Taylor went on blabbing about how she and Nikki had had a heart-to-heart and were now best buddies, and Nikki was giving Taylor pointers on working it at parties. "She said older guys like women who play hard-to-get, and powerful ones, like executives and stuff, like women who are kind of mean to them. So I can still do the bitchy ice-princess thing. I just have to get better at concealing my contempt."

It had certainly worked for Taylor at Bev Hills, where doofuses she wouldn't even talk to drooled over her in the halls.

"You know, I meant to tell you, I had lunch with Clive the other day," I said.

"Did he say anything about me? Oh my God, he must think I'm such a dork!"

The idea that anyone would think Taylor was a dork made me

want to laugh. A few years ago, sure, but now? Hardly. "No, no, he offered to take you and me out to a really good Hollywood party. And soon, like, next week."

I wish I had thought to hold the phone away from my ear, because Taylor's scream nearly deafened me. "Oh my *God*! Do you think he likes me? What should I wear? Did he say it like, 'Hey, I want to take Taylor,' or was it just, like, friendly?"

This was so weird. Taylor, man-eater Taylor, had it bad for a guy. "I don't remember. But he wants to do it—that's the important part."

"Maybe we could double-date. Me and Clive and you and your guy. What's his name?"

"Dax. But I don't know if he likes me."

"He will," Taylor promised. "We'll make him, whether he likes it or not. Know why?"

"Do tell."

"Because you are going to ask him to be your date to the premiere, silly."

After my conversation with Taylor, who gave me a pep talk that convinced me that not only would I make Dax fall in love with me, but I would also be able to fly the space shuttle single-handedly and eventually run for president, I was completely fired up to see Dax at work the next week. The problem was, I couldn't find him. And I didn't find him for two weeks.

"Maybe he's working," Kelly suggested on one of my school days. She'd been dating a guy in her art class, so she wanted to believe everyone got a happy ending.

"You should ask around for him," Jenna said. "You know where he works. Act like you have some document to give him."

"Like a FedEx. Or a subpoena," Kelly added.

"Not helping!" I was wondering if I should just give up hope. After all, Brandon was still cute and very available now that Taylor had given him the boot.

"Give it time," Jenna said. "If it's meant to be, he'll come back to you. Like that stupid, sucky Sting song."

I wasn't completely convinced that Dax would reappear, but at least I had a new distraction on the set. After Taylor told Julia my mother had died in a car accident, Julia decided that I should be part of their mother-daughter meetings, seeing as I didn't have one. A mother, that is. It kind of made me feel like one of those pitiful orphans you see on those Feed the Children commercials, but considering how few advantages there were to not having a mom, I went along with it.

"I want you two to tell me what the word 'mother' means to you," Julia said the first time Taylor took me to her trailer. We were all sitting on the floor, and Julia had soft music playing in the background. It felt like we were going to have a séance or something.

Taylor leaped right in. "Warmth. Nurturing."

I looked at Taylor. Sheila had never been warm or nurturing in her whole life, and it made me a little sad. I could tell Taylor wanted Julia to be her mom so badly that she didn't even smirk at all this hokey touchy-feely stuff. She'd even started wearing a red Kabbalah string around her wrist, just like Julia.

"What about you, Erin?"

I racked my brain. "Loss," I said finally. "Regret. Guilt."

Julia just looked at me for a moment. Then, without warning, she grabbed me and pulled me into a hug. I was shocked, but I could see why Taylor liked Julia so much. She seemed to really care about people, even relative strangers like me.

"Your mother would never want you to feel that pain," she said, releasing me. "For your own good, let it go. Look at Taylor. She's fighting her negativity. Turning away toxic feelings. And people."

I shot Taylor a look. Did she—?

"I told her about emancipating from Sheila," Taylor said.

"That takes so much courage," Julia said, her eyes tearing up a little. She looked to me. "And you, without a mother. That you've been able to continue on is such an inspiration." Julia reached out and took each of our hands. "You are both little orphans in a way, you poor girls. And so strong. Such vessels of light."

I liked Julia, but the idea of being a vessel of light made me want to crack up. The thing was, when I looked over at Taylor? Her face was wet with tears.

"I am an orphan," Taylor whispered. "I wish you were my mom."

Then Julia and Taylor hugged for what seemed like an hour, both of them crying and sniffling. It went on so long that I started feeling uncomfortable, partly because I think they forgot I was there. I was hugely relieved when they both got called to the set. They walked out of the trailer holding hands.

After a few weird sobfests like that, I decided that I should try to be busy during mother-daughter meetings. It wasn't even that I thought I might do something stupid like giggle out of embarrassment, though that was a very real possibility. The thing was, I could tell how much these meetings meant to Taylor. It was almost as if she needed them, like water or air. And the last thing I wanted to do was get in the way of Taylor bonding with her new "mom," even if she wasn't the real thing. After Sheila, Taylor deserved whatever mothering she could get.

When I finally saw Dax, of course I wasn't expecting it. I wasn't wearing any makeup, and my face had completely broken out. Plus, I was wearing sweats. I might as well have just put a bag over my head. That's how gross I looked.

Amazingly enough, Dax didn't seem to mind. "Hey, sexy," he said as I walked past him on my way to the set. "Haven't seen you for a while!"

"I know." God, I wanted to touch him so badly.

"Got a minute for your old buddy Dax?" he asked in a way that sounded like he was a lot more than my old buddy.

"You bet," I said, my voice shaking a little. Jesus, what was wrong with me? Now I really had no idea why he didn't think I was a complete idiot.

He reached out and grabbed my hand. "Follow me."

"Where are we going?" We were rushing past the soundstages, around the commissary, and towards the front gate.

"Shhhh," was all Dax said.

We turned a corner, and suddenly we were in this little shady garden area between two buildings I had never seen before. There was a green park bench under a tree. Dax gestured for me to sit down. "My lady," he purred.

I was glad I could sit down, because I wasn't sure I would have been able to stay standing up. We were together, in private, finally. "This is so cute," I croaked. *Cute?* Seriously, could I be more of a lame-ass?

"I thought you'd like it," he said, putting his arm around the back of the bench. I could feel his fingers lightly brushing the top of my shoulder.

For a long time—I don't even know how long—we just talked. Dax was so amazing, and not just because he was so incredibly handsome (okay, that helped). But he listened to me in a way that no one had ever listened to me before. Not my mom, not Taylor, no one. I mean, Taylor listened, sure, but she always seemed to have some news that was more important than mine, or some plan she needed me to go along with. I could never hold Taylor's interest for long. It wasn't her fault or anything. I know my life must have seemed boring to her. But Dax, Dax acted like what I'd eaten for lunch the day before was breaking news.

I told him about being an extra, and the party we went to with Nikki, and just stupid stuff, like how much I missed school (I never said high school, of course). Dax told me his dad had been giving him a ton of work to do, most of it stupid errands, so he hadn't been around. He was thinking of taking some online courses at UCLA's extension program to pull up his grades, and then get his act together to go back to Columbia, or maybe transfer. The past few months, he said, had been crazy, and not fun.

"The only good part," he said, "was meeting you."

And then, Dax leaned over and kissed me. Softly at first, but then more urgently, his tongue creeping into my mouth. I couldn't turn off the annoying voice in my head that kept screaming, *"He's kissing me, he's actually kissing me,"* but I didn't care. He was such an amazingly good kisser, I just hoped I didn't disappoint him.

Maybe I shouldn't have spent so much time thinking about it, because just as I was getting into it he broke away. "What are you doing this Saturday?"

I actually really needed to study for finals, but I wasn't about to tell him that. "Nothing."

"Let's go out. We'll do something fun, just kick back. Ever been to SpeedZone?"

Of course I'd been to SpeedZone. It was a fancy go-cart race-track, and every sucky birthday party for a boy I'd ever been to had been held there. "I love that place," I lied.

We exchanged numbers and I told him how to get to Taylor's house to pick me up. And then, he kissed me again. "Can't wait," he whispered.

That afternoon Taylor actually reached into her trailer fridge and pulled out a tiny bottle of champagne after I told her about the kiss. "You got kissed, and I've memorized my lines for the rest of the week. We have to celebrate."

"Wait, how did you get booze in your trailer?"

Taylor looked at the bottle and shrugged. "I guess the PA who stocks my fridge just forgot. Or Nikki left it here."

When I got to the part where Dax suggested we go to Speed-Zone, Taylor spit a mouthful of champagne all over the rug. "You are NOT serious!" she bellowed, running to the bathroom for a towel.

"He thought it would be fun."

Taylor came out of the bathroom and looked at me. "Erin, does this guy know how old you are?"

"I never told him."

Taylor sat back down on the sofa and gave me a hard look. "He could get arrested if you guys do it, Erin. I'm not kidding. He's got to be at least eighteen, so you're—"

"Jailbait, I know." This whole conversation seemed kind of stupid to me, considering Taylor was sucking down a bottle of champagne. "Speaking of which, how old is Clive?"

"Oh, Cliiiive," Taylor said, letting his name roll off her tongue. "He just turned eighteen. But he knows how old I am. We talked about that at one of the table reads last week. He knows how old everyone in the cast is, because he checked on imdb.com. Did you know Julia is thirty-five?"

"That means she would have had you at twenty. Young mom," I said. "Maybe she was in college and had to give you up for adoption, and Sheila isn't your real mom at all."

"Don't I wish!" Taylor squealed. It turned out today Sheila was hanging out with the makeup artists trying to see if they could give her suggestions on which makeup would make her look younger. Considering we were doing some unsupervised underage drinking, Sheila was turning out to be a pretty crappy on-set guardian.

The door opened, and Nikki stuck her head in. "Wish what?"

"I wish I knew what to wear to the premiere," Taylor sighed. "You've got to help me, girl."

Nikki zeroed in on the champagne. "How did you get Clicquot, you lucky dog?" she said, picking up the bottle and pouring the last few drops into her mouth.

"I thought it might be yours, actually," Taylor said. "Who knows?"

"Maybe it's Sheila's," I suggested.

"Eww," Nikki said, putting the bottle down quickly. "Look, you guys, I want to make up that craptastic party to you."

"With another craptastic party?" Taylor asked, a little sarcastic. Clearly, she still wasn't over the last one.

"No, I have a designer friend who said she'd dress us for the premiere," Nikki said. "If you're interested."

"I was just going to go to the Beverly Center," Taylor shrugged.

Nikki looked at her like she was stupid. "She'll dress you, Taylor. For free. You just have to give back the dress the next day."

"Are her clothes nice?" Taylor asked, which earned another look from Nikki. "Okay, okay, I'll do it."

"Next month. Before TCAs," Nikki said.

Taylor turned white. "Oh my God, I forgot about that entirely. What am I going to do?" "TCA" stands for the Television Critics Association, which has a big convention twice a year for critics and journalists. They come from all over the country to Los Angeles to see the new TV shows and interview the stars. Taylor was going to have to attend panels and parties crawling with journalists and do, like, a hundred interviews. It was like having an oral-exam final, but over and over and over again, and there was no way to study for it.

Nikki patted her on the arm. "You'll be fine. I'll help you pick an outfit." I felt kind of bad that I couldn't be useful in any way, but if Nikki was good for anything, it was fashion advice.

Nikki grabbed a Diet Coke out of the fridge and made for the door. "Look, this is the fun stuff," she said. "After this, it's back to work, business as usual." We didn't know it then, but Nikki was only half-right. The fun stuff was on its way and lots of it, but once the show debuted it was never going to be business as usual for Taylor again.

I was teasing some life into my hair for the hundredth time when Taylor finally took my brush away from me. "He'll be here any minute, but by then you'll be bald."

Dax was ten minutes late for our date, which had been enough time for me to change clothes once, change my shoes three times (and end up in the same sandals I chose the first time), and rip a good amount of hair out by the roots.

Finally, we heard the buzzer. "Mind if I don't come up? I'm parked illegally," he said, his voice still sexy even through the intercom.

When I saw Dax's car, I wondered why he wanted to go to SpeedZone at all. It was a slick red convertible Porsche. "Nice car," I said, in the understatement of the year, feeling the seat rumble beneath me as the engine roared to life.

"Yeah, it's a hand-me-down," Dax responded, changing gears. "My dad wanted a Hummer, so I got this." I tried to tell him the only hand-me-downs I ever got were from my big sister, Victoria, and they were mostly old stained jumpers and one pink prom dress, but he couldn't hear me over the wind whipping through the car.

At the SpeedZone, we tried drag racing, and I'm pretty sure he let me win both times. Then, we moved over to the miniature golf course on the grounds. "A bit more relaxing," he said, nudging me. "You little Speed Racer."

Talking with Dax was so easy, sometimes I almost forgot myself and blurted out really stupid things, stuff that would completely give me away as a high school student. Like desperately wanting to skip third period all the time, if only Mrs. Mendlen didn't hand out detention slips like candy.

"So, do you live with Taylor?" Dax asked.

"I live with my dad. I want to be there for him, since my mom died," I said, which sounded like a pretty good line to me.

Dax stopped in midputt. "As much as you're going through, you take care of your dad. I don't know if I could do that."

Now I felt kinda bad. I didn't really take care of my dad at all. Hell, I barely talked to him. "You could, I'm sure of it."

"You haven't met my dad," Dax said, not exactly joking.

I somehow ended up spewing the story about my mom's accident, and how we'd had a fight right before. And Dax started telling me how his mom had had breast cancer, and how awful that was, especially because it was right after his dad had gotten married to another bimbo. The conversation got so intense we just gave up on our game and went inside to get something to eat.

"Want a drink?" Dax asked. "I think I may need one." Speed-Zone has a full bar, and I could see the bottles of liquor behind the counter.

"Diet Coke," I said.

Back at our table, Dax whispered, "I'm guessing you're a little shy of twenty-one?" he asked.

I swear I turned completely white. "A little."

"I'll get you something if you want it." So much for my theory that Dax might still be a teenager. Unless he had fake ID.

I looked around. The bartender looked bored, and I have to

admit, I liked the idea of doing something a little bad. "A Cosmo," I said, hoping I sounded like I knew what I was talking about.

"Coming right up," he replied with wink.

The SpeedZone Cosmo wasn't as strong as the one I'd had at that party, but that was probably a good thing. As it was, it turned me into a chatty Cathy. I told Dax all about how Taylor and I met, and how she used to wear headgear and braces. God, it was like I couldn't shut up if I wanted to, just yammering on and on like a crazy person. I could have been wrong, but Dax seemed fascinated by all my blabbering, sometimes stroking my hand or my arm under the table.

"It's getting late," he said finally. "Let's blow this joint."

When the Porsche pulled up in front of Taylor's place, part of me just wanted to run into her apartment and tell her what a great date I'd had. But then I felt Dax's hand wrap around the back of my neck and pull me into a kiss.

"You are so hot," he whispered in my ear. And that's when I felt his hand traveling over my shirt, then unfastening the top two buttons of it. Before I knew it, he had pulled it completely off me.

"Won't someone see us?" I asked. I almost didn't care, but the last thing I wanted was for Taylor or, worse, Sheila to sidle up to the car and say hello.

"We're not doing anything so bad, are we?" Dax asked, reaching his hand inside my bra. I really wished I had worn a nice one, not the threadbare, ratty cotton one I'd bought with my mom, like, two years ago.

And then, I felt him unhook it in the front, pulling it away to expose me, totally.

I didn't want to do it, but I pushed his hand away and started pulling my bra back together. "Maybe this isn't the best place," I said, looking around for witnesses.

Dax stroked the side of my face. "You're right. You're absolutely right. You're just so beautiful, I couldn't help myself."

He kissed me again, sweetly this time, and took my hand. "I think you're really special, Erin."

"I think you're really special, too." I took a deep breath and decided now was the time to take the plunge. "Dax, I was wondering if you'd be my date to the show's premiere."

Dax continued stroking my face for a long time, but said nothing. "Erin, you know I'd love to," he said finally. "But I'm kind of working, if you know what I mean."

"Sure," I lied, pulling on my shirt. I couldn't believe it. Maybe I hadn't let him go far enough.

"I'm not blowing you off," he said earnestly. "But I have to meet network executives and talk shop, for my dad. I'll see you there—we'll totally hang out—but I'd be a lousy date."

I felt tears welling up in my eyes, so I let my hair hang over my face. "No big deal."

"Hey," Dax said, taking my face in his hands. "If I could, you know I would. I really, really like you."

He kissed me again, and I smiled. Maybe he did. God, I hoped so. I swore to myself right then that the next time he took off my bra, if he ever did, I wouldn't stop him again. I would do anything he wanted. And I meant anything.

"Is this too tight?" Taylor asked, spinning around in a white column dress. Taylor, Nikki, and I stood next to Veronique, Nikki's designer friend, in a tiny Hollywood boutique. As small as it was, though, the place was stuffed with amazing clothes. Gauzy summer dresses, tops made out of strips of raw silk, hand-beaded and embroidered jeans. Nikki, it turned out, hadn't led us astray. Veronique, who was French and just as disturbingly thin as Nikki, seemed a little snooty, but I didn't care. Her clothes were that cool.

"It is supposed to skim the body," Veronique said, studying the seams of the dress. "But yes, I think this is too tight."

"Can I get a six?" Taylor asked.

"Maybe you should try something else," Veronique said flatly.

Taylor frowned. "But I like this one," she said.

"I know, but I don't have it in a six," Veronique said. "I tend not to carry much above a four."

Just the way Veronique said that, in this tone that suggested a size four was superjumbo-size, I almost told Taylor we should jet to Macy's, where the junior section goes all the way to fifteen. But Nikki grabbed a gorgeous black dress off one of the racks and shoved it under Taylor's chin. "There's so much other stuff here," she said. "This would look fabulous on you."

"That, I can alter," Veronique said. "If it's too tight."

Taylor shot Veronique a look, but took the black dress.

While Taylor was in the dressing room, Veronique and Nikki looked me up and down. "You, you're perfect to dress," Veronique said. "Straight lines."

"As in, flat chest?" I joked, but Veronique reached behind her and pulled out a ruby red dress. The neckline, if you could call it that, went all the way down to the waist.

"You have to try that on, Erin," Nikki said. "If you don't, I will."

I took the dress and went into the other empty dressing room. When I put it on, it was so light I felt like I wasn't wearing clothes, which was kind of unnerving. "Come out!" Veronique cried. "I need to see it!"

When I walked out, both Veronique and Nikki burst out laughing. "*Without* the bra, Erin!" Nikki said.

Yikes. I felt weird not wearing one, even though I didn't really need the support. My mom had always said only tramps go braless, and I guess it stuck. But when I put the dress back on without it, both Veronique and Nikki nodded their approval.

"See," Veronique said to Nikki, as if I weren't there. "That is the body I like to dress. None of these fake boobs, no offense. Slim through the hips. Perfect." She turned to me finally. "If you were taller, you could do runway work."

When I looked at her blankly, she said, "You know. Runway model."

I didn't like Veronique much, but no one had ever told me I was model material before. I was so distracted by the thought that when Taylor finally emerged from the dressing room, I barely noticed.

"I can't pull up the zipper," Taylor said, desperately tugging at the side of her dress. "But otherwise, I love it." It really was gorgeous. The bodice was a flowing black fabric dotted with tiny silver beads, and the rest of the dress was jagged, crisscrossed layers of the same material. It looked like something I'd seen an actress wear at the Oscars last year, only better.

Veronique ran over to Taylor and grabbed her hands. "Don't pull! I'll alter it. I just need to let out a seam."

Taylor looked up at me. "Oh my God! You look hot!"

"Should I wear it?"

In unison, everyone said, "YES!" And the minute I slipped it off, Veronique grabbed it, put it in a plastic garment bag, and handed it to me. "Get photographed. A lot," she said. "And remember to tell them Veronique made it just for you."

After Veronique picked out a pair of shoes for me, Jimmy Choos(!), she finally turned to Taylor. The snooty bitch looked none too happy about it, either. "You can pick up your dress in a day or two," she said. "Good-quality undergarments. And no salt, no sugar, until after the premiere. Junk food makes you swell."

Taylor turned almost as red as my dress. "Okay," she said meekly. Veronique stepped back and looked at Taylor for a moment.

"The curves are more of a challenge," she said, "but you are still very beautiful. A very beautiful girl." I hate to say it, but it didn't sound like she really meant it.

In the car on the way home, Taylor turned off the radio and looked at Nikki and me. "Is a six too fat?"

"Of course not," I said.

"Well . . . ," Nikki said, trying to keep her eyes on the road. "It's just that designer samples are usually a size two."

"So I am too fat." Taylor looked absolutely crushed.

"It's not that you're too fat, exactly," Nikki explained. "It's just how the business works. If you get down to a size two, you'll get a lot of free clothes, Taylor. People will be lining up to dress you."

So what if you have to become anorexic, I thought. Free

clothes! I wanted to shake Taylor, but I didn't. I already felt like I was interrupting their conversation just by being there.

Nikki smiled at Taylor. "You know, I'm a zero, and I used to be a ten," she said. "I just started working out more. And eating better. It's not a big deal. I can show you the diet I used. It really, really works."

"Okay. Maybe on Monday. And no ice cream again, ever," Taylor vowed, squeezing the top of her thigh through her jeans.

Once we got back to Taylor's place and Nikki had left, I was desperate to tell Taylor Nikki's diet couldn't be a good idea when she turned to me. "You have to help me ask Clive to the premiere," she said matter-of-factly, as if she were ordering a sandwich.

"Why me?"

"I've been trying for, like, two weeks and I keep losing my nerve," she admitted, turning back and forth in front of her bedroom mirror, then sucking in her cheeks.

"So you want me to ask him for you?"

"No, you're supposed to facilitate it. Like, bring up the subject and see if he's got a date already."

I felt bad for Taylor, really, I did. I could see why she liked Clive, and I could also see why this was making her nuts. He was cute, he was funny, and he really seemed to like Taylor. But he never made a move on her. Considering Taylor had never had a problem attracting men, this had to be making her crazy.

But still, I didn't like the idea of being the "facilitator." "This is kind of weird, Taylor. I mean, I won't have a date. Can't we just go together?" I'd already told her about the debacle with Dax, and I'd kind of been hoping we could prowl the party together.

Taylor sighed. "I like him so much, Erin. I've never felt like this about a guy before. If I don't ask him now, when there's a really good excuse, I don't know if I'll ever be able to do it." She paused, and I could tell she was starting to get weepy. "Nikki told me his last girlfriend was a model, Erin. How can I measure up to that?" Taylor shuffled through a pile of magazines on her coffee table. She pulled out one and opened it to a dog-eared page. There was a scrawny, glassy-eyed model with big hair and bony arms.

"But you do," I said. "You're so much more beautiful than her. Why are you doing this to yourself?"

"I was cute by Bev Hills standards, maybe," Taylor said, really crying now. "But it's different here. I'm too fat, and I'm not beautiful, not like Julia or Angelina Jolie or any big stars. I'm just cute, that's it. I don't measure up. No wonder Clive won't date me. I'm just his fat, funny little sister."

I'll admit it, I was shocked. It was like the confident beauty queen who walked across the stage at Spring Fling had completely disappeared and the little girl with darting eyes and the headgear had come back to puke up her insecurities over some guy.

"Clive will be your date, Taylor," I said, desperate to do anything to stop the tears. "I'll make sure of it."

I was sitting on the steps of Taylor's trailer, pretending to read a book. "How long do I have to stay out here?" I whispered. Taylor opened the door a crack and poked me.

"He's not supposed to know I'm in here," she hissed. Once I'd agreed to help "facilitate," Taylor had concocted a plan. I would sit on her trailer steps, spot Clive, call him over, then ask him if he was excited about the premiere. And that's when Taylor would casually pop her head out of her door and jump into the conversation.

It all felt so canned, like we were reenacting an especially cheesy episode of *Days of Our Lives*.

"It's easier if you're there," Taylor had explained. "I won't chicken out that way."

"Or you'll still chicken out, and I'll just be a witness."

Surprisingly, Taylor didn't find that amusing.

By the time Clive walked past, I almost didn't notice because I had stopped pretending to read a book and was actually reading it.

Taylor opened the door a crack and whacked me in the head with it. *"Ow!"*

"Wake up, loser!" Taylor hissed.

"Hey, Clive!" I yelled in a singsong voice. I could hear Taylor groan, but she finally shut the door.

"My girl Erin!" Clive yelled back, bounding over to sit next to me. "Whatcha reading?"

"Schoolwork, nothing fun," I sighed. "But who cares about that? Are you all psyched about the premiere?"

"Are you kidding? I've never had a show get past the pilot stage. This is like prom, but better."

"Are you supposed to take a date? I wasn't sure."

Clive nudged me. "I'm thinking about taking my mom. Or do you think that's too weird? My publicist thinks it's sweet, but I think it may be too mama's boy geeky."

Taylor stuck her head through the door. "Hey, your mom could go with mine, and you and I could go together," she said quickly. "Sorry, I just overheard you talking."

Clive nodded, mulling it over. He didn't seem to think it was at all weird that Taylor just happened to pop into the conversation at the ideal time. "That could work. Or is that sick? I mean, you're my little sister. Someone might accuse me of incest." He winked at Taylor, who rolled her eyes.

"I promise to keep my hands to myself. No incest."

"Well, in that case," Clive joked, pretending to wipe the sweat from his brow. "That could be cool. We can stick the moms in one limo and the rest of us could get another, and that way we can party a little. But no incest, of course."

Taylor smiled, but she didn't look too happy. "Of course."

She was even unhappier later that afternoon in the Traylor. "No incest!" she wailed, clutching an embroidered pillow to her chest as she fell onto the sofa. "How did this happen?"

"You're still going out with him," I countered. "It's just a group date."

"Group date," Taylor said, as if this were a fate worse than food poisoning. "He doesn't like me at all!"

"You don't know that," I said, though I suspected it might be true given the whole incest thing.

"He's never going to like me," Taylor moaned. "I'm too fat!"

"You're not too fat," I said for the millionth time. Taylor was now complaining about her invisible fat nonstop, like whenever she ate something or put on a pair of jeans.

"I am. And my teeth are disgusting." Taylor leaned towards me, pointing to her two front teeth. "They still stick out. Still!"

Well, it looked like the geeky little girl in the ducky sweater and the headgear wasn't just visiting; she was here to stay. The worst part was, Taylor hated that little girl. Hated her so much she'd do anything to get rid of her, no matter how much it hurt. I could have said something then, but I didn't. I didn't want to upset

Taylor, didn't want to make her mad. I hate conflict, and it wasn't such a big deal, right?

But now I know that I should have said something. It might have made a difference. And I'll spend the rest of my life kicking myself for not doing it.

When Taylor's car came to pick me up a few days later, I could almost feel the tension the minute I walked out my front door. Something was wrong. Seriously wrong.

When I got into the backseat, I could see Taylor's face was red from crying. "The TCAs," was all Taylor was able to say before she started bawling.

Sheila, who was sitting next to her, just rolled her eyes. "The critics loved Taylor. *Loved* her. I have no idea why she's being this way."

"What happened?"

Taylor wasn't able to tell me, what with blowing her nose and snuffling, but Sheila was. "They had this panel, with the whole cast and the producers, and the journalists were all there to ask questions. And you know what happened? Almost all of the questions were for Taylor. They loved her. They kept talking about it being *her* show."

This just made Taylor cry harder. "It's *Julia*'s show," she wailed.

Sheila put an arm around Taylor, but Taylor shrugged it off. "Well, it *was* Julia's show. I don't think anyone's going to say that anymore. You could just see the producers getting it. Little light-bulbs over their heads, you know. I bet right now they're rewriting all of the upcoming episodes so Taylor's the focus."

Taylor dried her eyes with a knotted-up Kleenex. "I should apologize to Julia," she said. Sheila's head spun around like a rabid owl's.

"You will do no such thing!" Sheila said. "You can't help it that you're more talented than she is. Apologizing would just rub salt in her wounds anyway."

For once in my life, I kind of agreed with Sheila. I'd seen the pilot episode of the show after Taylor slipped me a tape. I'm sure I was biased, but the critics were buzzing about Taylor for a reason. There was just something about her on-screen, something even I hadn't seen in her, just being her best friend. In Hollywood they talk about people who have "it," who pop off the screen, and that was Taylor. She had it.

As for Julia, well, all that warmth and sweetness I'd seen in person just didn't translate. On TV she looked awkward and lost. I'd never been a big fan of her movies, but I kind of got what people liked about her. She seemed nice, and open. But on the pilot, that was totally missing. It was almost as if Taylor had sucked up Julia's star quality, and all that was left was a sad, empty shell. Harsh, I know. But it was the truth.

When we got to the set, you could tell something was different. No one spoke in the makeup room. Taylor hid in her trailer, and I didn't see too much of anyone else, either, especially not Julia. Even Clive was subdued, waving a quick hello to me before disappearing.

It was only later in the day, when I was walking back from lunch, that I saw how bad things had really gotten.

Two of the show's producers and a network executive were standing at Julia's trailer door. One of the suits banged on the door, waited, then banged again. "Julia? We just want to talk to you," he said.

When I walked into the Trayler, Taylor had her face pressed up against a window, watching the scene outside.

"What the hell is going on?" I asked her.

"Julia wouldn't shoot her scene today." Taylor looked at me with the saddest expression, I swear, I've ever seen. "It was a scene with me. Just the two of us."

Taylor looked outside again. *"Oh my God,"* she shrieked, then flew past me and out the door.

I looked outside. There was Sheila, right behind the executives, calling out to Julia.

"Honey, you can't take it personally," Sheila yelled. "She's just a very talented girl!"

I watched as Taylor grabbed Sheila and dragged her back to the Trayler. Once inside, she slammed the door. Taylor was so mad I almost thought she was going to hit Sheila, who seemed completely confused.

"What the hell are you doing? Are you trying to get me fired?" Taylor screamed.

"Don't be ridiculous. I was trying to help," Sheila spit back. "I thought a woman's voice would reassure her."

"*Stop* helping. All you ever do is embarrass me!"

"That is an awful thing to say to your mother!"

"What are you going to do about it, Sheila? Ground me?"

"That's not a bad idea!"

"Not while I'm paying the bills."

Sheila just stared at Taylor for a minute. I think it really hit her that there was nothing she could do to punish Taylor, not anymore.

"Go home, Sheila," Taylor said after a while. "Just get off the set and go home."

"I am your mother and you will stop speaking to me that way right now!" Sheila said in her best stern-mom tone. But Taylor wasn't having it.

"No, I really think you should go shopping," Taylor said, her voice pure ice. "Isn't that what you really want? To spend my money?"

Sheila's face curled up into a snarl. "I worked hard your whole life so I could provide you with everything. Braces, clothes, food on the table. You never wanted for anything, Taylor. Not once, you ungrateful little brat!"

"So now you're evening the score? Spending my money on Fendi purses and a house in the Hollywood Hills because you got me braces? Is that how it works?"

"I'm not looking for my house. I'm looking for *your* house. And you have never once shown any appreciation for how much time I've spent trying to find one for you."

"Because I don't want some big house! How can I afford a house when you're already spending every cent I earn! Look at you!" Taylor reached out and yanked Sheila's sleeve. "Gucci, is it? How much was that?"

"I didn't raise you to be so disrespectful," Sheila said, pulling her arm away. "You should be ashamed of yourself."

"No, Mom, you should." Taylor glared at her, then walked out of the Trayler.

Not wanting to stick around with Sheila, I followed her.

"Where are you going?" I asked Taylor as she stormed across the lot.

"To talk to Julia," she said.

"Are you sure that's a good idea?"

Taylor shrugged. "It's the only idea I've got right now."

Taylor walked up to the huddle of suits outside Julia's door. "I was thinking maybe I should talk to her," she said quietly.

The suits looked at one another, then at Taylor. One of them smiled at her. "That's a nice idea, sweetheart, but maybe—"

Just then, Julia opened her trailer door. "Let her in," she said simply.

The suits parted, and Taylor walked past them and into Julia's trailer. She was in there for a long time, but no one moved. We all just stood around, waiting.

When Taylor finally came out, she looked tired and shaky. "We can do the scene," she said. "Just give her a few minutes, and she'll head over to makeup."

And just like that, Taylor left for the set. The suits looked at one another with these big grins on their faces. "She's really something," one of them said, and they all nodded smugly, as if they had done something smart.

It wasn't until much later, when shooting was done for the day and everyone was headed home, that Taylor and I sat in the Trayler and she told me what had happened.

"She lost it, Erin. Just lost it. She was crying about being too old, and how her career was over," Taylor said. She looked sad and a little angry, as if she'd just found out Santa Claus wasn't real. "She said she was just going to retire and get a ranch somewhere in the desert and paint."

"Oh my God, she's quitting?"

"No. She just wanted someone to tell her she wasn't old and her career wasn't over."

"And you did."

Taylor nodded. "I just didn't think she was the type to lose it like that. I thought she was so together, you know?"

I did. It was hard for me to imagine Julia freaking out like that, even now.

"She said she might not be in the mood for our mother-daughter meetings for a while. Which I understand." But I could tell from the look on Taylor's face that she didn't, not really.

Taylor sat down in front of her vanity mirror and began wiping off her stage makeup. The thick foundation gave her this tan and healthy glow, and without it she just looked kind of sick. "Does it ever seem to you that adults are even more screwed up than we are?"

I thought about my dad, whom I almost never saw anymore, and Sheila, who was probably running around the set telling everyone about what an ungrateful daughter she had. "Every day."

"You know, sometimes I feel like I'm the only adult around. Julia's a mess. Sheila's a mess. The producers and directors fight like little kids. And you know something? I just want to be a kid. And I can't, or the whole world will fall apart."

As Taylor wiped more of her makeup off, I noticed the bags under her eyes, which I'd never really seen before.

"Is that what happens? We just all get crazier as we get older? Because I am so not down for that," Taylor sighed.

"I think life just gets more complicated."

Taylor wiped away the last spot of lipstick from her face. "You know something? I just don't see how that's possible," she said. "I really, really don't."

As the August premiere (apparently fall comes around a little sooner when you work in TV) inched closer, you could feel the excitement building on the set. The warm summer air almost crackled with nervous energy, fueled by all the hopes and dreams of the cast, the crew, everyone right down to the extras.

Part of the reason we were all so excited was because the reviews were in, and the news was mostly good. All the critics seemed to adore *Family Style*. They liked the writing, they liked the concept, and they loved Taylor. "Loved" might even be an understatement. The *Los Angeles Times* had called Taylor "an exciting new discovery," and the *New York Times* had labeled her "a sharp comedic talent."

There was only one problem. The reviews for Julia, well, they weren't as good.

TV Guide called her "worn and listless," and lots of other reviews barely mentioned her. One critic said he liked the show *despite* her.

That afternoon, Julia locked herself in her trailer again. But this time, none of the suits stood outside. Instead, they had her written out of the scene she was supposed to shoot that day.

New pages were delivered to Taylor before she even knew what was going on. All the lines that had been Julia's had been changed a little and given to her.

Taylor curled up on her sofa in the Trayler and scanned the pages. "This is so wrong," Taylor said, looking at the scene. "I can't believe they're doing this."

"I can," Nikki said. "Pout once, you get sympathy. Do it twice, you're a pain in the ass who's slowing down production. If she was getting rave reviews and generating buzz, they'd put up with it. But she's so not the star she thinks she is."

"She's still a huge star," Taylor said. "They should have let me talk to her first."

Nikki patted Taylor on the head. "That's so sweet. But so stupid."

Sometimes I couldn't stand the way Nikki talked to Taylor, like she was some mental reject. But Taylor never seemed to mind. I almost think she liked having someone boss her around, even if Nikki was only a year or two older than we were.

"Why is it wrong?" Taylor asked Nikki.

"Please! They want you to be the star of the show. Why would you want to waste your time making nice with Julia?"

I couldn't sit quietly a second longer. "Because Taylor's a decent person," I said.

Taylor didn't agree with me. She didn't say anything at all. She just started reading her revised script, trying to memorize all her new lines.

Getting ready at Taylor's house for the premiere was chaos, but fun chaos. Luckily for us, Sheila had already left with Clive's mom, who was just as bubbly and funny as her son. I kind of felt sorry for her, having to spend the whole evening with a mess like Sheila. But at least Taylor, Nikki, and I had the place to ourselves to get ready.

Taylor had a stylist come over to do her hair and makeup, and just as she left, Jenna and Kelly showed up. They were dressed to kill, Kelly in a sexy blue strapless number and Jenna in a goth corset dress and combat boots. I thought they looked pretty freaking amazing, but they both gasped when they saw my red dress.

"Your man is going to die," Kelly said, staring at me. "Just keel over and die."

"As long as he's straight, I'm sure he will," Jenna said. "I mean, look at the girl. Who knew?"

"Okay, enough about Erin's dress. My turn," Taylor said, pushing us away from her full-length mirror.

I'm pretty sure I gave her a dirty look right then, but I tried to remember it was Taylor's moment. "I have to look good, because the whole world is going to be there taking pictures," she said, almost (but not quite) apologetically. "GOD, I'm so nervous!"

"Don't be," Kelly said. "Everyone's going to love you. There is no cooler person on television than you, promise."

Taylor shook her head. "I should never have asked Clive to go to the premiere."

"What?" I could just imagine her asking me to go downstairs and uninvite him for her.

Taylor examined her makeup in the mirror. "It's just making me more nervous. It's like taking a date to your SATs or something." She grabbed a Kleenex in each hand and jammed them underneath her armpits. "Am I sweating already? I'll die if I'm sweating already."

Nikki handed Taylor her dress. "Sweetie, Clive will love you, the press will love you, and the Nielsen viewers will love you—don't worry. Just get dressed."

Taylor slipped into her dress, and not only did it fit; it was way loose.

"She must have let out the seams too much," I said.

Taylor hopped up and down in front of the mirror, then hugged Nikki. "It's working!" Taylor squealed.

"I told you," Nikki said, kneeling down to pin back the extra material in Taylor's dress. "You're totally, like, a four now."

I looked at Taylor in the mirror. Nikki was right. Taylor's hips looked a little slimmer, and her face seemed thin. I realized I hadn't seen her eat much of anything lately, except the occasional grapefruit.

The intercom buzzed.

"CLIVE!" Taylor screamed. She ran to the intercom and jumped up and down for a second, then stopped. "Oh my God, I think I started sweating!" she wailed.

"Just answer it!" Jenna yelled.

Taylor calmed down and answered the buzz with her best sexy purr. "Hellllo?" she said.

"I'm here to pick up a party of five?" the limo driver said.

I could see Taylor was already disappointed. "We'll be right down," she sputtered, then turned to us. "Why didn't he buzz himself? I could have invited him up!"

"Because he's probably already drunk in the limo," said Jenna, grabbing her purse and heading for the door. "To which I say, all aboard!"

Jenna wasn't completely off base, either. In the limo, Clive had already opened a bottle of vodka from the minibar and immediately handed glasses around to everyone. "I think we're going to have to settle for screwdrivers, or rum and Cokes," he said. "If I had known they'd have such a crappy selection in here, I would have brought my own stash."

Taylor was cuddled up so close to Clive, I was amazed he could lift his arm high enough to pour a drink. But Clive seemed completely oblivious to Taylor's goo-goo eyes.

"Clive, did you see Taylor's dress? Isn't it gorgeous?" Nikki said, trying to help.

"Magnificent! My little sister is going to be on a best-dressed list, I bet," he said. Taylor made a face when he said "little sister," and I think the rest of us did, too.

But we forgot about that awkward moment mighty fast, because once we convinced the driver to let us put on a mix CD that Jenna had brought and the vodka started flowing, we were having a pretty great time. I swear, I always have the most fun in limos. Kelly rolled down the window and practiced her royal wave on pedestrians, and Clive got us all playing an entirely stupid game of Simon Says, which is actually a bitch once you've had something to drink. Taylor even loosened up, laughing so hard at Clive's jokes she almost spit out her drink.

By the time we pulled up to the entrance of White Lotus, I'd almost forgotten the point of the evening. But the minute that door opened, there was no missing it.

I have to hand it to Taylor. As silly and punchy as we'd been on the ride there, and as shaky as she'd been in her apartment, when her toe touched that red carpet she was as calm and collected as a princess. And she needed to be, because everyone around us was going insane. And I really mean insane.

A publicist in a black suit introduced herself as Marie and told Taylor and Clive she'd escort them through the line. It may seem stupid that grown people need someone to help them walk down a red carpet, but the truth is, it's so overwhelming, you need someone to tell you when to walk and when to stop, because otherwise you could just end up standing there like a deer in the headlights. I had thought the camera crews at the Spring Fling were nuts, but this was a whole other ball game. There were so many flashbulbs popping it felt like we were in the center of a never-ending fireworks display, and photographers were screaming and waving. *"Taylor! Over here! Who are you wearing? Taylor! Clive! Clive! Over here! One of you two together! Over here!"*

Clive took Taylor's hand and kissed it as the photographers yelled for more. He wrapped his arm around her waist, too, and I swear you have never seen a cuter couple. Taylor looked so happy. Like a girl in love.

It took forever for Taylor and Clive to make it past the photographers, and Nikki posed for photos, too. Jenna, Kelly, and I waited off to the side, happy to watch the chaos instead of being the focus of it.

"This is so insane," Kelly whispered. "I feel like I'm watching Taylor become a star, you know? Like, just add vodka and, *pow!*" I nodded. I knew exactly what she meant.

Once Taylor and Clive were done, a photographer yelled at me, "Hey, you in the red dress, who are you wearing?" He got me to spin around for a few pictures, but no one else seemed to care. I figured if Veronique asked me, I could honestly tell her I'd posed on the red carpet.

After Clive and Taylor dealt with the photographers, there were still hordes of reporters to talk to, some from television shows and others from big magazines like *People* and *Us Weekly*.

Taylor and Clive had to stand there on the carpet with the publicist and get hammered with crazy questions you wouldn't believe.

"Taylor, what's your favorite eye shadow?"

"MAC, Purple Haze," Taylor answered.

"Taylor, what would you like to say to our teenage readers in Italy?"

"Ciao, *bella*?" she suggested.

"Taylor, what's it like having Clive for a big brother? Is he really like a big brother?"

I could tell Taylor didn't really like that question, but she just smiled. "He's just a great guy in general," she said, clutching Clive's arm a little harder.

Then Taylor got to the *Inside Edition* reporter, and the publicist took her arm and whispered in her ear. I don't know what Marie said, but I'm guessing she was telling Taylor to watch herself. Shows like *Entertainment Tonight* are pretty celeb-friendly, but *Inside Edition*, well, let's just say they dig for dirt.

"Taylor, we've heard there's been conflict on the set with Julia Hanson!" the reporter screamed. "Can you tell us what's going on?"

"I'm so honored to be working with her," Taylor said, nervously looking at the show publicist, who quickly cut in and began pulling Taylor away.

"We have to keep moving, sorry," the publicist said, and Taylor smiled sweetly and walked quickly to the next reporter. She looked genuinely sorry to be blowing off the girl from *Inside Edition*, but I'd known Taylor too long not to be able to read her face. The truth was, I think all the questions were starting to get to her.

It's one thing just to talk to people, but knowing they're recording it for millions of people to see or read, knowing that one airheaded moment can make headlines, or that one stupid little joke can offend tons of people? Even for someone as determined and focused as Taylor, it was a hell of a lot to ask.

It took us a full hour just to work our way up to the pair of stone lions that flanked the front door of the club, but even once we got that far it wasn't like things slowed down at all. Everyone wanted to talk to Taylor. Network executives. Producers. Directors.

An old guy in a suit walked up to Taylor. "Loved the pilot, loved it," he said, shaking her hand. "We should talk about plans for your hiatus."

Another younger guy in a jacket interrupted. "I'm with the network, Taylor, and I wanted to introduce myself," he said. "Welcome to the family!"

I managed to get close to Taylor, and she quickly grabbed my arm. "Oh my God, this is so crazy!" she whispered. "Great crazy, but still, crazy!"

Just then another guy in a suit practically shoved me out of the way to get to Taylor, braying about how talented she was. Clive caught me right before I landed in a potted plant.

"Jesus, you'd think she was handing out money," he said as he pulled me to my feet. "Screw this. Let's go."

Clive pushed through the crowd, and linking arms with Jenna and Kelly, we finally, finally got inside. I had no idea where Nikki ended up, but I bet she was still hanging out with the reporters, hoping to soak up some of Taylor's reflected glory.

Once we got away from the throng of people at the entrance, we could actually see the place we were in. It was amazing. There were bamboo screens and Chinese wooden sculptures on the walls, some of which were lined with red and purple silk. It was the coolest place I'd ever been to.

"I totally want to decorate my room to look just like this," Jenna gushed.

Jenna and Kelly grabbed a booth, and Clive offered to get us all drinks from the bar. Taylor had told us earlier that the pilot episode was going to be screened in about an hour, so until then we could just pork out at the sushi bar and relax.

"This is sweet," Jenna sighed, looking around the room. "I can't believe I'm really here."

"Oh, don't get all Cinderella about it," Kelly said. "It's unbecoming when you're wearing combat boots."

"Just because I'm goth doesn't mean I can't be excited," Jenna snapped. Then she looked a little worried. "Wait, does it?"

"I don't know about you, but I'm getting something to eat," I said. Jenna and Kelly could debate etiquette all they wanted, but I was starved.

I was loading up a plate with yellowtail and spicy tuna rolls when I saw Clive trying to carry all four of our drinks in his hands. I walked up and gingerly grasped mine, a plain old Coke. I'd already had plenty to drink in the limo.

"Thanks, Erin." Clive smiled. "You're a lifesaver."

We started elbowing our way back to the table. "So, are you nervous yet?" I asked.

"Yes and no. Everyone's excited about the pilot, and we may even get some good reviews. But if no one watches? It's all for shit."

"Taylor seems pretty confident it's going to be a hit."

Clive shook his head. "I know, I know. And I hope she's right.

But right now, it's all hype. It's like we're imagining all this, all the people kissing our asses and telling us we're great. Because it's just not real."

I thought about how Taylor took everything so personally, good and bad. How she was so convinced she was going to be a star. And I really did think she would be, but what if it didn't happen?

By then we were back at the table, and somehow so was Nikki. "You didn't get a drink for me?" she pouted.

Clive sighed and pushed his beer in her direction. "All yours, my dear."

Nikki started slugging it down like it was grape juice, scanning the room as she drank. "Is that Paula Abdul?" she asked. "Does that look like the guy who directed *40-Year-Old Virgin* to you? God, I can't remember his name. Shit!"

Suddenly, Nikki sprang out of her seat. "That's Jerry Bruckheimer! I've got to meet him," she said, practically walking on top of Kelly as she scrambled out of the booth, sloshing beer on Clive in the process.

"Great," Clive said, grabbing a cocktail napkin to dab at the front of his pants.

"I don't like her," Kelly said bluntly after Nikki was out of earshot.

"Me, neither," Jenna added. "And did you notice how thin she is? We could use her for tracing paper."

"Nikki has her good points," I said, though I was feeling kind of hard-pressed to think of any at the moment.

Suddenly Taylor came galloping up to the table.

"You won't believe who I met!" Taylor said, squeezing into

the booth next to Clive. "Adam Brody! Funniest guy ever! And I met one of those guys from *MADtv*. Can't remember his name, but great guy. He said the buzz on our show is the best he's ever heard. Ever!"

Clive shot me a look. Maybe Taylor really was getting too caught up in the hype.

"Oh, and get this," Taylor added. "Julia didn't show up. I overheard this one guy saying she might be recast. That has to be wrong, I'm sure." But Taylor didn't really look unhappy about it.

She started to tell us more, but then the screening started. Someone had put plasma-screen TVs all around the room, so you couldn't not see the show. Of course, I'd already seen it, so I was able to spy on everybody else as they watched. From the start the crowd was quiet, totally sucked in. Jenna and Kelly were, too. Kelly even gasped at one point, when Taylor's character threatened to steal her dad's car keys.

Clive, clearly bored, was scanning text messages on his cell phone. And Taylor couldn't take her eyes off him.

When the show was over, everybody in the place applauded, and people started swarming our table to talk to Taylor and Clive.

"Let's get out of here," I said to Jenna, but she shook her head.

"Are you kidding? Everyone at the party is coming to this table. It's like ordering pizza, except instead of pizza, you get celebrities, piping hot."

She was right, of course. A lot of the people who came up had faces I recognized, but right now I just wanted some air. It's funny, but once you've met a few celebrities, you start to realize they're just people. Better dressed than the rest of us, and prettier maybe, but in the end, just people.

I spent the next hour or two just kind of milling around the party, occasionally heading back to Taylor's table to see who was chatting her up. Most of the time, it was old guys in suits. I could just imagine what Taylor was really thinking behind her smile. "You are sooo boring," or maybe "Are those hair plugs?" But perhaps when old guys are telling you how great you are and how much they want to turn you into a big star, it isn't so bad.

I'd had all the sushi I could stand, and finally headed to the bar for something cold to drink. With all the people packed into the room, I was starting to sweat.

"Hey, gorgeous," purred a familiar voice next to me. Dax.

God, he looked good. A black suit, white shirt, and a skinny tie, just punk enough not to look like the getup of the old geezers around us. "Hi," I said, trying to be a little cool. He wasn't my date, after all, and I didn't want to act like some geeky schoolgirl. Even if I technically was one.

"Let's get some air," he said, taking my arm and leading me out to the patio. I was still thirsty, but I forgot all about my drink the minute we walked outside.

I thought we'd found the most romantic place in the world. A white tent hung high overhead so you could just see a sliver of the night sky, and stone Buddha sculptures lined the walls. Little candles flickered on the tables. I felt Dax run his hand up and down my naked back. The evening was suddenly looking a lot more exciting.

Dax glanced around the room, then fixed his blue eyes on

mine. "I can get out of here in about ten minutes," he said. "I want to take you to the beach house. We can fall asleep listening to the waves crash along the beach."

"You have a beach house?" I asked. It occurred to me that losing my virginity watching the waves in Malibu would be kind of ideal.

"Technically, it's my dad's, but he never uses it. Can you go? Ditch your friends?"

I nodded. Dax squeezed my hand. "I'll get the car. Meet me out front in about fifteen," he said, before disappearing back into the crowd.

I was so caught up watching him walk away, I didn't even see Nikki lurching towards me.

"Are you the new one?" she slurred, her enormous lollipop head wobbling back and forth. Clearly, she was drunk or high. Or both.

"What?"

"Dax's new little girl," she said. "Emphasis on little."

"What are you talking about?"

"Oh, sweetie," Nikki said, making a face. "You don't know, do you? Dax likes his girls young. He probably thinks you're thirteen or fourteen."

The moment I found out that my mother had died, I felt like someone had literally kicked me in the stomach. I couldn't even breathe; it felt so bad. This was like that. A sucker punch, plain and simple.

"What did Dax say, that he's still in college?" Nikki continued, laughing a little. "So he didn't seem so much older. Twenty-seven years old, and I bet he's still trying to pull that one off."

"It's a lie," I said, my voice shaking. "It's just gossip."

"Oh, no, Erin," Nikki said, teetering on her high heels. "How do you think I got this job? I was just an extra on his daddy's last show, that piece of crap *Our Little Corner*. But Daddy was very good to me once I promised not to press charges against Dax. I was only fourteen then. Best break I ever got."

What she was saying was so surreal, I felt like I couldn't absorb it. Random words just popped into my head, and I struggled to thread them together. Dax. Nikki. Charges. Fourteen. Little, little girls.

"You're drunk," I said. She had to be lying. I wouldn't put anything past Nikki.

"Not drunk enough," Nikki said evenly, waving to a waiter carrying a tray of drinks nearby. "You know, he doesn't even give me a second glance? It's the implants. I look too grown-up for him now. But you"—Nikki pointed at my chest—"you could be twelve years old in the right light. Goddamn Asians. You're all tiny like that."

I pushed past Nikki and headed for the door. This couldn't be true. Dax wasn't like that, no way in hell.

I saw the red Porsche waiting at the valet station, Dax behind the wheel. I ran over and got in.

Chapter Seven

Yeah, age is a big deal in this industry. No one wants to get old. But I don't know—I don't think I'd ever get Botox or a face-lift. I've lived a lot, and I'm going to earn every wrinkle, believe me. I'd never want to hide that.

—TAYLOR CHRISTENSEN in *CosmoGirl!* magazine

In the car, Dax kept looking at me. "You look pretty damn hot in that dress."

Believe it or not, I'd completely forgotten about my dress thanks to Nikki's drunken little rant. I looked down, hoping to God a nipple hadn't popped out or anything. "Thanks," I muttered. "Can I ask you something?"

"Ask me anything," Dax said, shifting into a higher gear.

"Did you ever . . . date Nikki?"

Dax looked at me for a moment, then tossed his head back and laughed. "Did she tell you that?"

I nodded, feeling a little stupid but mostly relieved. Why would I ever trust Nikki's word over Dax's? What the hell was I thinking?

"I bet she was loaded, right?" Dax said, shaking his head.

"She was definitely drunk."

"Well, that's an improvement for her," Dax said. Looking at me, he put one finger against the side of his nose, and snorted. "Her problem's bigger than alcohol. But you didn't hear it from me."

It made sense. Nikki always seemed kind of hyper, and then there was the super-bony body.

"Let's not waste time talking about that crack whore," Dax said. "Did you have a good time tonight?"

I told Dax about our ride in the limo and watching Taylor walk the red carpet, and he told me what a drag it was hanging around with his dad and all the boring studio suits. Pretty soon I almost forgot about Nikki. Almost. What she had said was like a mosquito buzzing in my ear. And no matter how hard I tried to swat it away, it just wouldn't disappear.

The beach house was tiny, just a one-bedroom bungalow, but the view was amazing, even in the dark. You could see the moon reflect off the black seawater in the distance, and the sky was a blanket of stars. The patio opened right out onto the beach, and the ocean was so close you could smell the salt in the air. It was hard to believe the city was just a few miles away, because standing there with Dax, I felt like we were alone on vacation somewhere exotic and perfect.

"Nice, huh?" Dax whispered into my neck. I felt a hand running down my back and his lips brushing the side of my cheek. Maybe this was the right time. It was definitely the right place.

I felt him unhook the back of my dress, and that was all it took for the flowing red silk to puddle at my feet. There I was, standing outside practically naked except for my thong and my jewelry. Tonight, at least, I had worn good underwear.

I had thought this was what I wanted. And on the surface,

it couldn't be any better. I was standing here with this gorgeous guy just a few feet from the beach, wearing (or not wearing) an incredible designer dress. It was like something you dream about when you're a kid playing with Barbies. I had always wanted to be Barbie, beautiful and blond and living in a Malibu Dream House, and this was about as close as I was ever going to get.

For a minute I tried to just stare into Dax's eyes, those beautiful eyes, and forget about Nikki. Maybe Dax wouldn't stick around forever, but maybe he was the perfect guy to help me get rid of my virginity. I'd never told him I was a virgin, and I hoped he wouldn't care.

Dax began kissing me hard. He pressed himself against me, and let's just say he was happy to see me. I wasn't really sure what to do about that, but I hoped I could just keep kissing him and he would do the rest.

And then my cell phone rang.

Dax ignored it, but I couldn't. At first, I was worried that Sheila had freaked out and called my dad when I didn't come back with Taylor. But then I realized that I felt kind of relieved. Saved by the bell. Or the ring tone, whatever.

"Do you have to get that?" Dax asked, kissing me again as I pulled away.

"I'm sorry," I said, running for my purse.

"What the hell happened to you?" Taylor yelled over the line. "I can't believe you bailed on my premiere party! The most important night of my life, and you go missing?"

"Now is not the time, Taylor," I said through clenched teeth.

"Why is it every time something good happens to me you have to spoil it? Do you really need attention that badly?"

I couldn't believe it. Here I was in a total mess, and somehow everything was all about Taylor. As usual.

"Well, you may want to tell that coke whore Nikki to keep her mouth shut!" I was yelling so loud it hurt.

"What the hell are you talking about?"

"Go ask her!" I screamed, snapping shut my phone and throwing it across the room.

I looked up. Dax was watching me from the sofa. He silently handed me my dress.

"I think you may need to go home and get a good night's sleep," he said. In the dark, I couldn't see his face. But after my little meltdown, I'm not sure I would have wanted to.

The next day at school, I filled Jenna and Kelly in on the dirty details of my evening. "That *bitch*!" Kelly screamed when I told her what Nikki had done. "Do you think she's lying?"

"I don't know," I admitted. "I hope so."

Jenna jabbed my chest with a black-lacquered fingernail. "It doesn't matter if she's right or not. That was bad party etiquette if nothing else."

As mad as I was at Nikki, I was pretty pissed at Taylor, too. She hadn't even asked if I was okay before ranting about how I had spoiled her important evening. Ha! I was so mad, I would have quit my job as an extra, if my dad wasn't counting on the money. Instead I decided to take the bus to the set the next day, which took a full two hours longer and involved sitting downwind from a creepy, homeless guy who smelled like rotten onions. But it was better than having to sit in a limo with Taylor.

When I got to the set, I stuck around the extras' holding area.

Not only did I not want to bump into Taylor; I was a little nervous about seeing Dax. Driving me home the other night, he hadn't said much, and when he dropped me off all I got was a chaste little kiss on the cheek. Ouch.

A bunch of extras were passing around a copy of *Us Weekly* and giggling. "What is it?" I asked, trying to look over their shoulders.

"Oh, nothing," a short kid with greasy brown hair said. "Except the star of our show wore a see-through dress to the premiere."

And there was a full-page picture of Taylor. That beautiful black dress she had worn turned completely transparent when exposed to the photographer's flashbulbs. You could see Taylor wasn't wearing a bra, but worse, you could see she was wearing these awful cotton granny panties, and they were even a little crooked on her hips.

The article next to the picture was just as bad. CHUBBY STAR-LET ALREADY OVEREXPOSED! the headline said. There was even a little illustrated thumbs-down in the corner just to drive home the point that Taylor was a fashion disaster.

As mad as I was, I felt awful for Taylor. This was like having a lousy picture in the yearbook, but so much worse. Granted, I'd had a rough night, too, but I didn't have it recorded for everyone and their dog to see. So I made my way to her trailer, crossing my fingers that Nikki wasn't already there.

As I expected, Taylor was curled up on the sofa, moping. And Sheila was there, too, with a copy of the magazine curled in her fist.

"You should have let me take you shopping, you little fool!"

Sheila screamed. "I could have picked out a decent dress. Who the hell is this Veronique woman?"

"You are *not* helping, Sheila!" Taylor yelled back. When I opened the door, Taylor ran up to me, turned me around, and pushed the both of us out the door. "I'm leaving!" she yelled back at Sheila.

"Thank God you're here," Taylor sighed. "Did you see my picture?"

I nodded. Taylor groaned and covered her face. "They called me chubby! I could just die, right here. This is the worst thing that has ever happened to me."

Of course it was. "It's not so bad, Taylor."

"Everyone's seen my underwear! I looked like an idiot. A big, fat idiot. I'm never going to live this down."

"People will forget about it by tomorrow. And you don't look chubby at all."

"I've tried so hard to lose weight, Erin. So hard. And it's not enough."

I had to get her off this fat rant. God, she never seemed to eat anymore as it was. "What does your agent say?"

Taylor shrugged. "She said this happens all the time and not to worry about it. That it was good I got a full page in *Us Weekly*. Even if it was as Most Overexposed Star of the Week."

I couldn't help it. I laughed. And, after slugging me in the arm, Taylor finally smiled a little.

"You suck," Taylor said.

"But you see, it really is okay. Any publicity is good publicity, right?"

"I guess," Taylor admitted, still moping. "She did say the ratings for the premiere were huge, though."

"That's great! You can get emancipated soon."

She looked back at the Trayler and scowled. "That will definitely be a good thing."

"Absolutely," I agreed. But then I stopped short. Somehow I'd forgotten all about what was bugging me so I could talk Taylor through her latest drama. And I couldn't just act like everything was magically okay. "Taylor, we haven't dealt with what happened the other night."

Taylor looked confused for a minute, as if she'd forgotten entirely. "Oh, yeah. I'm sorry I cussed you out. Are we okay?"

"No, we're not!" I was trying to keep my voice down, but it was hard. I told her about what Nikki had said, and how I ended up at the beach with Dax.

"Did you sleep with him?"

"No. I couldn't. It was too weird."

"Then it's a good thing Nikki told you, right? She did you a favor."

"That's not the point!" I said. God, Taylor could be so clueless sometimes! "I was in the middle of this huge disaster, and you called me up to bitch me out without even asking what you were interrupting. And you know that phone is only for emergencies."

"I didn't think of that," Taylor said. "I was just really mad—"

"I know, and I'm sorry. But the least you could have done was ask how I was before you tore into me. And you acted like I stuck a knife in you when all I did was leave a party early. You're my best friend. You could have thought about someone other than yourself for half a minute."

Taylor seemed kind of shocked by that. "Wow. I didn't know you felt that way."

"I didn't mean to yell. Sorry." I was suddenly very tired. "Just keep Nikki away from me and we'll be fine."

"Okay. I really am sorry," Taylor said in a small voice.

In the distance I could see the first AD waving for me. Time to work. "I gotta go," I said.

"We're cool, right?" Taylor actually seemed worried.

"Sure," I said before I ran off.

I'd almost forgotten my fight with Taylor until that afternoon. I was just wrapping up a scene, one where I opened and closed my locker and pretended to talk to a girl with bright orange hair, when Taylor waved me over to her director's chair.

"I was thinking about today," she said. "And there is a bright side, you know."

"Oh yeah?"

"Well, you got a lot more action than I did last night. Clive wouldn't even kiss me. Aaaaand," Taylor said, reaching into her pocket. "I got you this. To celebrate. And say thanks for being my best friend."

She handed me a cell phone. A slick Motorola number that made my little pay-as-you-go look like crap.

"It does everything," Taylor said. "You can shoot video, even. I got one, too. It's kick-ass. You've got unlimited-whenever minutes."

"Jeez, Taylor, this is too much," I said. I thought for a second maybe I shouldn't accept it, but I couldn't hand it back. I mean, video? Come on!

"Yeah, but you deserve it," Taylor said. "And I have a request."

"Anything," I said without hesitation.

"Don't use up all your minutes on Dax. He sounds vile."

"Okay," I said. How could I use up unlimited-whenever minutes anyway?

Taylor opened her mouth to say something, but just then one of the producers walked up to us and tapped her on the shoulder.

"Taylor?" he asked. "You got a sec?"

It turned out that transparent black dress might not have been a big deal to Taylor's agent, but it was a huge deal to the producers of the show. They wanted their shiny new starlet to have a wholesome, girl-next-door image. And that meant next time she went to some big event, she had to clear whatever she wore with the costume designer first.

"Whatever," Taylor said, shrugging, on the drive home. "It's not like I'm ever going back to Veronique's."

"Well, she did tell you to wear good undergarments," I said.

Taylor looked like she was going to scream. "But she didn't say *why*!"

Chapter Eight

How does fame change your life? How doesn't it?
—TAYLOR CHRISTENSEN in *Premiere* magazine

Even though we knew the show was a hit, and we'd seen the ratings right there in the trades in black-and-white, I don't think either Taylor or I realized what that really meant. I know that sounds weird, but when you spend all your time on the set, ratings are just numbers. You don't think about having fans or being a star.

And the truth was, Taylor was spending a lot of time with her lawyer and agent to move forward with her emancipation, which wasn't easy, considering how nosy Sheila could be. The only upside was that Clive was helping Taylor out with all the details. They still weren't boyfriend and girlfriend, but Clive had emancipated himself, so he was more than happy to show his "little sister" the ropes. He was even giving Taylor and me driving lessons, occasionally letting us take his Prius for a spin in the studio parking lot.

As for my being aware of Taylor's growing fame, I was still too caught up in my Dax drama to pay much attention. Instead of breaking up with him, I had become the wishy-washiest girl on the planet. When he called me we would end up talking on the phone for hours, but then I'd tell him I was busy when he wanted to make plans. I started avoiding him on the set, which wasn't hard to do, since his dad had him running around so much. He'd ask me if something was wrong, but I always said no. I wished I had an explanation for my actions, but I didn't. I still wanted Dax. I wanted to be with him. But then that mosquito Nikki planted in my ear would start buzzing, and I just got stuck in this weird limbo. I think I secretly hoped he'd just break up with me, or ask me to marry him or something crazy like that. And I'm not sure which one I wanted more.

But as far as Taylor becoming an overnight sensation, the only clue we really had was that Julia's role continued to get smaller as the weeks went by, and Taylor's just got bigger. They should have changed the title from *Family Style* to *Taylor 24-7*.

So, it wasn't surprising that there was more than a little tension on the set whenever Taylor and Julia had a scene together. Taylor tried too hard to be nice to Julia all the time, but it didn't matter. She'd say hi, and Julia would just nod, then ignore her. Apparently Julia's nutty-twiggy hippie crap worked only when she was the star of the show. Taylor even sent her flowers one day, but Julia just handed them over to the makeup artists. When Taylor walked into the trailer to get her face done, there they were, reflected a million times over in the wall of mirrors. I know that must have hurt her so much, but she didn't say a word.

Then there was the day that everyone is still talking about, even people who weren't there and get half the story wrong. But I was there, and I can tell you exactly how bad it was. And it was pretty damn bad.

Taylor and Julia had a scene together, and in it mother and daughter were facing off over something stupid the girl had done, like skipping school. And Julia's character was supposed to smack Taylor across the face. Whichever bozo on the writing staff came up with this bright idea, I hope he or she got fired right away.

Julia insisted that the director tape the rehearsal so their reactions would be "fresh." I think this was just so she could have an excuse to smack Taylor as many times as possible. Not that you're really supposed to smack the other person, not hard at least. But I guess Julia was a Method actor, because she wanted to make it look really, really real.

The first take, Julia hauled off and hit Taylor so hard, I thought she had broken Taylor's neck. Taylor's head jerked to the side so sharply she actually lost her balance and stumbled. But then, amazingly, Taylor just righted herself and delivered her next line. And boy, it sounded like she really meant it.

"That was low, Mom," Taylor hissed. "But I'm going to live my own life, and there's nothing you can do about it."

Usually when a director calls "Cut," there's lots of yelling and people rushing around, but this time everyone was absolutely still and silent. No one knew what to do next. Julia just walked off the stage as if nothing was wrong, plopped down in her director's chair, and read a magazine. Taylor didn't move. I think she was too shocked. Even a minute later I could still see Julia's big red handprint on her face.

Finally, the director spoke. "Um, let's do one more take. Okay, ladies?" he said in a very nervous voice.

Taylor and Julia nodded, and took their positions again. A makeup artist rushed onto the set to put foundation on top of Julia's handprint, but by then it was beginning to fade.

"Action!" the director called, and Julia said her lines. Then she slapped Taylor. And if anything, this time she hit her harder. And then Taylor did something no one expected.

Once she regained her balance, she reached out and shoved Julia so hard the woman went flying back into the prop sofa. Then Taylor stomped over to her and, like a pro, delivered her lines again. Julia just gaped at her like a fish, totally out of character. The director yelled, "Cut," and Taylor glared at him.

"Are we good?" she asked in a tone that implied he better damn well be done with that scene. I could actually see a little blood on her lip. Yeah, Julia had hit her that hard.

"Yes, we're good," the director said in a squeaky voice.

When the show finally aired, you could still see how hard Julia hit Taylor, and if you really looked, you could see that awful red handprint on her face. But not surprisingly, the shove in the second take didn't make the cut. And it's a shame, because to this day I think that's some of Taylor's best acting.

Two days later, Julia was replaced by another actress. The newspapers said it was because Julia wanted to pursue other interests. Just goes to show, you should never believe anything you read, especially when it's about Hollywood.

While we were hanging out in the Trayler the day after Julia's dismissal, I tried to get Taylor to talk about what had happened. So far, she hadn't cried, hadn't complained, nothing. I don't know why, but it was like she just wanted to forget the whole thing had happened.

"She's a bitch, plain and simple," Taylor said, drinking yet another Diet Coke, her billionth one of the day. "I was stupid to think otherwise. That's all."

"You looked up to her, though. That's got to hurt."

Taylor's eyes hardened. "I did. I don't anymore. And that's fine. She did me a favor. I'm never looking up to some stupid actress again. I've got to look out for myself. Because no one else will."

"That's kind of sad," I said, but secretly I was hoping this new attitude applied to Nikki, too. Ever since our encounter at the premiere, the girl just bugged me.

Taylor didn't say anything for a while, but when she spoke she didn't sound as tough. "Yeah," she said softly. "But growing up with Sheila, at least I'm used to it."

On the way home from work that day, Taylor nudged me in the ribs. "I am dying for a Double-Double," she said. That's what they call the double cheeseburgers at In-N-Out. "My treat."

When we saw the red and yellow In-N-Out sign in the distance, Taylor tapped on the driver's shoulder. "Can you stop here, just for a minute?" she asked. "I'll give you some of my fries, promise!"

When we pulled up, the driver turned around and looked at us. "Should I go through the drive-through, or would you prefer I go in?"

"Oh, we'll get it ourselves," Taylor said, opening the car door.

"Are you sure?" the driver asked, his eyes wide behind his round glasses.

"No problem!" Taylor said. "Why not?"

Well, it turns out the driver might have been trying to give us a hint. I mean, it never occurred to me that people would get all worked up over Taylor at a fast-food joint. Celebrities hang out all over Los Angeles, and hardly anyone pays any attention except the paparazzi, you know? But imagine what would happen if you were at your local McDonald's and Lindsay Lohan popped in for a Happy Meal, or Mischa Barton waltzed into the Taco Bell near your house. That's right. Total chaos.

So you kind of can guess what happened to our little In-N-Out run.

The minute Taylor walked in, I could see people turning around and pointing in our direction. One guy yelled, "Hey, Taylor! Love the show!"

Taylor smiled in the guy's general direction and gave a little thumbs-up sign. "Oh my God, I'm getting recognized!" she whispered in my ear. "How cool is that?"

It was the last thing I heard her say, because suddenly people were shoving me out of the way, trying to get to Taylor. A lot of them were snapping pictures with their cell phones or waving place mats in her face for her to sign. One little girl tugged desperately on Taylor's sleeve like an orphan begging for porridge.

"Can I get your autograph?" she squealed, and Taylor bent down to sign her napkin. Then someone else handed her a cup, and a kid who was probably our age pulled up his T-shirt.

"Write it on my chest!" he yelled. Taylor did, and the guy didn't even scream, even though it must have hurt like hell to have someone scrawl on him with a ballpoint pen.

I looked around. The restaurant hadn't seemed that full when we walked in, but when everyone including the employees clustered around Taylor, it was a mob scene. Taylor was smiling and talking to people, but when the crowd didn't get any smaller and more people kept pouring into the restaurant, I started wondering if maybe things were getting out of control. And that's just about the time the paparazzi showed up.

Suddenly there were guys with cameras screaming, *"Taylor, over here, Taylor!"* Flashbulbs were popping, and this just seemed to make the crowd more frenzied. Taylor had gotten backed up against a table, and she actually looked scared.

I ran out to the car and banged on the door. "She's being swarmed," I told the driver. "Please, can you help me get her out of there?"

The driver didn't think twice. He just got out of the car and stomped into the restaurant. He wasn't a big guy, but he was tall, and when people saw him in his black suit and black tie, they just automatically moved out of his way. I guess they thought he was her security guard or something, or that maybe he had a gun. Not that I cared. By the time we had walked back into the restaurant, the crowd around Taylor was fifteen people deep in any given direction, and she was looking ghostly pale.

"Excuse me, excuse me," the driver said, barreling through the crowd. And just like that, he grabbed Taylor by the arm and dragged her to the car. The crowd followed us, of course, but at a distance.

"I can't believe that," Taylor said, struggling to catch her breath. "That was unreal!"

"You're a star, Taylor," I said. "Get used to it."

"I AM a star!" Taylor started laughing, the color returning to her cheeks. "I mean, I've seen the paparazzi camped outside my building, but that's nothing compared to this. Nothing. Everyone in there knew my name, Erin. Everyone! Do you know what this means?"

"It means from now on you're going to have to use the drive-through if you want a burger."

We both laughed, but Taylor stopped short. "Oh my God, Erin. I'm that kind of famous," she said slowly.

"I know, duh." Apparently stardom was making Taylor a little slow on the uptake.

"No, no, I mean, like, I can't go to the mall and just hang out anymore. Or put out the garbage in my pajamas. Now I have to think about everything I do. And what I can't do. Like getting a hamburger." You know the look people on trial get on their faces when the judge hands down a life sentence? Sort of stunned and frightened? That was the look on Taylor's face right then.

"We can still get a hamburger," I said. I asked the driver to pull over at the next In-N-Out we saw, and when he did I dashed in to get our food. But after I handed Taylor her Double-Double, she just stared at it.

"I'm not hungry anymore," she said. "Besides, I'm on a diet."

There were other signs that Taylor was a big star. Namely, how she kept popping up in the tabloids. There were stories about what kind of makeup she wore, about whether she looked thin or fat, about what she ordered at Starbucks one day (with the catty headline "Iced blended mocha? Not with those thighs, girlie!"). There were pictures from our yearbook even. After the transparent dress, it seemed like the rag sheets were really hungry for any dish about Taylor, even if the stories were made up. And a lot of them were, mostly about how Taylor was dating other TV stars she'd never met. But there was one that was absolutely true. Unfortunately.

When I walked into the Trayler, Taylor was sitting on the floor with the tabloid spread out in front of her, reading and rereading every word, as if she couldn't believe it.

"What is it?" I asked, but Taylor didn't speak. I looked over her shoulder.

MALIBU BARFIE! the headline proclaimed in big, bold print. The article was short, but it was long enough to ruin a friendship.

A close friend of Taylor Christensen, Kelly Bend, gave our *STARZINE* reporter a scoop—that TV's sexiest new star had a nasty nickname in junior high. Poor Taylor was teased for tossing her cookies on her first day at a new school, but she didn't let that unhappy beginning get her down. The plucky aspiring actress actually made light of her nervous stomach by spiritedly reenacting that moment of infamy in the school cafeteria, inciting a food fight. Sounds like we know where her talent for drama came from!

"I can't believe she talked to the tabloids," Taylor said finally. "We joked about that, remember?"

"It's not a mean article, though," I said, trying my best.

Taylor didn't say anything. She just kept staring at the page.

I sneaked outside and called Kelly. I barely got a word out before Kelly lost it.

"I thought it would be a good thing!" Kelly screamed. "I've been trying to call Taylor all day, but her phone must be off. I had no idea!"

It turned out Kelly had started talking to some reporter on the red carpet at the premiere, and the lady gave her a call fishing for dirt one day.

"She called Taylor a prima donna, and so I told her that wasn't fair at all," Kelly cried. "I told her about Malibu Barfie to make a point! That she wasn't always this perfect diva, that she's really down-to-earth. They cut out all the good things I said, though."

One question still lingered. "Did they pay you?" I asked.

Kelly hesitated. "Three hundred bucks," she finally admitted. "But seriously, who cares? It's just a stupid little story!"

Well, Taylor cared. A lot.

I promised Kelly I would try to explain it to Taylor, but it didn't do any good.

"I don't care," Taylor said simply. "She wasn't even there, Erin. If she had been, she would have known how awful it was. That was one of the most humiliating things that has ever happened to me, and at the lowest point in my life. And that's the freaking story she has to blab?"

I felt my face flush hot. I was the one who had told Kelly about Malibu Barfie. I wanted to tell Taylor it was sort of my fault this happened, but I couldn't do it.

Taylor picked up the tabloid, wadded it into a ball, and threw it in the trash. "If you want to stay friends with her, fine," she said. "But we're over."

I did want to stay friends with Kelly. But after that, it was hard. I felt weird talking to Kelly and Jenna about what was going on at work, and I never knew what to say when Kelly would ask me if Taylor had gotten over the story yet, especially when I knew

Taylor wasn't going to, ever. Kelly and I were still friends, but I knew we'd never be as close as we were before.

I guess I could have told Taylor to snap out of it, or screamed and yelled at her until she forgave Kelly. It would have been for her own good. But I had to be loyal to Taylor. I mean, the girl gave me a cell phone, right?

Even though a new drama seemed to spring up on the set every day, the rest of my life actually wasn't so bad. Thanks to the on-set tutor, my grades were good, and since my dad had bitched out Victoria, she hadn't bugged me about much of anything. And finally, when I'd long since stopped hoping for it to happen, my dad started acting, if not totally normal, more like his old self.

When my sixteenth birthday rolled around, I didn't really think he'd notice. Birthdays were another thing my mom had handled when she was alive. She'd make *mi yeok gook*, this seaweed soup Korean people always eat on their birthdays, and before dinner we'd all sit down at the dining room table and I'd unwrap gifts. And, of course, there was cake, usually chocolate blackout fudge from Sweet Lady Jane, this place that makes cakes that are almost too pretty to eat (but one bite and you so don't care about messing them up; they're that good).

But without Mom around, I figured even a Twinkie was too much to hope for, much less gifts and homemade soup. When Taylor said she was going to take me out to Geisha House to celebrate, I figured I'd just ask my dad if I could go out to dinner and that would be that. So when I walked into the kitchen after school and saw my dad wearing an apron and pulling a pot out of the kitchen cabinets, I almost died of shock.

You've got to understand, when my mom was alive, my dad never lifted a finger in the kitchen. The guy wouldn't have known a dishwasher from an oven; he was that bad. And even after Mom died, Victoria had to show him how to use the microwave so he could heat soup and TV dinners.

I must have had an awful look on my face, because my dad kind of laughed and looked embarrassed. "I thought I could make *mi yeok gook* for you," he said shyly, like a kid who'd done something stupid. "Do you know where the oil is?"

I stuck my head inside the refrigerator and pretended to look for the sesame oil. I knew exactly where it was, but my eyes were tearing up and I didn't want him to see. I don't know why I was all weepy, exactly, but I think it had to do with a lot of things. Missing Mom, wishing she were here for my birthday. Understanding that every holiday, every celebration, would have this emptiness. But I felt happy, too, seeing Dad trying so hard to make everything okay.

After I collected myself, I handed him the oil and smiled. "Thanks, Dad."

I looked over his shoulder and saw a recipe he'd printed off the Internet and a plastic bag from the nearby Korean market. Looking at all the pots and pans, it was pretty clear to me my dad was out of his depth. "Maybe we should soak the seaweed," I suggested.

"Oh," my dad said, as if this was a surprise to him even though the recipe was sitting right in front of him. After that, I made a lot of "suggestions," which kind of meant my dad would hand me stuff and I'd end up doing it myself. Which was fine by me, because otherwise we would have been eating dry seaweed and burned garlic for dinner, if that.

When Taylor's car came to pick me up, I dragged her in the front door. "My dad made soup," I whispered.

"So?" Taylor asked, looking at me like I was stupid.

"Special Korean soup. My dad, in the kitchen. Cooking."

Finally, Taylor got it. This was officially a first for my kitchen-phobic dad. "Is he okay?"

"He is. Like, really okay."

Taylor craned her neck to look over my shoulder, as if she didn't quite believe me. But there Dad was, in his apron, humming and stirring the *mi yeok gook*. "I'll cancel the Geisha House reservation and tell the driver to take a break."

"Invite him in," I said. This was a celebration, after all. Maybe not the one I'd expected, but possibly the best one I could have asked for.

So that's how I ended up celebrating my sixteenth birthday with my dad, Taylor, and this nice guy named Haime, eating *mi yeok gook*. Taylor even called Sweet Lady Jane and had a studio messenger bring us a cake (yes, chocolate blackout fudge) in time for dessert.

No, it wasn't the Geisha House, but guess what? It was, in a lot of ways, so much better.

With ratings for *Family Style* just getting better and better, the good part of being a big star started to sink in with Taylor. She had money. And instead of letting Sheila blow it on a house in the Hollywood Hills, she was going to spend it. Just the way she wanted.

The first step was getting a car. Since Clive had been a pretty good driving instructor, we both got our learner's permits. Sheila was fine with that, since she was already pleading for a Mercedes.

Taylor let Sheila drag her to exactly one snooty car dealership before she put her foot down. "I want a Prius," she said as her mother lovingly stroked the leather seats of a red convertible.

"You've got to be kidding," Sheila spit back. "Those are cheap."

"They're environmentally conscious. Cameron Diaz and Leonardo DiCaprio drive them. So does Clive."

Taylor got her Prius in Salsa Red Pearl. Taylor 1, Sheila 0.

When Clive and I went with Taylor to pick up her car, I could have died of envy. "Oh my God, Taylor, it's so cute!" I sighed as she got behind the wheel. The car had a hands-free phone and a six-CD player that was better than anything I had at home.

"I'm glad you like it," Taylor said, grinning at me as she hung an arm out the window. "Because yours is black."

I looked at Clive, who had the same knowing grin as Taylor. *"Oh my God!"* I screamed. "Taylor, thank you thank you thank you!"

I practically jumped into the car to hug her. "I can't believe Sheila let you do this!"

"She got her stupid Mercedes, so she can just stuff it," Taylor said. "I got her car used, though. She was SO pissed."

When I got inside my new car, I swear, I wanted to sleep in it. It was the nicest thing I'd ever owned. All my life I'd been getting Victoria's old hand-me-downs, and now I had something not only new but better than anything else she had. And maybe it was childish, but that was absolutely the greatest.

Right then I promised that I would try to be a better friend to Taylor. If she wanted to talk about Clive until she was blue in the face, fine. If she wanted to hang out with that bitch Nikki, fine. Fine, fine, fine.

When I showed my dad my new car in the driveway, he kind of blinked as if he wasn't sure what he was seeing was real.

"She gave it to you?" he asked. "To keep? Not a loan?"

"It's mine. She signed it over and everything."

"You just pay insurance, that's it?" He still couldn't absorb it.

I hadn't really thought about insurance. Or gas. "Is it okay if I pay for it from my extra work? I'll see if I can get on some other shows if that helps—"

My dad shook his head. "It's fine. We'll make it work." He walked over to the car, opened the door, and got in. He ran his hands over the wheel.

"Your friend Taylor," he said, "she is a very, very nice girl."

I smiled, and then I thought of Mom. I wondered if now maybe, just maybe, she'd agree with him.

The first day I drove my car to the set, I made a beeline for Clive's trailer. "Want a lift?" I asked him when he poked his head out the door.

"Absolutely. Think I can get Taylor to buy me a car?"

"You've already got one, silly." I slugged Clive in the arm. Taylor might not have liked to think of him as a big brother, but I did. "Come on, you've got some free time, right?"

Clive looked at his watch. "Half an hour. That's long enough for you to crash into something, right?"

"Probably. And if you ask me to parallel park, I can do it in less."

After we made it out of the studio parking lot, I decided to ask Clive something that had been eating at me for a while.

"Clive, I noticed you and Dax didn't really get along."

"Oh, God," Clive groaned.

"Look, I heard a story, and I need to know if it's true."

Clive rubbed his eyes, as if trying to wake up from a bad dream. "Okay," he said finally. "Shoot."

I told him what Nikki had said, and he didn't seem surprised.

"As far as I know, it's true," he said. "She wasn't the first, either."

And then Clive mentioned the names of some other TV stars, child stars who are big enough names I can't even think about repeating them without getting sued. Let's just say that when they became big stars, they were young. Really young. Junior high, maybe even elementary school.

"They were Dax's girls," Clive said sadly. "You're probably the oldest. The closest he ever got to legal."

I felt sick to my stomach. The buzzing had grown to a roar I couldn't drown out anymore. As cute as Dax was, I had to admit there was something wrong with him.

"Why didn't you say something?" It suddenly hit me that every time Clive had seen me with Dax, he'd never said a word. "I thought we were friends, Clive."

"I wanted to. You have to believe that. I hated seeing you with that scumbag."

"That's not much of an excuse."

"If you had decided to tell Dax you heard this from me, I'd be pumping gas in Oklahoma somewhere." Clive sighed.

"Everyone has something to lose in this business. It's not so black-and-white."

"I never would have betrayed your trust. I'm a better friend than that."

Clive looked at me. "Really?"

"Absolutely."

"I am really, really sorry, Erin. I mean it." Clive truly did look heartbroken. "Please forgive me."

I sighed. "I do. Just promise you'll tell me next time I'm dating a pervert."

Clive crossed his fingers over his heart. "Will do." He paused for a moment. "Do you think you can do me a favor?"

"Sure, what?"

"I need you to get Taylor to give up on me. Introduce her to a new guy, anything."

"You're really asking the impossible," I said. "She's so into you it's sick."

"It's never going to happen."

"If it's the age thing, she's willing to wait."

"It's not."

I rolled my eyes. "Every other guy in the United States is hot for her, and you're not?"

"Not my type."

"You think she's immature."

"No, it's not that."

"What?"

"Erin, can you keep a secret? No kidding?" For once, Clive wasn't joking around, I could tell.

"What?"

"I'm gay."

I know what you're thinking. So what? Lots of people are gay. But being gay in Hollywood? Not so easy. Maybe you can come out if you're a character actor, or a comedian, or if you're old. But if you want to play a romantic lead? Not on your life. Think about it. How many really successful openly gay actors are there? You can probably name a few. But I'll bet they aren't starring in love scenes with the opposite sex. I mean, no one's casting Ellen DeGeneres in any romantic comedies with Brad Pitt. Crazy, isn't it? It's okay to play gay on TV or in movies, but only if you're straight. Being homosexual in real life can still be a career killer for an actor. Stupid, but that's the way it is.

So I knew I had to keep Clive's secret. I had to. Even from my best friend. My best friend, who loved him.

It wasn't long after that that Dax called me. I had stupidly given him my new cell phone number right after I got it, even knowing what Nikki had told me.

Before I answered, I slipped into the Trayler. I knew Taylor was on the set, and I wanted some privacy.

"Where are you?" Dax purred. "I want to see you. I'm five minutes from the lot."

"Dax, I don't think that's a good idea."

"You never have time for me anymore. Is this about that bitch Nikki?"

"No, it's just . . . I don't think I'm ready for a relationship, you know?"

"What the hell does that mean?"

"I think we should take a break."

"Oh, come on! How immature are you?" I'd never heard him like this before, his voice dripping venom and contempt. "What do you think this is, a game?"

"I gotta go." I hung up the phone, shaking. It rang again, and I turned it off. I could hear my mother's voice in my head, telling me that boys lied and would say anything to get what they wanted. And for once, I wondered if, at least in this case, she was right.

The first trip Taylor, Nikki, and I took in her little red Prius was to Rodeo Drive that Saturday. Taylor had determined that if Sheila was dressing like a high-class hooker on her paycheck, the least she could do was get a kick-ass designer outfit of her own.

Our first stop was the Prada Epicenter. It was more like a big art exhibit than a store. There was no front door, so it was like the whole place was open to the street, but you could feel the blast of air-conditioning when you "entered." You could change the dressing room doors from clear to opaque just by touching them, and mannequins were set up in the weirdest places. Pairs of legs wearing beautiful shoes sprouted from a staircase as if the rest of the dummy were stuck under the store, and one mannequin was buried in a porthole so you had to look down through the floor to see it. I figured most people who shopped at Prada liked that, since they were used to looking down at other people anyway.

I had no money of my own to spend, but I had still wanted to come along for the day. Even if I couldn't shop like a rich kid, I could at least see what it was like. And let me tell you, it's a lot cooler than the mall.

Sifting through racks of fifteen-hundred-dollar dresses and skirts, Taylor was too distracted to concentrate on price tags, even if they were totally boggling my mind. "Clive is so perfect for me," Taylor sighed, pulling out a beige skirt with aqua embroidery, barely looking at it, then flinging it over her arm. "Why isn't he madly in love with me?"

"Clive is a great guy," I said, trying to be as supportive as I could. "I mean, even if you just end up being friends—"

"What are you talking about? They're perfect for each other," Nikki snapped, giving me a condescending look as she gathered up piles of skirts to take into the dressing room. "She's so much better for him than his last girlfriend, that model from Bulgaria or whatever."

"Who was six feet and a hundred pounds," Taylor sighed.

"And she barely spoke English. Come on," Nikki replied. "Forget her. You look good in blue, don't you?"

I was going to tell Nikki we might want to gently try to talk Taylor out of her fixation on Clive, since he clearly wasn't making himself available to her, but I forgot all about it the minute I saw Taylor come out of the dressing room in a spaghetti strap slip dress.

Okay, obviously I knew Taylor had been losing weight since the debacle at Veronique's. I never saw her eat anymore, God knows. But I had no idea how much weight. She was always wearing long sleeves and sweats around the set and complaining about how cold it was, even when it was ninety degrees out.

But now, as Taylor stood there in her dress, there was no denying that her stupid diet had gone too far. Her upper arms barely looked bigger than her wrists, and her legs were just like Nikki's, spindly little sticks that didn't seem strong enough to support a human body.

Taylor had become a lollipop.

I couldn't help myself. "Oh my God, Taylor! You look so thin!" I screeched.

Taylor smiled and gave Nikki a high five. "I know! This is a zero, and it's totally hanging loose on me."

"I didn't mean that in a good way," I said.

Nikki looked at me like I was crazy. "You're insane, Erin. She looks great."

Taylor looked in the mirror, then turned to the side. Not that it mattered, since the Prada store had these freaky mirrors that let you see the front and back of your outfit at the same time. "I could probably use more tone. I haven't been working out at all."

"You don't need a workout—you need a freakin' sandwich," I muttered under my breath, but no one heard me. Another woman walked towards the dressing rooms, then turned around and left. Watching her totter away in ridiculous high heels, I could tell she was super skinny, too. What was wrong with all these people?

Taylor kept spinning back and forth before the mirror. "Clive won't think I'm chubby anymore, will he?"

"I don't think he ever did, Taylor." I wanted to grab her and pull her out of the store, take her to a doctor, something. But I didn't. You know why? I was thinking about my little black Prius and my new cell phone. I wanted to be a good friend to Taylor. And maybe that meant shutting up. That seemed to be the thing to do in Hollywood. Everything, even your opinion, was a secret here.

Still, I guess the look on my face gave me away. Taylor patted me on the head. "I'm fine, Mom," Taylor joked. Nikki and Taylor gave each other a look. A look that said that they felt a little sorry for me.

Taylor walked back into the dressing room. "Now, Nikki, do you think this would look better in the green?" she asked, pulling Nikki in with her. Through the door I could hear them talking about colors and cuts and styles, see ghostly shadows moving inside. Without me.

It's funny. I didn't know it at the time, but looking back, I can see that this was the day when everything started to change between Taylor and me. It just seemed like there was this wedge being driven in between us. And there was Nikki, waiting to jump into the empty space.

Taylor and Nikki walked arm in arm out of the store, swinging bags of size-zero skirts and five-hundred-dollar shoes, and I followed behind, empty-handed, missing most of their conversation. At first I'd ask them what they'd said, but after a while I stopped. They didn't seem to care whether or not I was included, and some little part of me suspected that I might not like what I heard anyway.

The day Taylor served Sheila with her emancipation papers was probably the most stressful of my life. Sitting in the Trayler with Taylor, her agent, her manager, and, of course, Nikki for an hour waiting for Sheila to show was almost as bad as that day when Taylor and I had to wait to see the principal after our food fight. But worse, because on the crazy scale, Sheila had Principal Zinner beat.

Caitlin, Taylor's agent, looked at her watch. "Should I call her again?" she asked. "I have a three o'clock I can't reschedule."

When Taylor first started talking about calling in her "people" to give Sheila the news about the emancipation, I thought it was a recipe for disaster. Sheila was going to freak no matter what, so why bring in more witnesses?

"Caitlin is trained in dealing with difficult people, Erin," Taylor had explained. "She can defuse the situation. And you know Sheila will need defusing." I had to admit, if Caitlin could make a lunatic like Sheila quietly accept that her meal ticket was kicking her to the curb, I was going to be pretty darn impressed.

Taylor nodded yes to her agent. I could just see it, Sheila flaking out on this big meeting because she was too busy spending Taylor's money on Gucci shoes or whatever. Of course, Sheila didn't know it was a big meeting. She just thought Caitlin wanted to brainstorm about Taylor's movie career. She had no clue that movers were already at their apartment picking up Taylor's stuff to take it over to Nikki's condo in West Hollywood, or that Taylor had withdrawn all her money from the checking account she shared with Sheila. No more Fred Segal for her.

When the door finally blew open, there was Sheila in yet another trashy new outfit. It took a second before her eyes adjusted to the dim light inside the Trayler. "What's going on?" she asked, putting down her purse.

"Sheila, I'm glad you're here," Caitlin said coolly. "Have a seat."

Sheila perched on the edge of the sofa, her spine totally erect. "Why are you all here?"

"We just want to have a conversation about some changes that need to be made to help Taylor's career," Caitlin continued. "You see, Sheila, in order for Taylor to have more opportunities, she's decided she needs to be emancipated. And we just wanted to inform you of all the benefits."

"What?" Sheila said, leaping to her feet. I could tell she wanted to haul off and hit Taylor, but couldn't with so many people around. "What are you trying to do, take away my daughter? Is this the scam you're trying to pull?"

"It's a purely practical matter," said Bradley, the tall man who was Taylor's manager. "It allows her to work more hours, which could have a huge impact on her feature film career. I'm sure you can see the advantages."

"Taylor?" Sheila asked, trying to find her daughter's face in the crowd. "Who put you up to this?"

"It was my idea," Taylor said. Her voice sounded a little shaky, but she was looking at Sheila dead on. I wouldn't say she was unafraid, but I think she was ready for anything her mom might dish out.

"What does this mean? Who's going to manage your money?" Sheila squawked. Of course money was the first thing she thought of.

"We have a great accountant we work with," said Brad. "Everything will be taken care of."

"What about me?" Sheila glared at Taylor. "After all I've done for you, this is how you repay me? This is the gratitude I get?"

Caitlin reached out and took Sheila's hand, trying to look sympathetic, although I knew she felt otherwise. Taylor had told me that Caitlin hated Sheila with a passion. "Sheila, you will always be Taylor's mother. Nothing will change. But for the sake of her success on this show, she needs more flexibility in her schedule. And Taylor isn't that far away from eighteen in any case, so all she's doing is speeding up the process a little. It doesn't mean she doesn't love you or she wants to abandon you. Not at all."

I knew for a fact that was a big stinking lie, but it seemed to calm Sheila down.

"I'm going to move in with Nikki," Taylor said.

Sheila started turning red, but before she could speak, Caitlin cut in. "For the emancipation to clear, it helps if we can prove she can live on her own, Sheila," she said. "It's just a technicality."

Sheila seemed to be pretty okay with everything, but Taylor couldn't resist getting her licks in. "Just think, you don't need to come to the set anymore," she said drily. "You can go back to your career."

Sheila's mouth gaped open, and I almost laughed. I knew she'd rather die than get another secretary gig.

Suddenly, Sheila pointed at me. "I'm the guardian of your little friend!" she shrieked, as if she'd found the loophole that would save her. "What about that?"

"Taylor's new personal assistant will be taking over that responsibility," Caitlin said smoothly.

"I want to talk to my daughter ALONE," Sheila said, and I saw Taylor's eyes go wide. The whole reason all of us were here was specifically so that couldn't happen. Taylor knew Sheila would bully her until she broke down and changed her mind about the emancipation. But luckily, Caitlin knew that, too, and she wasn't about to let it happen.

"Surely you realize this is very hard on Taylor, and I think you just need to give her some quiet time," Caitlin said, taking Sheila firmly by the arm and steering her to the door. "Why don't you and I go have lunch and talk this over?" I have to say, Caitlin was good. Very, very good.

Sheila looked over her shoulder at Taylor, but Taylor was whispering with Brad, and neither one of them looked up. Caitlin opened the door, and just like that, they were gone.

The rest of us sat in silence for a few minutes. I knew we were all thinking the same thing, that Sheila might come running back inside, yelling and screaming. It had almost been too easy. But after a while, we relaxed. Taylor thanked everyone for coming and gave each one of us a big hug. Sheila was finally out of the picture. At least, that's what we thought.

Once Taylor and Nikki were living together, it seemed like I hardly ever saw either one of them anymore. Now that I had my own car, it didn't make sense to get a lift from Taylor, especially since she was living closer to the studio than I was.

I did get to spend some time with Taylor's new assistant, a sweet, heavyset woman named Lila, who mostly seemed to run errands for Taylor and talk to Caitlin on the phone about parties and events Taylor needed to attend. But as far as her being a guardian to me, Lila and I seemed to take a live-and-let-live approach. I wouldn't get arrested, and she'd let me do whatever I wanted.

Lately I'd been hanging out with Clive. Now that I knew his little secret, we spent a lot of time talking about cute boys and what we wanted in relationships. It was a little weird at first because it was hard for me to picture Clive with a guy, but after a while I got used to it. And Clive was more like me than I realized. He wanted a boyfriend who would love him before they slept together, too.

One day when I dropped in on Clive, he looked entirely freaked-out. "Taylor just asked me to dinner at Crustacean," he said. "This is a disaster."

"Don't go."

"I tried. She practically put me in a headlock. Every excuse she had an answer for. She was determined, Erin."

I knew what Taylor was like when she wanted something. I couldn't imagine what it was like to be the something she wanted. "So you go. That's not so bad, is it?"

"Oh, come on," Clive said. "You know how uncomfortable it is. It's like you and Dax."

Oh yes, Dax. After he screamed at me on the phone, he called back and left about a hundred apologetic messages, telling me he loved me and he was just upset and frustrated and how I needed to forgive him. I think on the last few messages, he was drunk. Just a few weeks ago hearing him say he loved me would have made me insanely happy. But now it skeeved me out.

"Come with us," Clive said, grabbing my hands.

"On your date? Are you high?"

"It's not a date, not officially. Please, Erin? You've got to save me. Maybe if I bring you along, she'll get the hint that I don't want to date her."

"Why can't you just tell her you're gay?" I hated keeping a secret from Taylor, and if Clive would just get some guts, I wouldn't have to. "You can trust her."

Clive hesitated. I guess he was trying to find the right words. "Taylor's not like you, Erin. She's an actress. She's . . . dramatic. Maybe once she's moved on to someone else, I can tell her. But right now, I think she'd be so mad about it, she'd punish me."

I rolled my eyes. "You can't help being gay."

"I know that, and you know that, but in my experience, a woman scorned is a woman who goes to the tabloids."

I wanted to say Taylor would never do something that mean, and then I thought of Alexandra and Brandon. Maybe she really was mean enough to drag Clive out of the closet and ruin his career.

"Fine, I'll come to dinner," I said. "But I'm ordering lobster, and I'm not paying."

I don't know why I did it, but I immediately went over to the Trayler. I think I was feeling bad about what I'd just thought about Taylor, that she was mean and untrustworthy. But when I tried the door handle, it was locked. Taylor had only ever locked the door when Sheila was on a rampage, and since the emancipation proceedings began, Sheila hadn't been on the set.

I knocked. "Taylor?"

The door opened a crack, and Taylor poked her nose out. "Oh, Erin," she said, opening the door and pulling me inside.

The Trayler was dark and smelled kind of musty, as if it hadn't been cleaned for a while. "What's up?" Taylor asked, not smiling. She looked kind of jittery, and I noticed the piles of Diet Coke cans stacked around the kitchen counter.

"I just wanted to say hi," I said. "I haven't seen you in a while."

I heard the toilet flush, and Nikki came out of the bathroom, smoking a cigarette. "Hey," she said before flopping onto the sofa.

I felt uncomfortable, but it seemed rude to leave so quickly. "How's emancipation treating you?"

Taylor pulled a cigarette out of a pack sitting on the sofa. "It's fine, I guess," she said in a bored voice.

"When did you start smoking?" I asked. No wonder Taylor looked so sick. Well, that and the fact she was perhaps even skinnier than when we went to Prada Epicenter.

"I don't really smoke," she said, stuffing the cigarette back in the box. "Just sometimes. It's not a habit."

"And don't tell the producers," Nikki said. "They'll cream her. They're already mad about this." Nikki shoved a copy of the *Star* over to me.

There was a picture of Taylor and Sheila on the cover, with a big tear down the middle. A headline screamed, TAYLOR DUMPS PENNILESS MOM FOR THE PARTY LIFE!

"Oh my God," I said. "Sheila did this?"

Taylor took the paper and opened it to a dog-eared page. "They quote her and everything. She says she sacrificed her career in real estate for me, and now she can't even afford a place to live."

"Is she really homeless?" I couldn't believe it. I knew Taylor had given her a big chunk of cash after the emancipation went through, so she could buy a house. Or at least that's what Sheila claimed she needed the money for.

"Of course not," Taylor said. "She's got a condo in Encino. But somehow they overlooked that."

"You should sue," I said.

Taylor shrugged and tossed the rag aside. "Nah. Sheila would enjoy that too much. Oh, hey, did I tell you I'm getting my GED?"

"No more classes, no more books, no more teacher's dirty

looks," Nikki muttered while flipping through TV channels with the remote.

Taylor nudged me. "Hey, Clive finally asked me out on a date," she said, smiling. "We're going to Crustacean. Nice, huh?"

It was so hard to keep my mouth shut. Taylor couldn't even admit to me that she'd asked him instead of the other way around. I started wondering if Taylor's obsession with dating Clive had more to do with winning than actually dating. The less he wanted her, the more she had to have him. What Clive said about a woman scorned was making sense to me.

"That's great," I lied. "I hear the food is good."

"Who cares? I'm not eating it. Seafood's totally fattening. And I don't want to have a full stomach if we finally get together. I want to look good naked."

"Lie on your stomach," Nikki suggested. "That way they only look at your ass." She got up and stretched, then slouched towards the door. "Later," she said, walking out.

I was so distracted thinking about how the hell I was going to explain crashing Taylor and Clive's date that I didn't even notice that the conversation had sputtered and died. It was so weird. I'd always felt like Taylor and I could talk about anything, but now it felt like there was nothing to say. Nikki's presence hadn't helped, but it wasn't the problem. Things were just different between us.

Taylor's cell phone rang, and she picked it up. I waited for a minute, but it was clear she was going to have this conversation whether or not I was there. I waved as I walked out the door, but Taylor didn't even notice.

———

As Clive and I walked into Crustacean, I was feeling so nervous, I swear, I could feel the sweat trickling down the back of my neck. I could already predict what was going to happen. Icy cold stares from Taylor, awkward conversation, and after it was all over I was going to be in the doghouse just for having shown up. Good times.

"Cool place," I said to Clive, trying to take my mind off what was to come. And it really was cool. Crustacean is this expensive Vietnamese restaurant in Beverly Hills that has a little stream buried under the floor so you can see koi fish swimming beneath your feet.

"Order lobster, order anything on the menu," Clive whispered. "I so owe you one for this."

When we got to the maître d' station, Taylor was already standing there. She was dressed in a gorgeous pale green cocktail dress, and I was sure she'd hired someone to do her makeup and hair. You'd think she was going to an awards show, not out on a date. "Hey, girl," Clive said in his friendliest voice.

Taylor turned around and hugged him, just as she spotted me over his shoulder. I seriously thought her eyes might pop out of her skull. "What are you doing here?" she asked in a voice that was barely civil.

"I forced her to come with me," Clive said, putting an arm around my shoulder. "I thought it would be good fun, the three of us hanging out together."

"Oh," Taylor said, still glaring at me.

The poor maître d' just stood there watching us for a minute. "Three for dinner, then?"

"Yes, three," Taylor muttered through clenched teeth.

We followed the maître d' to a table in the middle of the restaurant. "Taylor, your stock must be pretty high now," Clive said, looking around. "This is the A table." In Hollywood, where you sit in a restaurant is almost as important as getting in. You want to see and be seen. And here, right in the middle of the action, was the best spot.

"Well, it doesn't hurt that I'm with my big brother," Taylor said. She was trying to joke around, but it just came out bitter and angry.

Once we sat down, I opened my menu and started reading like I'd just gotten the latest issue of *Teen People*. If I could just keep reading through the whole dinner, I might avoid melting under Taylor's death-ray glare.

"I need to go to the restroom," Taylor announced. "Come with me, Erin."

"I don't need to go." No way was I getting in a confined space with this girl.

"I like the company," she said, digging her nails into the fleshy part of my upper arm.

"Okay, okay," I said, reluctantly grabbing my purse.

Once inside the bathroom, we waited for everyone else to clear out. When one woman walked out of her stall, I tried to grab it, hoping to barricade the door against Taylor. But Taylor nailed my sandal to the floor with one pointy stiletto heel.

"I have to pee," I whined.

"Hold it," Taylor hissed.

After a while, it was just the two of us. I've never wished so badly to be interrupted in my whole life.

"Why are you here?" Taylor hissed. "You're ruining my date!"

"Clive insisted I come. I don't want to be here, trust me."

"Then go home. I'll call you a cab. Say you're sick." Taylor reached into her purse for her phone.

"I can't—I promised."

"Why did he make you promise? Are you dating him?" Taylor looked like she might actually haul off and hit me; she was so mad.

"God, no. He just said he thought it would be more fun for the three of us to hang out."

Taylor sighed and put her phone back in her purse. "He has to get over this age thing. I mean, it's not like I'd turn him in."

This is the time, I thought to myself. I'm going to tell her the truth. It's not that big of a deal, really. I'll just say Clive's gay, and she has to keep her mouth shut. Simple. We're best friends. She can keep a secret, right?

But Taylor opened the bathroom door, ready to go. "If this is the way he wants it, fine," she said. "But he should know he can't put me off forever."

I should have pulled her back into the bathroom and spit it out. I should have, but I didn't.

Back at the table, I stuck my nose in the menu and let Clive and Taylor chatter on about work and which director was more incompetent and the worst thing they'd read about themselves in the tabloids.

I had memorized the description of what I planned to order (whole Maine lobster, angel-hair pasta with tamarind, basil, and Roma tomato sauce, $37.95) when I sensed someone staring at me. It wasn't Taylor's acid glare, or Clive silently pleading with his eyes for me to save him from Taylor's flirting (I'd been ignoring that for a full fifteen minutes). I looked around.

There, at the bar, was Dax. He was as handsome as ever, wearing a relaxed brown blazer over yet another of his rock T-shirts that probably cost him a couple hundred dollars. And he was coming over, a drink sloshing in his hand, his eyes dark. Unreadable.

I kicked Taylor under the table. "OW!" she squealed.

I nodded in Dax's direction. Taylor looked over her shoulder, then sighed with exasperation. Clive was the last to spot Dax, and I saw the muscles of his jaw tighten. Glad I wasn't the only one feeling uneasy.

"Hello, ladies," Dax purred, moving behind me and lightly putting his free hand on the back of my neck. "Fancy seeing you here."

"Hi, Dax," Taylor said flatly, giving him a bored look. "What's up?"

"Nothing at all, nothing at all. Mind if I join you?" He didn't wait for an answer, instead grabbing an empty chair from a nearby table and squeezing himself in between Taylor and me.

"I don't think there's enough room," Clive said, giving me an "Are you okay?" look.

"Really, Dax, maybe some other time," I said.

"No time like the present. I'm starved," Dax said, putting his hand back on my neck, harder this time. He was grinning, but in a way that seemed forced, his lips pulled back tightly over his teeth. "So, what do you recommend, my little China girl?" Dax asked me.

"I don't know. I've never eaten here before," I said, totally confused.

But Taylor got it. "She's Korean, Dax," she said in an icy voice. "Just because she's Asian she's supposed to know about Vietnamese food, is that it?"

"My bad," Dax said, closing the menu. "They all taste alike, you know? The cuisines, I mean."

I think all of us were so appalled by that, no one knew what to say. I shook my head, forcing Dax's hand off my neck. Dax looked at me with a pouty expression on his face. "You know, you're very, very bad at returning phone calls, Erin."

All of a sudden, the mood at the table spiraled from tense to downright hostile. "Do you have to do this here?" Taylor hissed. "She'll call you later."

"No, I won't," I shot back. "We broke up, Dax."

"Silly girl," Dax said, still smiling. He picked up a menu and leafed through it. "You got your feelings hurt, and you're punishing me. I understand."

"Take a goddamn hint, Dax," Clive said, leaning across the table, his hands gripping the edge tightly. "Drive home while you're still sober enough."

"Oh, aren't we butch tonight!" Dax tossed back his head and laughed loudly. People at nearby tables swiveled around and stared at us. "Funny to see you here, Clive. Didn't think you liked . . . fish."

Clive didn't say anything. The two men just glared at each other, silently daring the other to make his move. "You want to take this outside?" Clive said finally.

"What is going on?" Taylor asked, waving away the waiter who was walking towards our table.

Dax looked at Taylor. "So, Taylor, what do you and Clive like to do together, now that you're such good buddies? A little shopping? Get your nails painted? What?"

"That's it," Clive said, and just like that, he reached across the table, grabbed Dax by the shirt, and punched him in the jaw. I saw people at other tables turning around, and at least one camera phone flashed.

Dax sat back in his seat and wiped the thin trickle of blood coming out of his mouth. "Now, now, Clive," he said. "You really think no one knows about your little dalliances in Boystown? Get real."

Taylor looked like she was the one who'd been hit. "You're gay?" she whispered. Behind her, I could see the maître d' and all the waiters in the restaurant descending on our table. Great.

"How did you know?" I asked Dax, who only shrugged.

The maître d' hovered over Clive's shoulder. "I'm afraid we can't allow fighting in the restaurant," he said, wringing his hands.

Clive grabbed Taylor and me by the hand. "That's fine. We're getting out of here," he replied.

Dax grabbed my other hand so hard I almost screamed. "She's not going anywhere. We need to talk."

"NO!" I yelled, pulling myself away. *"Leave me alone!"*

Well, if everyone in the place hadn't been staring at us already, they were now. Dax just held his hands up in the air, shaking his head. Like I was the crazy person, and he hadn't done a thing. The bastard.

Standing out on the sidewalk waiting for the valet to bring Clive's Prius around, the three of us huddled together, trying not to attract the attention of the paparazzi clustered outside the restaurant.

"Are you gay?" Taylor whispered.

"Not the time," I whispered back as Clive fished around in his wallet for a tip.

None of us saw Dax coming towards us until it was too late.

Dax pushed Clive so hard he almost flew through the air, slamming him up against the side of the building near the valet table. Then Dax was on him, showering Clive with punches as the paparazzi gleefully snapped away.

Taylor stood up and started screaming, *"Get off of him!"* I tried to pull Dax back, but I wasn't strong enough. Finally a few valets ganged up on Dax and dragged him off Clive, who didn't look so good. He had a black eye and a bloody lip. "If you broke my ribs, I'm suing you, you asshole," he wheezed, clutching his chest.

But Dax was looking at me. "Erin, let's talk. You know we need to talk. Five minutes, that's it."

Clive was on his feet, and the Prius was at the curb, waiting. Taylor took me by the arm. "We're leaving, Dax," she shouted. "Just go home."

Dax grabbed me around the waist and pulled me away from Taylor. "I love you, Erin. You know I do," he said. It wasn't the seductive growl I was used to, but a desperate plea.

It was so hard to look into those beautiful blue eyes and think that Dax was a violent creep. But he was. There was no denying it, not anymore.

I saw Clive opening the passenger door of the Prius and wave to me to hurry up. I ran toward the car.

Then I heard Dax yell, "You *bitch! You stupid little bitch!*"

I didn't look back until I was inside with the door locked. I know it sounds crazy, but even as we pulled away, some part of me wanted to get out and run into his arms. I wanted Dax to wipe away the tears that were streaming down my face. And more than anything, I wanted to pretend this night had never happened.

Chapter Nine

When you're famous, everyone wants a piece of you. So you tend to shut people out. No one thinks you could ever be lonely, but you can be lonely in a room full of people. You can be lonely surrounded by people who claim to be your friends, who claim to love you. People talk about the price of fame, but no one ever mentions the isolation.

—TAYLOR CHRISTENSEN in _Elle_ magazine

"So you knew," Taylor said to me, slowly smoking a cigarette as she sat at Nikki's dining room table. Clive, Taylor, and I had come back to Nikki's place to talk things over. And yes, Clive had come clean about being gay. He didn't say a word about our conversation, not even a hint, but thanks to my little outburst at the table, Taylor knew I'd been keeping his secret. But I don't think it would have mattered what I'd said, because Taylor knew how to read my face just as well as I knew how to read hers.

"Yes, I did," I said, watching as Taylor's eyes became red and angry.

"I made her swear to secrecy, Taylor," Clive said. "You can't blame her. This is my fault. Entirely my fault."

Taylor spun around, jabbing her cigarette in Clive's direction.

"What the hell were you thinking? You must have known I liked you. Did you think I'd just figure it out?"

Clive sighed. "It's not like that."

"Okay, then, what is it like?" Taylor snapped.

"Seriously? For a little while I thought I could make it work with you. And by the time I knew I couldn't, it had gone on too long."

Taylor dropped her head onto the table, as if what Clive had said was simply too much for her to bear. "What, you felt that sorry for me?"

"No, I liked you that much. I really thought maybe I could do this. For the longest time I've been trying to convince myself I'm bisexual, you know? Obviously I've had girlfriends before."

"Great," Taylor said to the table.

Clive leaned over, trying to catch her eye. "I couldn't fake it with you, Taylor. You're kick-ass. You're, like, one of my best friends now. If you were just some girl, it would have been different. But I knew you deserved better. I just didn't know how to tell you."

Taylor looked up at me. "You told Erin."

No one said anything, and Taylor kept looking at me. "You're my best friend, Erin. That should have trumped any promise you made to Clive."

"I'm really, really sorry," I said. There was nothing else I could say.

"This whole disastrous evening is going to be in the tabloids now. God knows what story they'll come up with. We'll be lucky if we don't all get fired by Dax's dad."

Taylor found a pack of cigarettes on the kitchen counter and lit another one. "You don't know what it's like for me at all, do you? You have no clue what it feels like to have everyone watching everything you do, just waiting for you to screw up. And I have all these people being nice to me, people working for me, but I can't even trust my own mother not to rob me blind."

Taylor took a long drag on her cigarette. I could tell she was trying not to cry. "Still, I figure it's okay, because my friends care about me. I can count on them. But that's bullshit. I can't even trust my best friend. I'm all alone. You know that? I don't have family, I don't have friends. I'm just alone."

Clive put a hand on Taylor's shoulder. "You do have friends. You do. Come on. We love you, Taylor. Please, let's just move on, okay?"

No one answered, because at just that totally awkward moment Nikki blew through the door. She was dressed in a spangly minidress and heels so high, I was surprised she could walk in them. "Hey, what's up?" she asked as she galloped past us. "Where's my wrap? Oh, here it is," she said, snatching a black pile of fluff from the sofa and heading back for the door. "Anyone want to go to Privilege? Taxi's waiting outside."

Taylor stubbed out her cigarette in a dirty coffee mug and slowly got up from the table. "I'll go," she said, grabbing her purse and following Nikki. "Lock up when you leave." She didn't look at us, just grimly followed Nikki out the door.

Just like that, they were gone. Clive looked at me. "Think she'll ever forgive us?"

"I have no idea," I said. Hell, I wasn't even sure if I would be able to forgive myself.

Taylor did forgive me, kind of. She didn't have me fired, or ban me from the Trayler or anything. We even laughed a little when the tabloids reported on our "bizarre love triangle" with a picture of Clive smashing Dax in the face and a story about how both of them were trying to win Taylor's love. But things were different between us.

It was mostly little things. Sometimes I'd knock on the Trayler door (which was always locked now) and she wouldn't respond, even though I knew she was inside. Lila started answering Taylor's cell phone to tell me why she was too busy to talk. And then I would see Taylor and Nikki talking together on the set and ask them what was up. "Nothing," Taylor would say, either nattering on about dumb stuff like the weather or falling silent. But the minute I left, I could hear them whispering behind me.

I kept thinking things would get better with time. Weeks passed. They didn't.

One time I waited until I knew Nikki was busy on the set; then I knocked on the Trayler door and waited. I wanted to talk to Taylor alone, see if there was any chance we could patch things up. It was a long time before Taylor answered the door. Her skin looked gray, and her eyes were puffy, as if she'd been sleeping.

She didn't say anything, but just walked away, leaving the door open for me to come in.

I watched as she walked over to the sofa and flung herself onto it as if it had taken the last drop of her energy just to get up.

"Are you okay?" I asked. "You look awful."

"I don't feel so great," Taylor said, closing her eyes. "Probably the flu."

"Let me call you a doctor. Or I can go to the drugstore, get you some DayQuil."

Taylor waved a hand in the air, as if pushing the idea away.

"Stop being a pain in the ass, Erin," Taylor muttered. She looked at me. "Hey, guess who I slept with."

"Slept with?" As far as I'd known, Taylor was a virgin, but the way she said it, so casually, it was like she'd already scored with the entire sound department.

Taylor told me the name. It was a big star, a name I can't ever repeat. But I'll tell you right now, I'll never see one of his movies again, not even the big summer action flicks.

"We were hanging out at Dolce, just talking, and he offered to give me a ride home, because I went with Nikki," Taylor explained. In the same tired voice she told me how he opened up bottle after bottle of champagne, and it seemed like they were driving around for hours. She was feeling pretty drunk when he started kissing her.

"I didn't really want to, but then I started imagining he was Clive, and it was okay," Taylor said. Then she described how he pulled off her panties and held her down by her wrists. She was pretty drunk by then, she said. Maybe she blacked out for a second, she wasn't sure. But before she knew it, it was too late to say no.

"Then he just dropped me off at Nikki's," Taylor said with a shrug. "So, now I can say I slept with a guy who makes fifteen million dollars per movie."

"Was that . . . did you lose your virginity?"

"Sure," Taylor said. "I had wanted to save it for Clive, but that didn't work out. So this is fine."

This was awful. But looking at Taylor, I didn't know what to say. She was so blasé about it, like it was no big deal. I looked at Taylor's hands, so bony and old-looking sticking out of her sweater. "I'm worried about you, Taylor."

"Then you should have cared enough to tell me about Clive. Or have you conveniently forgotten about that? Whatever. Just leave, will you?"

"Taylor—"

"GO!" Taylor screamed. She lunged off the sofa and pushed the door open. *"Get out!"*

I left, hearing the door slam behind me, the lock clicking into place.

After that, I mostly kept up with Taylor by reading the tabloids. It's weird checking up on a friend by reading about her, but I felt like I knew a little more about what was going on that way, even if most of the stories were total nonsense. I saw pictures of her sitting next to Snoop Dogg and Gwen Stefani at one party, and even dancing with Wilmer Valderrama in another. No more of Nikki's craptastic parties.

At first I thought the nonstop partying was just about Taylor being mad and trying to prove she didn't have to hang out with Clive or me anymore. But then I'd read the stories that went along with the pictures. They said Taylor was drinking, and they said she was much too thin (duh). They linked her to every single guy she was in a photo with, but I guessed those stories were probably pure fiction. Still, even from a distance I could tell she was partying too hard, and I'd known for a long time she was scary skinny.

Looking back, I know I should have been more worried.

I shouldn't have cared so much about being a pain in Taylor's butt, or having her hate me more. The truth was, I was too busy moping over my breakup with Dax to really think about anyone other than myself. I heard that Taylor had had him banned from the set, but I never found out if that was true. But if it was, I'm grateful.

It wasn't until Clive pulled me aside one day that I really got it that something was wrong with Taylor. "Have you talked to her lately?" he asked after we'd stepped inside his trailer and shut the door.

"Not much," I admitted. "She's usually hanging out with Nikki, and you know how much I love her."

"Things are not good with her, Erin," he said, shaking his head. "We need to do something."

Then Clive told me that Taylor had been showing up late and blowing her lines. The producers had been dumping a lot of her dialogue on Clive and Peter, the guy who played her dad, because Nikki wasn't doing so well, either. And the wardrobe people were going crazy trying to hide how much weight she'd lost, putting her in long-sleeved dresses and billowy circle skirts.

"She keeps telling me she's just stressed-out, but we're all stressed-out. This isn't stress," said Clive. "She won't talk to me, but maybe she'll talk to you."

"I wouldn't bet on it." I hated the idea of having to confront Taylor. Next she'd be telling me I was doing the producer's dirty work or I was just jealous of how thin she was. As crazy as it sounded, I still wanted to be a good friend. I wanted to make it up to her for keeping Clive's secret.

"We've got to talk to her, Erin," Clive said, serious as a heart attack. "Because whatever is wrong with her, from the looks of it, it's killing her."

I'll say it right up front. Clive and I came up with a lousy plan for our little intervention. But hey, hindsight is always twenty-twenty, right?

"Why do we have to go to this club?" I whined as Clive drove us into Hollywood.

"There's no bigger buzz kill than getting caught in the act," he said. Clive had a point, but I didn't see how it would help. Taylor would just look at us, shrug, and keep doing whatever she wanted to do. Having us look down our noses disapprovingly at her wasn't going to change anything. She was just living the life every other Hollywood starlet already lived. Or wanted to live.

The club wasn't one of the swank buildings in Beverly Hills or Santa Monica where the networks had parties. This place was an old office building in a funky part of town. A Mexican market was in the minimall across the street, as well as a paycheck-advance place. I bet the people inside had no idea that celebrities were partying just a few feet away, close enough to touch.

There was a long line snaking around the building, but Clive just waved at the bouncer, who lifted the velvet rope and ushered us in. "Have you been here before?" I asked, impressed.

"Once. Gave the guy an autograph. He's writing a screenplay. Yada yada yada."

It was dark inside the club, and it took me a moment to get my bearings. The place was packed, and the music, all thumping bass and drums, was pounding. Clive grabbed my hand and dragged me towards the back of the building.

"How are we supposed to find her in this crowd?"

"Not a problem," Clive said, pointing to where an enormous bouncer, much bigger than the one at the entrance, stood outside a closed door. The VIP section. Of course.

Clive walked up to the bouncer and whispered in his ear. I just tried to look bored. If you act like you want to get into a VIP section, bouncers are automatically suspicious of you. You might be a fan, horror of horrors. Celebrities talk all the time about how much they like meeting their admirers, but the truth is, they go to great lengths to keep away from them.

Whatever Clive said to the bouncer, it worked. The door was opened, and we slipped inside.

It was less crowded in here, and there were enormous sofas pushed up against the walls. The music wasn't quite as loud, even though a DJ was busily spinning away in the corner. A few women who looked like models were dancing together in one corner, champagne flutes in their hands. A group of men watched them, nodding to the music. I recognized one as a rapper I'd seen on MTV. The rings on his hands glittered under the room's reddish light as he reached out and stroked some girl's thigh. She smiled, and moved closer to him.

Before I could ask Clive if he remembered the rapper's name, he dragged me on to another room. More sofas, more faces I recognized. One guy looked like Ashton Kutcher, and I think I saw Paris Hilton and Tara Reid laughing in a corner, but it was hard to tell. We walked past a chaise lounge, and I saw a mirror covered with white powdery lines sitting on the coffee table. A thin girl in a tube top leaned over the mirror and snorted up a line of coke so fast I almost wondered if I had really seen it.

Clive saw them before I did. Taylor was slumped in a corner sofa next to a good-looking guy who appeared to be fast asleep and a girl with pink hair. Nikki danced on the coffee table with about five other girls. At Nikki's feet was a pile of vodka bottles, all tipped onto their sides. Empty.

Taylor barely looked up when we sat down on the sofa, and it took a little while for Nikki to notice us. "Whassup!" she slurred.

"Hey, it's Mom and Dad!" Taylor said, raising the glass in her hand. "Cheers!" The other people on the sofa stared at Clive and me as if we were curious zoo animals dropping by for a visit, but reluctantly scooted over so we could sit down next to Taylor.

Even though Taylor's glass was almost full, she tossed it back, gulping it down so fast I thought she'd choke. "Did you know a jigger of vodka is only one hundred calories? If I don't eat all day, I can drink, like, ten of these. Although that means I have to dance for two hours."

"You haven't eaten all day?" Even I knew drinking so much on an empty stomach wasn't a good thing.

Clive stroked Taylor's arm. "I bet Swingers is open. We can get you a turkey burger or something. Come on."

Taylor yanked her arm away. "Don't touch me! If you want to make yourself useful, get me another drink."

Clive looked at her the way my mom used to look at me. Disappointed, and a little sad. "I can't do that, Taylor."

"Fine." Taylor wobbled to her feet. She had only one shoe on, a red spiked stiletto. She looked around. "Where's my shoe?" she asked no one in particular before she shrugged and hobbled towards the bar.

Clive tapped Nikki on the foot. "How much has she had to drink?"

"I'll never tell," Nikki said, looking down at us with a crooked grin.

Taylor came back from the bar with a full bottle of vodka and four glasses. "Let's all have a drink," she said, falling backward onto the sofa. "I want to celebrate my so-called friends coming to babysit me." The pink-haired girl picked up the bottle of vodka and took a slug, then passed it around.

"Taylor, we're just worried about you," I said. I hated this. I felt like I was in the middle of one of those cheesy Lifetime movies about addiction. But what else are you supposed to say when your best friend is drinking herself sick? "Rock on, hope you didn't drive"?

Taylor ignored me and grabbed the bottle of vodka away from a skinny white kid with a Mohawk. "Don't drink out of the bottle, dumb-ass. That's tacky," she growled. She poured the vodka into the glasses, gesturing for Clive and me to join her drunken spiral. "Come on, where's your manners? I'm buying! I'm always buying, aren't I, Erin?" Ouch.

"Taylor, this isn't good," Clive said. "You're just hurting yourself."

Taylor stuck out her tongue, and when we didn't pick up our drinks, she shook her head and laughed at us. "Oh, so you're just going to sit there and give me dirty looks? When the drinks are on me? Very rude." Taylor picked up another glass of vodka and downed it, licking her lips.

I looked at Clive. I don't know what he was expecting, but it clearly wasn't this. So much for hoping the shame of being exposed as a drunken party animal by her friends would send her running to rehab.

Nikki nudged Taylor. "They are sooo bringing me down," she whined. "Come with me to the bathroom, okay?"

Taylor grabbed her purse and stood up. She eyeballed Clive and me like we were the lowest form of scum, worse than pedophiles or talent agents. "You prissy little bitches should stay here and make friends. Maybe you can find another soul to save. But stay the hell away from me."

Both Taylor and Nikki exploded into giggles as they wobbled out of the room, grabbing the now half-empty bottle of vodka out of the pink-haired girl's hands as they left.

"Well, that was fun," I said.

"Don't take it personally," Clive said. "She's drunk." He stood up and reached for his wallet. "Well, we're here. Let's hang out, have a drink, come up with a new plan." He went to the bar and returned with Cokes.

Instead of coming up with a new plan, we sat there in silence. I didn't know what we would do if Taylor and Nikki came back our way. But I didn't need to worry about it. Hours passed, and they never showed up.

"Let's see if they've passed out in a corner somewhere," Clive said.

We walked around the VIP section, but we couldn't find them anywhere.

"We should go," I said. "This was pointless."

Clive flopped back on a sofa, defeated. "They're here somewhere. And at some point she's going to be puking up all that vodka that's been sitting on an empty stomach, and she's going to have a change of heart—I know it. We just need to take advantage of it."

"It's almost three in the morning. I don't know about you, but I'm not sure I have the patience to sit around waiting for her to throw up."

Clive looked at me. "Did you see what I saw? Aren't you worried about her?"

"Of course I'm worried about her. But she can make her own choices. I'm not her mom, and neither are you."

"She doesn't have a mom. That's why she needs us."

"That's not true, actually. She has one, a crappy one, but that's more than what I've got and I'm not drinking myself sick." I was being a bitch on wheels, but I didn't care. I was tired, my head was starting to throb, and my feet ached. And yeah, I was pretty goddamn angry on top of it all.

"Why are you so pissed off? Taylor's drinking has nothing to do with you."

It occurred to me that that was exactly the reason why I was pissed off. Taylor's drinking didn't have anything to do with me, and lately it seemed like nothing in her life had anything to do with me. I wasn't even sure how much we really had in common anymore. And the thing was, I couldn't talk to her about my feelings, not honestly. Taylor had gotten me my job; she'd bought my car; she paid my cell phone bills. I owed her too much to be honest with her. Instead, I felt I had to be nice.

That's when it hit me. I was mad at Taylor, but I was even angrier at myself. Because I knew, deep down, I'd been a crappy friend. I had thought keeping my mouth shut and going along with whatever she said was the right way to support her. Even coming here and blathering on like some sort of sappy Hallmark card come to life about how worried I was and how much I cared about her was crap, because it didn't mean anything. We weren't really confronting her, not with the kind of wake-up call that gets results. We should have told her that she needed to stop or we wouldn't be friends with her. I should have told her I was giving back my car and my phone. Clive and I hadn't even discussed what to do if Taylor actually admitted she had a problem. Our goal had really been to act concerned, but not so concerned that she got pissed at us.

It's easy to think that being a good friend means sucking it up and going with the flow. No one likes to fight, except Sheila. But sometimes you need to tell the hard truths, because if you don't, it's the same as lying. Lying to your friend, and to yourself. For a long time I'd blamed the distance between Taylor and me on Sheila, then Nikki, even the TV show. But now I saw a lot of it was me. I'd stopped being real. I'd stopped being myself.

"Tell me something, Clive. Are you here because you feel guilty about what happened with Taylor?"

"I'm here for Taylor, period," he said, his voice tight. "What's past is past."

"I think that's crap, Clive, I really do." I got up from the sofa. "I'm going to find them."

"Erin," Clive said. Even over the thudding disco, I could hear his exasperation. He didn't get up to follow me as I walked away. Which was probably for the best. No one would have wanted to see what I saw in that club bathroom, at least not without some warning.

At the bathroom, there were two other girls waiting in line, their arms folded across their chests. "Don't bother," one of them said. "We've been standing here for almost twenty minutes. Hope you don't have to pee or anything."

"It's so insanely rude. Like, it doesn't take that long to do blow off a toilet seat," said the other, who reached over to the door and banged her fist on it. *"Get out of there!"* she screamed, though she didn't seem that loud because of the music.

"Maybe I can solve this," I said. I banged on the door, too. *"It's me, Erin! Let me in!"*

Just like magic, the door popped open and Nikki's skinny arm grabbed my hand, pulling me in.

The first thing I saw was Taylor, crying and curled up in a ball next to the toilet in the middle of the bathroom. Her dress was soaked with sweat, and the air reeked of vomit and God knows what else. I think there were even chunks of puke in her hair, but I wasn't about to get close enough to check. "I think I'm having a heart attack," she said, wiping the snot running from her nose with the back of her hand.

"I'm outta here," said Nikki. I hadn't even noticed her standing next to me. "This is way too much."

"Nikki!" I grabbed her skinny little arm, but she fiercely yanked it away.

"You get cops in here, and I'm so busted. I didn't give her anything, hear me?" she hissed before flying out the door.

I looked at Taylor. "Don't move, okay?" Like that was going to be a problem, but still, I had to say it.

I popped my head out the door and looked at the two girls waiting for the bathroom. "I'm really, really sorry, but someone's had the stomach flu in here, and it's severely gross."

"Eww," the girls said, walking away.

I shut the door and turned back to Taylor, who was still crying. "Are you sure it's a heart attack? Not anxiety or something?"

"My heart is beating out of my chest, Erin," Taylor sobbed.

"We have to call an ambulance," I said, reaching for my cell phone.

"I'll be fired!" Taylor moaned. "It'll be all over the tabloids. Everyone will think I overdosed."

"Did you?"

"No. Nikki does drugs, but I don't."

"Seriously?" I hated to say it, but a drug overdose made a lot of sense looking at the shape Taylor was in.

Taylor looked me dead in the eye. "I swear to God, Erin. I'm not saying I've never used, but I didn't today. That's why I'm scared. If it was drugs, at least I'd know why I feel like this."

The truth was, I was scared, too. "Forget about your stupid job. Let me call the ambulance."

Taylor winced in pain. "If the producers freaked when I wore a stupid see-through dress, what are they going to do about this?"

"You'd rather die than lose your job?"

Taylor looked at me. The answer was clearly "yes."

I hesitated. As sick as Taylor looked, she was still breathing and conscious. She said she hadn't done drugs, and I believed her. And even I had to admit she was right about her career being ruined if an ambulance pulled up out front and some ass with a camera phone snapped pictures of her being loaded into it.

I hoped Clive drove fast.

"Stay right here. We'll figure something out."

Taylor nodded weakly, and I ran out of the bathroom. There

were already two more girls waiting for it. "Someone's in there throwing up," I said as I flew past them. "Try the men's room!"

It was hard to find Clive in the near darkness, but I did. When I told him what had happened, he snapped into action. I couldn't believe I ever thought he was a man without a plan. "Get her ready to go. I'll get the front-door bouncer to help you get her to a back entrance, and I'll pull the car around to the alley. Have you got any money?"

"Yeah, why?" I handed him what I had, about eighty bucks. Clive fished out his own roll of bills and combined them.

"We'll need it to keep the bouncer quiet until a publicist can deal with him. Just go to the bathroom and wait for him. But if at any time she stops breathing, you call 911. Nothing's worth dying over."

I went back to the bathroom, hoping to hell Taylor was okay. When I walked in, she was kneeling in front of the sink.

"I want to get cleaned up," she whispered. "Don't make me go out like this."

I picked her up off the floor and propped her against the bathroom counter. She was so light it wasn't hard for me to do. Then I wet a paper towel and began wiping her face. No makeup was better than smeared makeup, I figured.

"I thought my life was supposed to be good now," Taylor said, starting to cry again. "I thought I was supposed to be happy."

"Shhhh," I said. "Just calm down." I found a comb in my purse and ran it through her hair, trying to ignore the stuff that got caught in the teeth. Using an elastic I had on me, I tied her hair back in a ponytail. I looked at Taylor's reflection in the mirror. Her face was gaunt, and the circles under her eyes were darker than ever. She looked so frail and sick it made me want to cry.

"You know you have a problem, don't you?" I asked.

There was a long pause. Taylor was looking at her reflection, too. "I know," Taylor said, finally.

Just then there was a pounding at the door. "It's Benny! Open up!" a booming voice yelled.

I opened the door, and the bouncer slipped in, walking right over to Taylor. "This is the way it's going to go. I'm going to pick you up, and you're going to wrap your arms around my neck, and we're gonna smile and laugh and act like we're having a party, okay? Can you do that?"

Taylor nodded. She was an actress, after all.

"You get her stuff," he said to me. "Let's go."

Benny lifted her up, and kicked open the door. Once we were in the main room, he let out a big laugh, as if Taylor had said something funny. Taylor giggled back. I didn't even mean to laugh, but I started in right along with them. You know how when you're nervous sometimes you can't help giggling, like at a funeral or in church? I think I was laughing so I wouldn't have a complete mental breakdown.

In a minute we had breezed out a back door I hadn't seen before, and there was Clive, waiting in the Prius. Benny put Taylor in the backseat like she was a priceless doll, and Clive discreetly slipped him the wad of bills. "You be okay, you hear?" Benny said to us. And then he pointed at Clive. "I'll send you my action script next week."

"Can't wait!" Clive yelled as I climbed in and we drove off, wheels squealing against the pavement. I had to hand it to Benny. At least someone was making the best of a bad situation.

At the hospital, Clive pulled up to the entrance to the emergency room. "Help her in. I'll go park."

Taylor and I got as far as the automatic doors before she collapsed.

Her eyes rolled back, those famously blue irises disappearing so that all I could see was spooky red-rimmed white. Her knees buckled beneath her and her entire body went limp. I will never forget that rag-doll body, those dead eyes, the grayish tint to her skin. The pallor of death. I tried to catch her, to hold her up, but I couldn't. Lifeless, she became surprisingly heavy—at least, too heavy for me to carry on my own. I screamed for help, but I didn't really have to, because about four nurses rushed over. They scooped Taylor onto a gurney and wheeled her away, yelling medical terms I didn't understand at one another.

One woman stayed behind and asked me a lot of questions that freaked me out. No, she wasn't on drugs. No, she hadn't attempted suicide. Yes, she'd been drinking. No, I didn't know how much, but it was a lot. No, she hadn't thrown up blood, or at least I hadn't seen it.

"Does your friend have an eating disorder?"

The question hit my like a fist. Hearing the words somehow made it real, this hulking elephant in the room that I'd been trying so hard to ignore.

"Yes, she does," I said.

Then there were more questions from the receptionist. I didn't know the name of her insurance carrier. I didn't know Nikki's address. The only thing I thought to do was give them her name, her real name. Maryanne Fedderbit. At least that would make it a little less likely some nosy hospital employee would leak Taylor's whereabouts to the press. But I don't think anyone would have mistaken her for a celebrity, what with her blond hair matted to her head and her skin so pale it seemed blue.

Clive finally came in and sat down next to me in the waiting room.

"How is she?" he asked.

"I have no idea."

Clive asked the receptionist if Taylor was okay, but she wouldn't say anything. Since I wasn't a relative, they couldn't release any information to me, even though I was the one who brought her in. I almost thought about calling Sheila or a producer from the show, but I got over that idea pretty quick. Taylor really was alone. Except for us.

After we'd been sitting there for about an hour, Clive leaned over and whispered in my ear. "Don't look, but is that girl over there staring at me?"

I darted a glance to my left. A morbidly obese teenage girl was sitting with her equally overweight mother, and they were both looking at Clive and whispering to each other.

"You've got to get out of here," I said. "If people realize you're in the waiting room, it's only a matter of time before Taylor's cover gets blown."

Clive got up. "Want me to take you home?" he asked.

"No. I'll get a ride."

Clive kissed me on the cheek. "Hang in there."

"You, too," I said. I felt bad for thinking Clive had just wanted to help Taylor to feel less guilty about hurting her. He was a really decent guy. No wonder Taylor was so heartbroken to find out he was gay.

By six o'clock, I'd almost drained the vending machine of Cokes using the change in my pocket and it was pretty clear to me I wasn't getting home anytime soon. I hated to do it, but I called my dad. I didn't want him to panic if he got up for work and realized I wasn't in my bed.

"Hello?" he said, already sounding worried.

"Everything's okay," I said quickly. "But Taylor's really sick. I had to take her to the hospital."

"Which hospital?"

"Cedars, but Dad—"

The line went dead. Great.

Either my dad was coming to yell at me in person, or he was just going to save his rage until I got home. I guessed I should have told him about Clive's intervention plan, but parents tend to freak out when you talk about interventions. Like if your friends have problems, you must, too.

I was still trying to think of good excuses when I felt someone sit down in the chair next to me. "Are you okay?" my dad said in a soft voice.

I jumped. I'd expected screaming or crying, but that didn't mean he wasn't mad. "I'm really sorry—"

Dad put a finger to his mouth, shushing me. "What happened?"

"I don't know. She said she was having a heart attack. The nurse wanted to know if she had an eating disorder. . . ."

I don't know why I started crying. I think I was just so tired. I'd been running on adrenaline all night, and I was shaky from all the sugar and caffeine I'd been sucking down. And sure, I was worried.

I'd like to say I thought Taylor was going to be fine, but honestly, I really thought she might die. When she collapsed at the hospital doors, her eyes rolling to the back of her head and her body limp, it was the scariest thing I'd ever seen. I couldn't imagine dying at sixteen, but I couldn't imagine my mom dying, either. Until it happened.

Through my tears, I tried to tell Dad about the club, about Benny and Clive and everything else (all right, I left out the stuff about Nikki being loaded—sue me), but he cut me off.

"It be okay," Dad said. "Taylor a strong girl. Have faith."

I nodded. I hadn't had much faith in Taylor lately. But then, I don't think Taylor had had much faith in herself.

I looked at my dad. "I'm really glad you came," I said. "I'm surprised you're not mad at me."

He put his arm around me. "I know you do the right thing, Erin," he said. "You very responsible girl. That why Taylor ask you for help."

I started getting all blubbery again. "*Ah ppa, sa rang hae*," I muttered into the shoulder of his jacket. Telling Dad I loved him, even in this awful setting, was something I had to do. Maybe I hadn't said it to my mom in time, but at least I could say it to him. And maybe I needed to say it a lot more.

"*Sa rang hae*," he whispered back.

We didn't say anything for a long while. That wasn't unusual for us, God knows. But this time, it wasn't awkward or weird. This time, there wasn't anything either of us needed to say. And that was just fine.

The receptionist called my name, and my dad and I walked up to the front desk. "She's resting now, but she asked to see you," she said, gesturing for another nurse to lead us to Taylor.

Walking down the corridor, I realized why I hate hospitals. Even when you're not the one who's sick, just being inside one of those places makes you feel unwell, from the flickering fluorescent lights to the drab beige walls to the smell of disinfectant mixed with other things you don't want to think about. I always feel a little afraid at a hospital. I wondered if Taylor felt afraid, too.

Taylor didn't have a private room, probably because I'd registered her as Maryanne. A thin curtain hung between her and someone who kept making these wheezing noises. It was like having Darth Vader for a roommate.

Taylor had an IV in her arm and she was hooked up to some machine that took her vital signs. Even with all the electronic upgrades and an awful baby blue hospital gown, she still looked better than she had at the nightclub.

"Hey, girl," I said, squeezing her fingers, careful not to touch the big needle in her hand.

"Hi, Mr. Kim," Taylor said, smiling at us. "I'm really sorry to drag you guys down here."

The nurse who'd come in to check Taylor's IV drip raised an eyebrow. "Don't be sorry. They did you a big favor, sweetie."

"What happened? Was it a heart attack?"

Taylor shook her head. "I was having a heart arrhythmia. My heart was beating too fast. That's why I passed out when we got here."

My dad frowned. "That doesn't sound good."

Taylor squirmed a little in her hospital bed. "The doctor said it was a couple of things," she said, looking at her IV bag drip, drip, dripping into her vein. "Dehydration, stress, you know."

Considering the girl was more Diet Coke than blood, I wasn't buying it. "Dehydration and exhaustion are lies celebrities tell the press," I said.

A tear trickled down the side of Taylor's face and disappeared into her pillow. "I just wanted to lose a little more weight. Nikki had been giving me these diuretics that were supposed to flush toxins out of my body, but they weren't working. And I didn't want to do drugs with her. So I'd been throwing up. And then, with the vodka making me sick—"

"Why would you take diuretics? You're already too thin," I said, feeling myself getting angry. I was going to go on, but my dad patted my shoulder and shook his head. Now was not the time.

"When can you go home?" I asked instead.

Taylor sighed. "They want to make sure my electrolytes are back to normal, and they want to make sure I'm eating. So a few days."

I'm no doctor, but I knew a few days in the hospital weren't going to cure Taylor of an eating disorder. "That's it?" I pressed.

"The doctor recommended some therapists, said I should take some time off," Taylor finally admitted. "Apparently I've gone crazy."

"You work for crazy people in a crazy industry. Go figure," I joked, and Taylor smiled. "But you're not crazy. You're just out of control." Maybe this wasn't the right time to tell Taylor what I really thought. But maybe there was never going to be a right time. "Look, I've been keeping my mouth shut way too long," I said, trying to remember the interventions I'd seen on cable TV.

Taylor looked a little afraid, but I kept going. "I can't be your friend if you do these self-destructive things, Taylor. The drinking, the starving yourself. I can't make you do anything you don't want to do. But I need you to know I care about you, and I can't stand by and watch you ruin your life. I'll give back the car, the phone, anything you've ever given me. They're not worth having to watch you commit this slow suicide. You really are killing yourself."

"I know," Taylor said quietly.

"You have to get into therapy. You have to lay off the alcohol. And I swear I will help you with that any way I can."

"Okay," Taylor said. "I can do that. I *want* to."

"But after tonight, I think you have a pretty solid reason to stop living with Nikki."

"*Not* a problem," Taylor said, an edge to her voice. "We're strictly coworkers now. Not friends, not roommates." Taylor shrugged. "So, I guess now I'm crazy and homeless."

My dad smiled at Taylor. "That's okay. You stay with us. We make sure you take care of yourself. Then you just be crazy, not homeless." Had to hand it to the old man for breaking out the gallows humor when we didn't even know we needed it.

I looked at Taylor, waiting for a reaction. I was sure she would beg off. Here she was, rich, successful, and totally independent. Why would she want to live with me and my dad, surrounded by IKEA furniture and sad memories?

But Taylor, well, she never failed to surprise me. "That sounds really good, Mr. Kim," she said. "I'd like that. I'd like that a lot."

"But we have rules in our house," my dad said. "Curfews. Chores. Just because you're a big TV star doesn't mean you're off the hook."

Taylor reached out to take my dad's hand, and then she took mine. And then she started crying.

"I'll wash every dish you've got," she said, wiping her tears on the back of her hand that didn't have a needle in it. "I'm so sorry I got mad at you, Erin."

"It doesn't matter now," I said.

"But you're my best friend. You're my family. Even when I had buckteeth and braces, you stuck up for me. I don't know how I lost sight of that. I'm so sorry."

Taylor was crying really hard now, and through the web of tubes and wires I did my best to give her a hug.

"I'm so glad you came, both of you," she sobbed. "I'm so glad."

I didn't have much of a family, God knows, but it was more than what Taylor had. And it was definitely more real than what she had with her fake mom Julia or even her real mom, Sheila. And I think Taylor knew, no matter what, we'd be there for her, whether or not she bought us stuff.

I hadn't really appreciated it, my little broken family, but to Taylor, the girl who had everything, it must have seemed like something she'd always wanted, something that had always been out of reach. Right until then.

Of course, we all know that's not the end of Taylor's story. It's really just the beginning, before the movie deals and the celebrity boyfriends, the video scandal and the shiny awards that line every inch of her mantel. But now you know what the tabloids and her fans will never know.

It's funny to me—people always talk about how they can relate to Taylor because they feel like they've grown up with her. They say they know what she's gone through from reading about her, and they envy her for all the money and fame she has. But they have no idea. Even I can't truly grasp all she's faced, what it's really like to live her life. But I know this. She is stronger than most people will ever realize, and she will survive, no matter what this city throws at her. And she's so much more interesting than anything the tabloids have ever written. Trust me.

Okay, so Taylor was really motivated to turn her life around after playing human pincushion at the hospital. The thing was, I was itching for a little transformation, too. But sometimes change comes at you in ways you don't expect. Like my chance to work for a big-time production company—and spend my afternoons with Jeremy, the smokin' hot but jerky college intern. Like Taylor's new boyfriend, Todd, a skater who made her heart beat faster—but gave her an appetite for risky business. And then there was *Family Style*, the show that had made Taylor a star—but was imploding right before our eyes. Change can be good, sure, but were we ready for so much of it?

Find out in *Pretty on the Outside*
Coming from NAL Jam in May 2007
Read on for a sneak peek

Here's the honest, embarrassing truth: I'm a sucker for happy
endings. Total, unrepentant sucker. I even watch bad movies on
basic cable late at night, the really lame ones where you know exactly how they're going to end in the first five minutes or whenever Tori Spelling walks onto the scene. Yeah, I'm that bad.

So you can forgive me if I assumed that after Taylor's ultimate slim-down plan (Food-free and all the alcohol you can puke
up—can't imagine why I haven't seen an infomercial for *that* one)
landed her in the hospital, the happy ending was just around the
corner. After all, she'd sworn she was ditching the self-destruct
mode, and to make sure she didn't backslide, she was moving in
with my dad and me. No partying or table-dancing at our house,
that was for sure. There are monasteries that were more fun than
the Kim residence. Anyway, things couldn't get any worse, so they
had to get better, right? I know, I know, life is never that simple.
But I'm a sucker, remember?

The thing is, I think Taylor was really hoping for that

cheeseball happy ending, too. Things had been rough for her. Sure, she was the star of her own television series, she had money and fame, and she wasn't even old enough to vote. But all that good stuff doesn't protect you from heartbreak and pain. In fact, I think it actually causes a lot of it. I mean, I'm positive Taylor never, ever would have developed an eating disorder if she hadn't become an actress.

So, sure, both of us had our fingers crossed. We were ready for the good times, some smooth sailing. Of course, it was a little more complicated than that. But let's face it, nothing is ever as happy and sugarcoated as it is in the movies. I mean, even if you live the whole happily-ever-after, you still have to die at the end, right?

Okay, fine, so I'm a little dark. Sue me.

When Taylor finally got out of the hospital, she and I sat in the backseat of my dad's crappy old Kia, watching the moon rise above the 10 freeway, holding hands as he drove us home. Holding hands was something we hadn't done since we were terrified middle school geeks, but I didn't care. I felt like I'd almost lost Taylor, really lost her, as in dead and gone, and I wasn't about to let go now. I was just so damn grateful she was here and okay (mostly) and that everything was finally, finally going to be alright.

Taylor's hand in mine was bony and birdlike, but she was still strong enough to squeeze my fingers so hard that she cut off my circulation. She didn't have to say it, but I knew she was thinking, too, about how close she'd gotten to being lost.

My dad looked at us in the rearview mirror and nodded. It's a Korean thing for everybody to sit in the backseat and let the driver chauffeur; don't ask me why. "So, Taylor, you call the doctor tomorrow morning, first thing, yes?" he asked. But it wasn't really a question.

At the hospital, Taylor's doctor had given her a referral to a shrink, and he even pulled my dad and me aside to tell us how important it was that Taylor get into therapy, saying all this scary stuff about anorexia being the most lethal mental illness there is and how it's the hardest to treat. It was weird to think Taylor's dieting sort of made her crazy, but when I remembered how she complained about looking hugely fat in size 00 dresses, I got it.

My dad's a pretty low-key guy, but once he heard that Taylor's condition was serious, I knew for certain she would never miss a therapy appointment, even if he had to drag her to the shrink by her hair. After my mom died, my dad never assumed the worst couldn't happen, the way most people do. To him, the worst had already happened. And he wasn't about to add an actress starving to death in his spare bedroom to the list.

"Yes, Mr. Kim," Taylor said meekly. All the attitude she'd been throwing at me for the last couple months was gone. Honestly, I think she liked the idea of someone bossing her around. She'd made such a mess of running her own life that I wasn't surprised.

Still, it was kind of shocking when Taylor walked into our dumpy little house and started following my dad like a puppy. "Is it okay if I use the phone? I have to charge mine," she asked, obediently trailing him into the living room. She was so thin that she looked like a little kid, and now she was acting like one, too. It gave me hives.

"Yes, to call the therapist," he said, patting her on her skinny shoulder. "After that, you should rest. Nap time." My dad was enjoying the good-daughter shtick a little too much. God knows he didn't get it from me or Victoria, his real kids.

I grabbed Taylor's arm and dragged her towards my room. "Seriously, make yourself at home, because the Little Miss Suck-Up routine is creeping me out," I hissed, pulling fresh sheets out of the linen closet and shoving them into her arms. They were ugly, pink flannel with little gray and green flowers, but Taylor, the diva who ordered her assistant to buy nothing less than five-hundred-thread-count Egyptian cotton, didn't make a peep of protest. "You can sleep in Victoria's room."

"What about the inflatable mattress? That way I can sleep in your room."

I wasn't really up for a sleepover, but I could tell from the look on Taylor's face that it wasn't like she wanted to have a three a.m. pillow fight or something. She just didn't want to be alone.

That night, I must have woken up at least twenty times. I know it was partly because I wasn't really used to sharing my room, but that wasn't all of it. I kept looking over at Taylor, checking to see if she was still breathing. Crazy, I know. But some part of me was dwelling on how I'd stopped paying attention before, and she'd practically died in some stupid nightclub bathroom. This time, I was keeping my eye on her, whether she liked it or not.

Considering what a crappy night I'd had sleeping with one eye open the whole time, surprise surprise, I didn't wake up until noon. But by then, the Taylor Spin Control team was already in full effect.

When I walked into the dining room, Taylor was already sitting there, dressed in her pink Juicy tracksuit. Next to her were her agent, Caitlin, and her manager, Bradley. There was also another woman I didn't recognize, but I guessed it was probably Patty, Taylor's personal publicist, who was different from Andi, the network publicist I'd met before. (Of course, I thought Taylor didn't need a publicist at all, since she was getting too much exposure in the tabloids without even trying.)

Patty was almost as wide as she was tall, with bright red hair and tiny gray teeth. She and everyone else but Taylor and me were wearing suits, which somehow made me feel even goofier in my sushi-print flannel pajamas. (Okay, I know, it's like, hey, she's Asian and she's got sushi pajamas, ha ha, but one, I'm Korean and not Japanese, and two, no one ever sees me in them. Except right at that moment.)

Everyone looked up quickly when I walked in, as if they were worried I might be a terrorist or, worse, paparazzi; then they got right back to their conversation when they realized it was only me. They could have given half a crap about my PJs.

"As I was saying, exhaustion is so last year. Let's tell the press it was an upper respiratory infection," Caitlin said to the group, running a perfectly manicured hand through her razor-cut black hair. The woman could have been a department store mannequin. "Bradley, what do you want to tell the producers of the show?"

Bradley, a good-looking guy whose exhaustion showed in the dark shadows under his eyes, shrugged. "I think they can be trusted with an eating disorder. That kid on *The Sopranos* got a lot of great publicity after she recovered. Of course, that's a show for adults, not families."

"But there was that anorexic on *Growing Pains* a hundred years ago," Patty said, waggling a finger at Bradley. "That girl got a lot of play in *People*. Anorexia is much cooler than it used to be. It's something teen girls can relate to."

Caitlin looked at Taylor. "Taylor, after you're over this little . . . snag, Patty can go to all the major players and get you a cover story. You can talk about your battle with anorexia, maybe do a fund-raiser or two, great stuff. This may be the best thing that ever happened to you."

I'm pretty sure my jaw was scraping the carpet at that point, but no one, not even Taylor, blinked, as if it was just fine to use a hellish disease as a nifty marketing tool.

Unfazed, Caitlin kept going. "And I like Patty's idea of playing up your having a father figure in Mr. Kim. It takes the edge off of kicking Sheila to the curb."

"Page Six will eat it up with a spoon," Patty said eagerly, leaning over the table. To me, she looked like a fat little hamster hovering over its dinner.

Taylor patted the chair next to me, gesturing for me to sit down. "We're trying to figure out our game plan. How to spin the whole hospital stay, in case the media gets a hold of it."

"Which they will," Patty said sternly. "The hospital we can play down pretty easily, but we need to think about the partying. Did anyone see you carried out of the club?"

Taylor shrugged. "Everyone. But the bouncer was smart. He made it look like we were just goofing around."

Patty shrugged. "Okay, I can work with that. There are worse things than people thinking you're screwing a bouncer." She turned to Taylor. "Honey, we need to do some serious image rehab here. I don't want you walking out of this house for anything, not even a coffee run, until I give you the all-clear."

"I'm supposed to see my therapist," Taylor said, pouting a little.

"Talk to her on the phone," Bradley shot back. The sternness of his voice meant business.

"When do I go back to work?" Taylor asked.

"Just as soon as we sort out our game plan," said Patty. "Actually, working may be the best way to put the rumor mill to rest."

"She just got out of the hospital. Shouldn't you wait until her doctor says it's okay?" I said, my voice more indignant than I intended.

Everyone at the table looked at me like I was from outer space, then looked away. No one said a word. It was like I'd just done something really embarrassing, and they were all too polite to call attention to it. "Well, I think we're about done," Caitlin said, reaching for her purse.

"Wait," Taylor said. "What about Nikki?"

"What about her?" Bradley asked.

Taylor rolled her eyes. "She left me to die at the club."

Everyone just stared at Taylor, utterly confused. "And?" Caitlin said.

Taylor crossed her scrawny arms over her chest. "Didn't you hear me? She left me there to die. D-I-E. Like roadkill. I can't work with her. She's got to be fired."

Caitlin sighed. "I completely understand how you feel, Taylor. Of course you're hurt. Of course you don't want to be around her. But . . ."

Taylor's eyes almost bugged out of her head. "*But*? There's a but? Are you serious?"

Bradley reached out and put his hand on Taylor's. "This isn't a good time to be making demands, sweetheart."

Caitlin nodded. "You've noticed how thin your scripts have been lately, haven't you? Looking like death and stumbling around like a junkie didn't exactly give the producers a warm, fuzzy feeling about you."

Taylor shot Caitlin a look so cold that even I felt the chill down my spine. Caitlin smiled quickly, as if that would smooth things over. "I know. None of this is pleasant to hear. But right now we need to worry about you keeping your job. And that means no problems, no diva behavior, no fighting on the set, none of that. You're going to kiss and make up with Nikki and put this behind you. She's nothing. Just act like you don't hate her guts. You're talented; you can do it."

Taylor looked like she'd swallowed a bug, but she nodded. "Fine. Whatever."

After Taylor's "people" filed out, she and I just sat at the dining room table for a while. "I can't believe you have to work with Nikki," I said.

Taylor nodded. "It's so unfair, it's sick. If you hadn't shown up that night, the bitch would have let me croak in a puddle of my own puke. She's probably sorry I didn't, because she would have gotten more screen time with me dead."

My dad walked into the room and sat down at the table, all smiles. "These people, they help you work everything out?"

Taylor shrugged. "I hope so." She looked at us, as sad-eyed as a dog in a bad velvet painting. "And I hope you guys like me, because apparently I can't even walk outside for a while. I'll totally pay rent, by the way."

"Outside is overrated," I said. "So, what do you want to do now?"

Taylor let her forehead drop with a light thud onto the table. "Is it possible to rewind? You know, go back in time?"

My dad patted her on the back, and his smile faded. I bet there was a time he'd like to rewind to, back before my mom died. "No," he said. "But if you find a way, you let me know."

Taylor had disappeared into my room to call her shrink, and I was still debating what to wear instead of sushi pajamas, when the doorbell rang. This time, I couldn't see anything through the peephole except an explosion of flowers: dahlias, roses, orchids, the expensive stuff. They were gorgeous, but I felt a shiver run through me. I'd broken up with Dax a while ago, but knowing how psycho he got towards the end, I couldn't rule out a sudden reappearance.

I opened the door a crack, making sure the safety chain was firmly attached. A delivery boy's head peeked out above a pink dahlia, and I sighed with relief. I grabbed the bouquet and shut the door with my foot, desperately fumbling with my spare hand for the tiny card marked TO ERIN KIM.

But when I opened it, the note inside was for Taylor.

Dear Taylor, Clive told me you got out of the hospital, and I'm so glad you're okay. Let's talk. Love, your pal, Nikki.

Nikki. At least she had the common sense to address the bouquet to me and not to Taylor, which would have given a delivery boy a really great scoop to leak to the tabloids. Still, she was pretty stupid. There was no way a pricey bunch of plant life was going to smooth things over.

Later, Taylor walked into the living room and spotted the flowers, which I'd put in a vase on the table. "New guy?" she asked me.

I shook my head and handed her the card. She didn't say a word as she read it. She just gently pulled the flowers out of the vase, walked over to the kitchen floor, and threw them down with a big wet splat. "My shrink says I have to start expressing my anger instead of internalizing it," she said.

And with that, she started jumping up and down on the flowers, grinding the heels of her sandals into each blossom like she was doing a dance step. She paused. "I'll totally clean this up, promise," she said, then got right back into her flower smashing. Her hands were balled into angry fists, and after a few moments I could see a trickle of sweat drip from her forehead. "Are you going to help me or just stand there?" she panted.

I almost hated to help. The flowers had been so beautiful despite the ugliness of the person who sent them. But I certainly wasn't against externalizing a little anger myself. I walked over to the nearest rose and pictured it as Dax's head. And when I ground it into pulp with the bottom of my slipper, I'll admit, it did feel good. I was mad at him for being such a screaming ass, and I was mad at myself for falling for his crap. I was mad about a lot of things, the more I thought about it.

I was mad at my mom for dying, even though I knew it wasn't her fault. I was mad at my sister for being so busy at UCLA, even though she drove me crazy when she was around. Oh, and I was still kind of mad at Taylor. She'd pretty much shut me out after she'd realized I'd kept Clive's secret from her. I couldn't blame her for that, but it didn't mean I wasn't a little pissed at her for holding a grudge.

Before I knew it, I was sweating all over my pajamas and struggling to catch my breath. I looked down. There was pink and yellow mush all over the floor and my slippers. Just a few broken stems were left to suggest there had ever been a bouquet of flowers. We looked at our handiwork. "Feel better?" I asked.

"You know, I do," Taylor said, giving me a big grin.

"Me, too." And then we both started laughing, laughing so hard we ended up on the floor in the pile of dead flower mush, holding our sides and gasping for breath.

"What is going on? What is all this mess?" My dad was standing over us, hands on hips, looking at us like a math problem he had no clue how to solve.

"Sorry, Mr. Kim," Taylor said, sobering up instantly. "We'll clean this up right away."

"Sorry, Dad," I chimed in, scraping up little piles of flower mush and dumping them into the garbage.

My dad stared at us for a minute, completely confused. "Okay. But don't get so excited. Bad for your health." As he shuffled out of the room in his slippers, I heard him mumble in Korean, *"Yeo ja deul eun hwei mal eul an deut ji?"*

"What did he say?" Taylor asked me.

"Why are girls so difficult?" I translated.

That just made us crack up all over again. When I caught my breath, I peered down at my poor sushi pajamas. They looked like they'd been used as a float in the Rose Parade. But I didn't care.

"Oh my God," I wheezed. "Nikki should send flowers all the time."

"I know!" Taylor yelped. "It's so much more fun than therapy!"

It was weird, but I felt so good, like I'd gotten rid of all this rotten stuff that had been festering inside me. I took a deep breath and stood up, wiping flower guts off my ruined pajamas. I'd have to throw them in the laundry, but I didn't care. Inside, I felt clean, like a brand-new girl, openhearted and pure.

I wish I could have stayed that way.

Liane Bonin has written for *Entertainment Weekly*, the *Los Angeles Times*, *Mademoiselle*, *Teen People*, *Flaunt*, *Maxim* and lots of other publications. She lives in Los Angeles with her husband and three intermittently stinky dogs. Visit her and find out more about Erin, Taylor, and the whole Fame Unlimited series at www.lianebonin.com.